life after lila

life after lila

A NOVEL

by

GINNA MORAN

For Eric Hall, my oldest brother. I was once told to write what I know, and I blew off the advice because all my para-normal books have been about things I couldn't have possibly known, like creatures and magical powers. But in writing this book, I did take that advice to heart in a way that I hope I captured how much your life as my brother has inspired me. I hope I did Xander's character justice, because without you, he'd have never existed. This book is for you, big brother. Love you lots. Love you always!

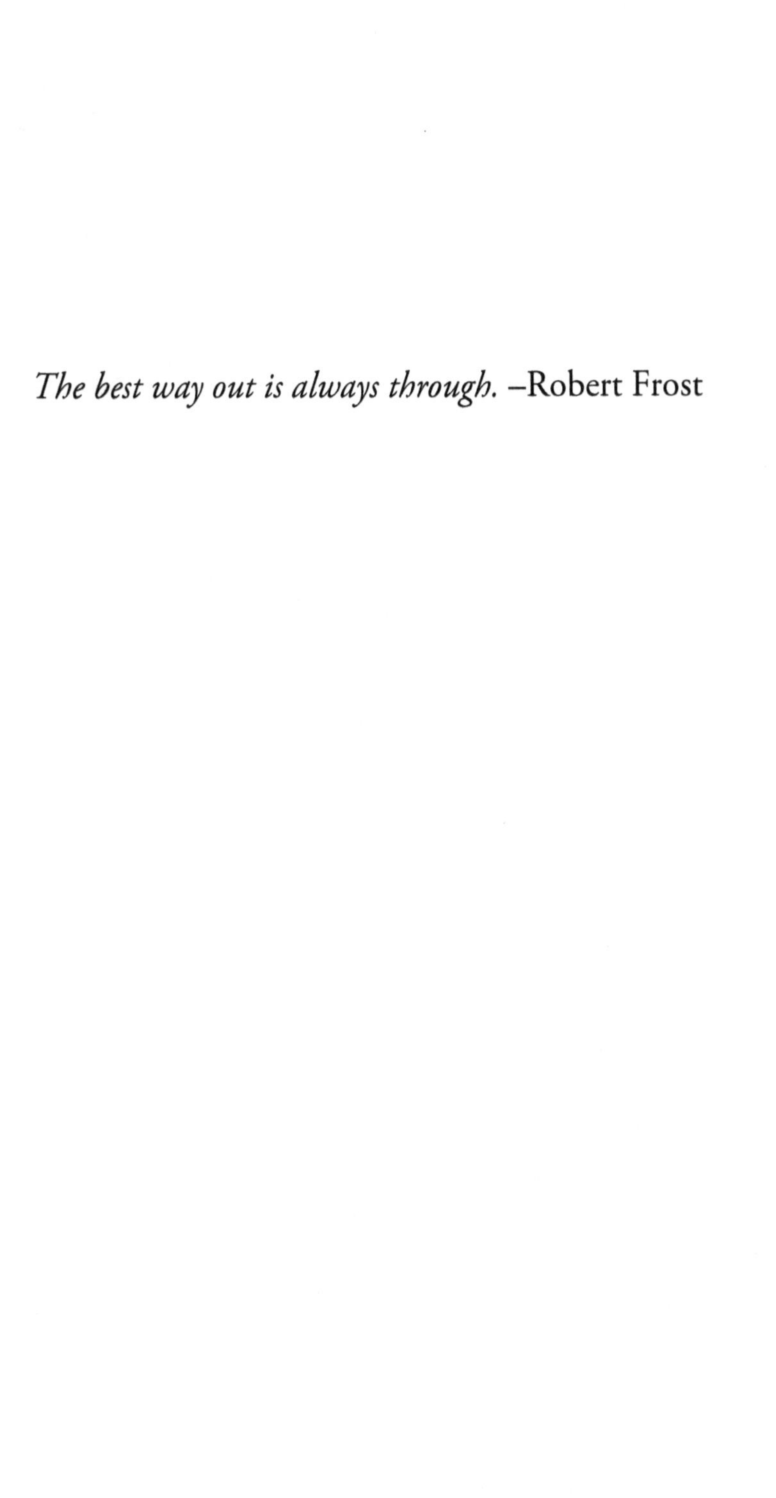

The best way out is always through. –Robert Frost

Prologue

life with lila

COOL, RAINBOW MIST sparkles through the air the moment the sun peeks through the clouds, turning the overcast day into something magical. Lila dances in the wet grass and waves the hose around like she can will summer to come early, though it's still the middle of winter. My twin brother, Caleb, laughs, watching my best friend in the entire world from where he washes what Mom calls my Barbie Mobile.

Standing just out of reach, I hold my camera in my hands, waiting for the perfect moment to capture to add to the pile of all the other moments I knew I wanted to remember forever. And hanging out with my two favorite people in the entire world is always a perfect moment in my book.

Lila's musical voice echoes through the quiet neighborhood. A mischievous look crosses her face, and she wags her eyebrows at me before glancing back to my brother. She covers the hose with her thumb, double checks to see if I'm ready, and then sends an arc of cold water directly in my brother's face.

I snap the picture.

Lila and I laugh in unison, and I run a few feet back and take a seat on my swing set when Caleb lifts the bucket of suds up, causing Lila to squeal. She screams, spraying him with the hose again, and he sends a wave of soapy water over her, drenching her shorts and legs.

"Come on, babe! Snap another picture!" Lila calls, waving the hose in my direction, pelting my jeans with freezing droplets. Only Lila would wear half a bikini while playing with the hose in weather this cold.

I laugh, rocking back and forth from my place on the swing set in the middle of the front yard, the one that has been here since we were kids. Lila covers the nozzle of the hose with her thumb again, shooting the water above us so it rains down in an icy mist. A second later, I snap the picture.

Staring at the tiny screen, I take in my best friend as she smiles with her eyes closed, the rainbow mist cascading in front of her. The pale sunbeams hit her perfectly, setting her dark hair aglow with streaks of caramel. Behind her, Caleb smiles just as widely. I know I'll caption the picture Winter Water Fun when I print it out later to add to my memory box.

Lila drops the hose before running to my side. She plops down on the swing next to me and leans over, dripping water onto the sleeve of my shirt.

"Ugh, my eyes are closed," she says.

"No retakes."

"Then let's take one together." She steals the camera from

me and turns it around. We both grin, the sun shining in our eyes, but neither of us complains. When she flips it back over to look at the screen, she bumps her shoulder against mine. "God, I love my best friend."

"I love mine, too."

Her smile lights her entire face as she stands before pulling me to my feet. "Forever?"

"Promise."

"Me, too."

Chapter 1

sixty days

"SIXTY MORE DAYS, Lila," I whisper, drawing a thick X on today's date on my calendar. The mark on shiny paper matches the small X-shaped scar on my forehead that I spend nearly two hours a day concealing with makeup, along with the dozens of other imperfections left on my once flawless skin from the worst day of my life.

The first moments of every morning are the hardest as I sit down and stare at the stranger in the mirror. She'll never be familiar to me, because the girl who stares back at me isn't how I remember myself. The puckering scars still sting with the memory of all the pain and suffering I went through just over a year ago.

Now, my reflection taunts me every morning. My face doesn't even compare to my chest and stomach though, where my skin has been burned, ripped open, and sewn up a few times by doctors whose names I've forced myself to forget. But the damage to my body doesn't matter much. That's easy to hide. My face? That's another story.

I'll never forget how much Mom cried the weeks after the accident. She was so devastated over what happened to me that she ended up spending over six hundred dollars at a beauty counter in a department store, searching for the best of everything.

After I refused more reconstructive surgeries, she wouldn't let me leave the house until the scabs fell off, the bruises faded, and I healed as much as my body could, with exception to the first time she let me visit Lila. She swore that I'd become self-conscious or depressed from all the insensitive people bound to stare at the damage. But I think she was the one who was scared to let people see me—embarrassed might be more like it.

"Sweetie," she once said, "If God intended for you to be ugly, you would've been born that way. But he didn't. So make sure to do all that you can not to disappoint him. He wanted you to be beautiful."

I cried for a week.

I still cry sometimes.

So now, every morning I wake up two hours earlier than I used to and sit in front of my overcrowded vanity table, applying layer after layer of concealer and foundation and then top it off with pressed powder. It's thick, uncomfortable, and heavy—unbearable sometimes—but I wear the makeup mask to please Mom, and I guess it does help hide the real me from the world, the one I don't want anyone to see.

Explaining to someone how I got my scars is something I

never like to do. Just knowing is enough to make me cross off one day at a time on my calendar. It's almost unreal that I have just sixty days to go.

Sixty days until I die.

A quick knock sounds on the door, pushing the thought away. It swings open, and I glance at my brother's reflection in the mirror. His messy, dark brown hair hangs over his brown eyes. They're the only features that we now share since the accident, even though we're twins.

He flashes a smile, his dimples peeking out on his smooth cheeks, and he slings his backpack over his shoulder. I used to have dimples like him before the metal plates were implanted in my cheeks to fix my facial damage. I never thought I'd miss something so small but I do.

He leans on the wall, and we make eye contact in my vanity mirror. "Done putting on your mask, Cee?"

I dab my favorite shimmery lip gloss onto my lips, pucker once, and say, "Yeah, just about." The jokes about my makeup used to bother me, but Caleb only says them because he thinks it's ridiculous how much product I use. What he doesn't get is that Mom wouldn't have it any other way. He'll never understand, and I wouldn't expect him to.

Scooping my makeup off the table, I drop it into my zebra-print purse. Caleb swipes my backpack from the floor by my closet and holds it out for me while I pull a pale pink hoodie over my head and slip into my Converses.

He gives me a once over. "It's hot out today."

I push my sleeves up and then place my hands on my hips.

"Not hot enough for me to care."

Sliding past him, I snatch away my backpack and make my way down the hall, stopping by the kitchen to grab a banana off the counter. Caleb reaches the front door before me and holds it open to let me out first. Bright sunshine beams through the trees and peppers the walkway in small bursts of sunlight. Caleb was right about the heat on this spring day, but there's no way around long sleeves. I'll never willingly show my scars if I don't have to.

"Want a ride yet?" he asks, unlocking his white Mustang. It's eight years older than us but looks like it had been sitting behind a glass case until my brother got it last year from an old man who lives down the street. Our parents wanted to buy him something new, but Caleb insisted on it, and Dad didn't argue because the price was a steal.

I shake my head and stroll past him, giving him the same response I do every weekday. I've given up hitching a ride with anyone, even Caleb, because I'm afraid. I'm afraid of getting in another wreck and having to go through the pain all over again. But it's not like I haven't tried.

On day two hundred and twenty-seven to go, Caleb convinced me to ride to the mall with him, bribing me with a new fragrance by Sara Nova that I smelled in a magazine the week before. I'm not the type to turn down a bribe, especially if it's a sixty-five dollar fragrance that would take a month's worth of allowance to buy, so I swallowed the tight knot in my throat, plopped into the passenger seat, and buckled up.

I took shallow breaths when Caleb started the engine, the

vibration shaking memories of the accident from my mind. My fingers turned white as I gripped onto the arm rest and braced the dashboard. I tried closing my eyes, but it only made my fear worse, because I could see the flash of the headlights blinding me, and I expected the Mustang to fold in half from an imaginary impact.

Caleb patted my knee, attempting to calm me down. "Ten more minutes, Coco. Hang on for ten more and it'll be over."

Tears leaked out of my eyes, and I could feel their salty wetness penetrate through the layer of makeup Mom had made me practice putting on until it was perfect, and I panicked.

A high pitched wail erupted from my lips, startling Caleb, and he swerved. The quick motion scared the crap out of me, and I screamed harder, clawing at anything I could grab onto. One of my nails snapped on the door panel and pain seared through my hand.

"Stop!" I yelled.

There was nothing Caleb could do but stop. He pulled over to the side of Sunbright Drive, and I jumped out, tripping on the curb, and scraped my hands as I fell onto the sidewalk.

The walk home that day was long, hot, and painful. My hands were on fire from my broken nail and raw palms. I bled on my favorite pair of jeans.

Caleb drove next to me, blaring his music loud enough so I wouldn't have to walk in silent shame. When we got home, he helped bandage my hands and stayed with me until my tears finally dried, and I was able to pull myself together.

"It'll get better, I promise," he said as he left me half asleep on my bed.

I wanted to yell at him for that, for making an empty promise that he could have no idea whether or not it would be true. Instead, I closed my eyes and tried my best to fight the nightmares away. I ended up not sleeping.

The roar of the Mustang starting up sends a shiver down my spine, pulling me from my memories, and I ignore the stalking car trailing behind me. I turn at the end of the block, taking the long way to school.

Between songs playing on my brother's stereo, I hear familiar voices a few houses down. I stop, listening to them for a second before turning around. I'm not in the mood to walk by Trent Wood or his sidekicks.

Caleb notices me turning around and pulls into a driveway, cutting me off. "What's wrong?" he calls through his open window.

I maneuver around his Mustang and continue walking without answering. If I told him, he'd get out and cause problems, and the last thing I need is for my overprotective brother to get involved in a matter I simply want to avoid.

Caleb backs up and drives to the end of the block ahead of me. He turns the corner and pulls next to the curb to wait for me to catch up.

"I don't want any trouble, man."

"You think I care what you want?"

I look over my shoulder. Trent pushes a guy into Jonathon Davis, who grips him by the T-shirt. The guy's outnumbered, though he doesn't let it stop him from trying to hold his ground. Paul Ortiz laughs from next to Trent, and they knock their fists together before picking up the guy's backpack from the ground.

The guy elbows Jonathon before he swings out at Trent, catching him in the shoulder. Trent stumbles forward, bracing himself against a mailbox, though he wobbles on his feet. The guy picks his backpack up and tries to push past the group of jerks. Paul takes a swig from a water bottle and spits it at the guy.

"Look at him flinch," Jonathon says, laughing. "You'd think he was scared we'd mess up his face."

Trent tries to push the guy again, but he's too fast and dodges him, clearly just wanting to leave without starting a fight he probably won't win with how many he's up against. He holds himself pretty well.

"Come on, Monster Face. Let us make it even," Trent says.

Squaring my shoulders, I face the group of guys as Trent spits water next. I can't get a good look at the guy, because he turns around to block himself and his hood obscures him.

"God, Trent. What are you? A child? Just leave him alone." My hand flies to my lips, my brain catching up to my mouth as the words spill out. I don't know why I said it, but it's too late to take it back now. I just couldn't stand here and let Trent be a jerk.

Four pairs of eyes stare at me and no matter how much I beg the universe, it won't let me fold in on myself and disappear.

Trent's lips curl into a cocky smile. "Whoa, Coco. Did you

say something to me?"

Come on, Universe. Don't make me stay here. I steel myself and roll my eyes. I haven't said much to anyone in a while. I thought no one noticed, or if they did, that they didn't care. "Weird, right? I hate wasting my breath on you."

My words only make him smile wider. "Now that's the girl I remember, but she wouldn't care about losers like this guy." He licks his lips, shifting his eyes between me and his friends. "What would Lila think?"

Trent fakes a shocked expression, holding his hand over his heart, and his friends both laugh like he's the funniest comedian in the world.

I look away before they catch the hurt sweeping across my face. Swallowing hard, I compose myself, mentally putting up a wall to keep my emotions from getting the best of me. "She'd think you were an asshole," I whisper, hiding the tremble in my voice.

Trent struts closer, and I tense as he drapes an arm over my shoulders. He smells like alcohol and mint gum, and I hold my breath when he whispers, "I'm just messin' with you, babe. I know you don't really care about that piece of trash." His fingers dig into my arm, and he holds me tighter.

"You wouldn't be such a jerk if you were ever sober," I mutter. "Maybe try eating breakfast instead of drinking it."

Trent grabs my chin and looks down at me. His dark blue eyes shine red outside his irises, and it looks like he's having a hard time focusing. It definitely wasn't water they were spitting. "What did you say?"

"I said—"

"Let her go." Caleb yanks Trent's hand from my face and punches him in the shoulder to push him away.

Trent raises his hands. "Coco knows I was just messin' around."

"Just get out of here," Caleb says, narrowing his eyes. Standing a few inches above six feet with the shoulders of a linebacker, no one messes with Caleb.

"Whatever, man." Trent jerks his neck, and Paul and Jonathon push the guy they were bullying onto the sidewalk.

Instead of trying to retaliate again, he shifts his face away to peer at Trent leave, but I can see him watch me for a moment in the corner of his vision.

"You okay?" I ask the guy, taking a step closer.

He shrugs but still doesn't look at me. "I'd have been fine. Those guys couldn't even stand straight. Sorry you got involved."

Before I have a chance to say any more, Caleb grabs my hand. "Come on, Cee. We're going to be late." Yanking me toward the Mustang, he looks like he's about to toss me in the front seat, and there's no way I'm going to let him. I don't care if he wants to protect me. I'm not getting in.

"Stop, Caleb." I dig my heels into the grass. "I can take care of myself. You don't need to follow me around all the time, acting like I'm a porcelain doll."

Caleb drops his hand to his side. "I was only trying to help."

I squeeze my eyes shut for a second. "I know, but just stop, okay?"

He hunches his shoulders and looks behind us at the boy Trent was harassing before bringing his eyes back to mine. "Fine, whatever, but I'm still following you to school. Trent's crazy, you know."

Strolling back to his Mustang, he hops in and starts the engine. I know he won't really stop trying to protect me from the world, but I'm sick and tired of him acting like he knows what's best for me.

What's best for me is that the calendar hurries up, because on mornings like this, I'm reminded how cruel the world is and how miserable it makes me knowing that people like Trent find the need to remind me of who I used to be.

I turn my attention back to the boy. He's already strolling away, but I don't move to follow him. "Hey..." My voice trails off.

He glances over his shoulder at me and offers a smile, his face half hidden by his hoodie. "No worries. I'm going to be late, too."

I only nod as I watch him turn the corner and disappear. Caleb revs his engine from behind me, and I wrap my arms around myself. *Take a deep breath.*

Even that doesn't settle my nerves. Not with the last few minutes racing through my mind and how Trent brought up Lila the way he did.

I push his words away and turn on my heels.

"Cee, where you going?" Caleb calls from his window.

"Home," I say. Sixty days can't come soon enough.

Chapter 2

fifty-five days

MY MORNING CLASSES suck. They're the boring, mandatory classes all seniors have to take. First period Calculus is the hardest because my brain doesn't process useless information that early, and I barely manage to understand anything, making my grade the entire semester a constant C-. Second period Government isn't as bad. Mr. Z manages to breathe some life into politics by streaming humorous TV shows that pretty much make fun of every politician imaginable. Third period English involves a lot of discussion, and I can sit back and just listen most of the time because the discussions are always dominated by the smartest ones in class.

The only time I ever had to speak was during a book presentation on *Things Fall Apart*, which lasted about thirty seconds and happened to be one of my favorite reads this year, because I totally understood Okonkwo's decision at the end.

Now that the morning madness is over, I head to the quad

to meet Yessica Vargas and Bridget Dune. I was never really friends with them before the accident, but they invited me into their group on day two hundred and six to go.

The day I met Yessica is a day I'll never forget. I had been sitting by myself against the science building for about a month at the beginning of this school year because Caleb took up playing basketball during lunch, and I didn't feel like cheering him on from the bleachers. He already had a herd of pretty girls desperate for his attention, who could be deemed his own personal cheer squad.

It was a humid September day, and I was sweating under my hoodie, even in the shade created by the building. I had my ear buds in, but I was only listening to silence. It was my way of keeping people from bothering me.

I could hear two people arguing around the corner. A lover's tryst gone wrong is how Lila would've described it, with the girl babbling incoherently as the boy whispered angrily. The voices stopped for a minute, and then the girl started bawling. I could imagine her shoulders shaking, black mascara running down her cheeks, her heart breaking. I felt bad for her, but I didn't attempt to move or intervene. It wasn't my business.

Two seconds later, Yessica careened around the corner and tripped over my feet because she was crying so hard she didn't even notice I was sitting on the ground. She hit the smooth concrete with a thud, and her tight black tank top rolled up to her bra line where I could see a small flower tattoo on her lower back.

She pushed up on her hands and turned to look at me. I

expected her to start yelling at me for interrupting her heart-wrenching exit, but she smiled, wiped her eyes, and sat down.

"My boyfriend's an idiot," she explained. "He loves to start fights so we can make up later and you know..." Her voice trailed off, and she blew her nose into a crumpled tissue she pulled from her bag.

I yanked my ear buds from my ears and just watched her until her eyes stopped being glassy. "Who's your boyfriend?" I asked, uncomfortable that Yessica had chosen to sit next to me of all people and cry her eyes out.

She tugged her folder from her tote bag and handed it to me. "Damien Valadez," she said, pointing at a collage of photos of her and who I assumed was Damien the Idiot. I had never noticed him before, but now that I had seen his picture, I was sure I'd see him everywhere.

"He looks more arrogant than stupid," I said, handing back the folder.

Yessica laughed as she stuffed her folder back into her tote bag. "You got that right." She stood up and offered her hand out to me. "You're new here, right? Wanna hang out with me?"

I wanted to tell her that we'd been in the same class since third grade, but I didn't feel like explaining why I looked so different this year since it wasn't like we talked before, even though she'd probably heard what had happened.

Instead, I just nodded and followed her to the table where Bridget sat, the same table we still eat at today. A couple of days had gone by before I admitted I was *the* Coco, the girl that everyone whispered about when they thought I couldn't hear them.

But they didn't ask any questions, just nodded like they knew, and that's the reason I no longer sit alone. Because these two girls care too much about what's going on in their own lives to care about mine.

Yessica slams down her bag in front of me, pulling me from my thoughts. "Have you two seen the new guy?" she asks, nodding her head in the direction of one of the food carts stationed in the quad for those students too lazy to go to the cafeteria. "His name is Xander Romano. I heard he was in a major plane crash and was the only survivor. You guys should see his scars."

Bridget leans across the table and whispers, "I heard he was involved with drug dealers, and they locked him in a burning house for not paying up."

I stare over Yessica's shoulder at the backside of a guy wearing black jeans and a T-shirt with a messenger bag slung across his back. His black hair curls around his ears, and he looks pretty hot from behind, but from the way Yessica and Bridget describe him, he sounds more scarred up than me without my makeup.

He turns around, shielding his eyes from the sunlight, and I don't see anything wrong with his face. That is, until he searches around the quad for somewhere to sit. Half of his face shows signs of being burned, the skin shiny and knobbed, and half of one of his eyebrows is missing. He has a lip piercing in the center of his bottom lip and his eyes are so green against his tanned skin that I can see them sparkling from where I'm sitting.

And I recognize him.

He's the boy that I stopped Trent from messing with last week before I decided to ditch. The one who looked like he didn't want anything to do with me. He shuffles closer, slightly frowning when he realizes there is nowhere to sit unless he joins one of the packed tables of students who gape at him, just like I am.

Bridget frantically waves at him, and he raises an eyebrow, walking in our direction.

"What are you doing?" Yessica glances around to see who is staring at us.

She shrugs her shoulders and mumbles, "You know I have a thing for bad boys," through her smile at Xander who approaches us.

Yessica tosses an empty bottle of soda at her, and she swats it away, hitting the back of some freshman boy who starts to burn us a look and then smiles like we meant to get his attention.

Xander comes up behind Yessica, and she jerks her head up to look at him. He smiles, one corner of his mouth rising higher than the other, showing off his straight teeth and a really cute dimple.

Bridget scoots over and makes room for him. "You look like you need somewhere to sit, new guy." She pats the seat next to her, and he pulls his messenger bag over his head before sitting down.

"Thanks." Xander locks eyes with me from across the table.

My cheeks warm, but I doubt anyone can see me blushing under the layers of foundation. He recognizes me, and I can't stop my hands from shaking. Not because I'm nervous, but because of how intently he's staring at me. It almost feels like he can see past my makeup mask.

He doesn't glance at Bridget even though she's leaning into him, and she glares at me from under her thick eyelashes.

Xander pushes his wavy, black hair from his forehead and then leans on his elbows. "Nice to see you again."

I bob my head and drop my gaze to my bright blue nail polish. If I don't initiate conversation, I'm sure he won't try to pursue it, like every other person at my high school.

"So, you two know each other?" Yessica says, flicking my shoulder.

"I bumped into him Friday." I don't elaborate the fact that I went out of my way to stop Trent from acting like a jerk. That's one of the things I learned from my brother—a guy never likes to be called out on a situation like that.

I watch through the grates in the table as Xander's Converse shoe taps the toe of mine. I don't know why, but I find it funny that we have the same shoes with matching black laces.

"Everything work out okay with your boyfriend?" He says it like we're alone, having an intimate conversation, even though my friends watch us.

Yessica lifts an eyebrow. "You didn't tell us you had a boyfriend." Her eyes light up like she's just discovered a dirty little secret.

I slide my legs over the bench and turn away from them. "That's because I don't." I get up and sling my backpack over my shoulder before the conversation goes off into dangerous territory. For once, I don't want to have to explain my brother's overprotective attitude, or why we look nothing alike.

I make it five feet away before I hear Bridget say, "Was the guy, like, six feet tall? Dark brown hair and coffee brown eyes? A total dreamboat?" She giggles, and I assume Xander must've answered her, but I couldn't hear it over Yessica's laughter. "Yeah, that's Caleb, my future boyfriend."

Crossing my arms over my chest, I head in the direction of my fourth period Ceramics class even though the lunch bell won't ring for another twenty minutes. Unless there's a substitute, Mrs. Grayson is probably in the classroom, firing up the kilns from this morning's classes.

As I turn the corner of the Art building, I see the door open to the Ceramic's room. Classical music drifts through the open door, and I reach into my backpack for my phone. I adjust the ear buds hanging around my neck into my ears, and turn up the volume until I can't hear anything over my music and the blood pounding in my ears.

I step a foot into the classroom when my backpack catches on something, and I stumble back, grabbing onto the doorframe for support. I look behind me and see Xander standing just outside the door, motioning for me to yank the ear buds from my ears.

I push the pause button on the cord of my ear buds. "Can I help you?" I cross my arms. My voice is higher than usual, and I feel guilty as Xander takes a step back and shoves his hands into his pockets.

"I wanted to say thank you for, you know, Friday." He

kicks a loose piece of gravel from the rock garden and stares past me into the classroom.

"I only did it 'cause Trent's a jerk." I sling my backpack off my shoulder and place it between my feet because it looks like Xander wants to say more with the way his lips twist to the side. He's staring at me like I'm more interesting than Mrs. Grayson as she carries small slabs of wood with ugly clay figurines from the metal shelves to the kiln.

Shifting on his feet, he says, "Yeah, I kind of got that."

He looks just as awkward as I feel, and I turn around to save us both from humiliation, but he reaches out and brushes his hand against mine. I freeze.

"The bell doesn't ring for—" He glances at his black leather wristband watch. "Another fifteen minutes."

"That's fifteen minutes I can work on straightening my lopsided coil pot."

He laughs. It's deep and raspy, almost like a smoker's laugh, but he doesn't smell like cigarettes. He smells pretty good now that he's only a foot away. Like a mixture of woods and spices, completely different from most guys here who smell like cheap body spray or nasty B.O.

I breathe deeply, drawing his scent to the back of my tongue, and hold it there for a second. "Are you wearing cologne?" I don't know why I blurt that, and Xander blushes like he's thinking the same thing. It's really cute, and I feel a smile crawling onto my lips.

He steps back. "Is it too strong?"

I shake my head. "It's just nice not to smell B.O for a

change." *God.* This conversation is turning from uncomfortable to embarrassing.

He glances behind him, and it looks like he's about to make a break for it, probably scared off by my inability to make normal small talk, which I'm okay with if he is. *Now's not the time to make new friends when you don't have much time left.*

"Good to know," he finally says, bringing his attention back to me.

My smile falls, and I can tell he's only hanging around because he doesn't want to be rude. I've seen Caleb do that with Melissa Cruise before he finally let her down as gently as he could, telling her he didn't have time for a girlfriend.

It's not like I'm looking for a boyfriend or for another friend for that matter. I'm fine being alone. But it bothers me that Xander assumes that my feelings will be hurt if he leaves. He's just making this situation worse by hanging around.

I grab my backpack off the ground. "I should probably head inside."

He reaches for my hand again, and I tuck my fingers into the nooks of my arms. It's like he wants, but doesn't want, my company, and it's starting to annoy me. He needs to make up his mind before I make it up for him. With the clock counting down, I don't want to waste more minutes than I have to on unimportant conversations like this.

I blow out a breath between my lips. "I'm trying to save you from feeling guilty about wanting to leave. I get it. I really do. Now if you'll excuse me, I'm going to class."

"It's not that," he says before I can turn away. "I was just trying to figure out how to ask you to show me where my next class is without sounding like a loser."

He digs through his bag and pulls out a folded piece of white paper, handing it to me. I read over his class schedule, noticing that we don't share any of the same classes, but our sixth period is next door to each other.

I hand his schedule back to him. "I wouldn't have thought you were a loser. I know you're new."

He rubs a hand over his scars. "I was also a little afraid you would tell me to get lost. With a face like mine, most girls figure out ways to avoid having to be seen with me." His honesty surprises me, leaving me frozen.

I study his face for a second, not obviously, just making it look like I'm looking into his eyes. I wonder how he got this way—if either the plane crash or drug dealer story is true. I don't ask because I know I wouldn't want to be asked if a stranger saw my scars.

"Everyone has scars. You just can't always see them," I say after a moment.

He tilts his head to the side, a dark curl falling onto his forehead, but he doesn't say anything.

"Come on. Your class is the building over. I don't want to be late because some new guy couldn't find his way around."

He smiles, trailing next to me, and I show him to the door of his fourth period Economics class. We part ways and I head back to the Art wing and Mrs. Grayson's repetitive classical music.

At the end of sixth period, I look around for Xander, but

he's either still inside his classroom or already gone. Caleb meets me halfway to the parking lot. He doesn't follow me like usual, though. He waves as he drives past and leaves me to walk home alone for once.

Chapter 3

fifty-two days

ON DAY THREE hundred and sixty-five to go, the first time I was allowed to visit Lila, was the worst Saturday of my life. I remember how my tears burned my still scabbing cheeks, how I could only see out of one of my eyes and only breathe through my mouth. I remember how the hospital psychiatrist suggested I write my thoughts down, how putting them out into the world was better than holding them in, but it didn't make a difference to me. Because on that awful Saturday, it was the first time I knew for sure that I'd never see Lila again. It was on that day that I wrote my first letter to Lila, the words forever branded into my mind.

I wrote, *The next year will be excruciating without you, Lila, and I'll be marking the days until we can see each other again, but I have to at least try. You know how pissed Caleb would be if I joined you now. He'd never forgive me. If I wait a year, I can leave him a note and tell him I gave it my all, but my all wasn't enough.*

Like your all wasn't enough.

I'm sorry for not paying attention and for not dying instead.

I'm sorry for asking you to make a promise you couldn't keep. I know you hate that as much as I do. And lastly, I'm sorry I can't see you sooner, but I will. Only three hundred and sixty-five days to go.

I wrapped the letter around the roses I had left for her even though I knew she'd never enjoy them.

And that day, I had never been so angry with Lila and myself. Because Saturdays were our favorite day of the week. Lila and I would hang out almost every Saturday, either just catching up on a week's worth of our favorite TV shows on one of our DVRs, or we'd hang out at the mall and window shop when we were both broke, go to the movies when we weren't, and went to every party we found out about whether we were invited or not.

We did everything together, even had our first kisses on the same day—not with the same guy of course. It was during winter break of our freshman year, and we had been invited to Jared Hall's house for his annual Chrismakkah party because his dad was Christian and his mom was Jewish. It was held on a Saturday between the two holidays, and we were both stoked because Jared was a senior and totally out of our league.

His house, a huge, newly built, modern mansion, sat at the very end of Crescent Street, surrounded by avocado trees. It was the first time we'd been there, but not our last, and I was mesmerized by all the Christmas lights strung through the trees, from the ground to the roof on the house, and twined around everything and anything that had a surface. It was a glowing contrast to the dark night. Even the stars were jealous of the way the house shined.

Lila and I were in the backseat of Mom's black Mercedes E55, and Caleb had shotgun. She parked in the circular driveway and let us out, handing her cell to Caleb for when we wanted a ride home.

Lila was out of the car first, and she ran to my side and yanked me out, laughing and smiling, and then dragged me to the open door. Caleb shuffled behind us, and we broke away from him the moment we entered. He was surrounded by a group of sophomore girls who didn't care he was only a freshman, and I could tell by his smile that he'd have a fun time without me.

"Come on, Cee. I heard Jared and his friends are hanging out upstairs."

I didn't ask Lila who she heard this from, but I knew she was right because I didn't see him or any of his friends mixing with the adults and lower classmen like us.

Lila led the way up the wide staircase. We followed the rock music coming from the last room on the left of the simply decorated hallway that had one wall table and a few Impressionist paintings hung evenly apart on the wall.

"In here," Lila said. She pressed her ear to the door, a smile lighting up her dark eyes. "Definitely in here."

She adjusted her top, showing off more cleavage than her shirt was intended to, and locked her fingers with mine. She flung the door open, and I held the door frame to keep my knees from shaking. I was terrified that we'd walk in on Jared and another girl getting it on, but when the door smacked against the wall, we were greeted with startled expressions that quickly melted into flirtatious smiles.

Jared pushed off his bed and held out his arms, wrapping one around each of us, before pulling us forward and shutting the door. "Glad you two made it," he said. His breath smelled faintly of alcohol and peppermint bark, but it wasn't bad smelling, almost like the peppermint schnapps my mom drank all through the winter months.

"Wouldn't miss it for the world," Lila said in her flirty voice, which was low and whispery and worked on all the guys.

Jared kissed her cheek and she giggled, dragging me with her to the bed. I noticed Tommy Bradford, Scott Solomon, and Jorge Rodriguez crowded around a bottle of vodka, taking turns pouring shots.

I brushed my light mahogany brown hair behind my ear, showing off my sweetheart neckline. "Hey guys," I said in a sweeter voice than Lila's sexy voice. With guys, I was always sugar and Lila was spice, both worked well with most guys we had crushes on.

Scott smiled while pouring a shot, and I remember my heart working in overdrive because I'd been crushing on him since the start of school, and he was interested in me. He was also just as hot as Jared. Scott used the desk to get off the floor, and he only spilled a drop of the vodka before the shot glass was offered to me.

I held my breath before tipping the glass to my lips. The vodka burned my throat, and I coughed, my eyes watering, and then I laughed out of embarrassment. Scott plopped down next to me, trailing his warm hand along my lower back, and I sank into him. We didn't even say anything before I found my lips pressed against his, and he slowly pushed his tongue into my mouth and slid his fingers into my hair.

The kiss was good for my first time, and I managed not to slobber all over the place. Scott tasted of vodka and strangely of orange, and I felt like I was floating in his arms because of the alcohol.

When it was time to leave, I gave Scott my number and had to drag Lila away from Jared. All four of us hung out off and on for a few months, and then after graduation, Scott and Jared went off to different colleges, and Lila and I had already moved on to new crushes.

So now every Saturday, even though she's gone, I still hang out with Lila, leaving flowers and my weekly letter on her grave, and today isn't any different.

I enter the quiet cemetery with a tote bag slung over my shoulder and follow the black paved road into the back section. Counting four rows past the giant angel statue, I turn and walk through the soft green grass, careful to avoid stepping on headstones.

Lila's grave is the sixth one down, and I tug a blanket from my bag and lay it out in front of her marker. The calla lilies I brought last week have been removed along with my last letter, probably by the groundskeeper who cleans up the dead flowers every Thursday.

I pull out a spiral notepad and a pen and carefully set the

bouquet of white carnations aside. Turning to the next empty page, I draw a heart before I begin to write.

I wish you were here, Lila. This week has been weird, and I don't know how I feel about it. There's a new guy at our school, and he's scarred just like me. I know what you're thinking and wipe that thought out of your head right now, because there's nothing going on between us. He's friendly enough and now sits at lunch with Yessica, Bridget, and I, but I think it might be because he's still new and doesn't know anyone yet.

Well, Lila, I'm sure you have better things to do than read this letter about my week. It's never fun anymore without you. Only fifty-two days to go...

I rip out the sheet of paper and wrap it around the carnations I brought this week before I stick them in the underground vase. I touch my fingertips to Lila's warm headstone before flipping onto my back to stare at the clear blue sky. I love warm spring days. It was miserable coming here in the rain because I'd be soaked down to my underwear by the time I got home. But today is perfect, and I could stay here for hours if I wanted to.

Closing my eyes, I enjoy the calm quiet of the cemetery. I feel myself nodding off until I hear the sound of a phone ringing. I sit up and look around, momentarily confused by the sudden noise, and then reach to the bottom of my tote for my cell phone.

I yank it out, expecting to see a missed call from Caleb, but I have a text message from a number I don't recognize. I swipe the screen and open my messages.

Unknown: *Hey, Coco. Got your # from Jaz. What're you doin?*

A frown crosses my face, and I text a reply.

Me: *Who's this?*

The response flashes on my screen within seconds, and I barely have time to read Xander before my cell starts ringing again—this time with a call.

I stare at Xander's number for a second, tempted to let it go to voicemail, but because I just responded, he'd think I was blowing him off or something. I just wish he'd text me back instead.

"Hello?" I mumble when I finally get the nerve to answer.

"I hope you don't mind me calling," Xander says. "I just wanted to see what you were doing today."

I try to think of something better to say than hanging out in a cemetery with my dead best friend, but the only thing that comes quick enough is, "Nothing."

"Cool. I figured since you were nice enough to show me to my class, then maybe you'd be nice enough to show the new guy around town?"

I twist my lips to the side. "I don't know how much I can show you. I don't drive."

He chuckles, the sound making static into the phone. "What kind of guy would I be if I made you drive me around? I'll pick you up. What's your address?"

My voice sticks in my throat. How am I supposed to tell Xander that I don't ride in cars either?

"You still there?"

"Yeah, sorry. It's just...I'm not at home." It's the only thing I think to say that won't make me reveal one of my debilitating fears that most people laugh at. The last thing I want is Xander to laugh at me.

"Where are you at? I can pick you up." There's an anxious edge to his voice, and I'd feel terrible if I told him he couldn't pick me up.

I swallow. "I'm on Fire Mountain Road, near the cemetery."

"That's only a few streets from my house. I can be there in a few minutes."

I squeeze my eyes shut, forcing myself to speak. "I have to warn you—"

"No warning necessary. See you soon."

The line cuts off before I have a chance to tell him about my fear of cars. I chuck my cell phone into my tote bag and stuff the blanket and my notepad on top of it.

I maneuver around the headstones until I reach the road and break into a sprint, running the entire way to the gate leading out. My chest heaves as I try to catch my breath, but I keep running until I'm a block away. My side cramps, and I bend over and clutch my knees. I dab my sleeve over my sweaty forehead, careful not to smudge my makeup.

Dropping to the curb to sit, I tug my compact from my zebra-print purse to double check how I look, just in case. I look as I did when I left the house, except maybe a tiny bit red on my neck.

A horn blares, and I nearly jump out of my skin when a

Mini Cooper screeches to a stop in front of me. Xander rolls down the window and smiles. He looks perfectly normal from this angle, and it's hard to imagine him any other way.

He reaches across the seat and pushes the door open. "You ready?"

My hands tremble, and I remain sitting on the curb. I force myself to smile, but it falters when he raises his eyebrows. We stare at each other for a moment, and then he turns the engine off and gets out.

Jetting around the car, he squats next to me. His black hair shines in the warm afternoon sunlight drifting through the trees, and the metal of his lip ring sparkles. "What's wrong?"

I suck in a breath to hold myself together so he doesn't think I'm a freak and keep my eyes trained on his dark jeans and our matching Converses. It was easy to play it off at school, but now that we're alone, it's hard for me to even look at him without feeling my eyes prickle.

I draw my gaze to his. "I'm cool."

"Then why are we just sitting here?"

"Because I don't drive...or ride in cars." The last three words don't come out louder than a whisper. I expect him to give me a funny look and tell me how crazy that sounds, like on day one hundred and twenty to go, when Yessica called me and asked if I wanted to go dress shopping for winter formal. She wanted to go to The Garden, an outlet mall two towns over, and not in walking distance, so I told her no. She tried convincing me for an hour and gave up when I said no for the hundredth time. She told me I was weird before hanging up the phone.

Xander's quiet for a moment, and I can feel his eyes on me. In my peripheral vision, I watch him blink a few times, and then shrug. He stands, grabs my hands, and tugs me to my feet. "Then I guess we walk."

***

I'm the lamest tour guide ever. I show Xander the grocery store, the playground, the train station, and the liquor store on the corner of Glacier and Vineyard, where Old Man Marcus hangs out and buys alcohol for under-aged kids for money. I almost suggest grabbing something to liven things up but don't. Xander's shoulder bumps mine, and we walk to Sage Avenue to a small strip mall with the nail salon my mom goes to every other week, a bridal shop, and a diner, and then we head in the direction of my house.

He strolls next to me, brushing his hand against mine every so often, but never attempts to grab it. He talks about his two brothers, Justin and Bradley, and his two sisters, Elaina and Tonya, all of which are older than him, and who all still live at home with his mom and dad. I just listen, occasionally asking questions when necessary but don't offer anything about myself.

I point to Ridgecrest Lane, and his eyes follow my finger. "This is my street. I can walk you back to your car if you want."

He pushes his hair back from his forehead. "I'm tempted to say yes so we can have a couple extra minutes together, but I'd feel guilty for making you walk home alone."

"If you haven't guessed, I walk alone all the time. I don't mind."

He takes my hand for the first time, twining his fingers through mine. "Or you could come to my house for dinner tomorrow, and we can pick up where we left off. I feel like I've been doing all the talking."

I press my lips together, running through at least twenty excuses that would sound lame coming out of my mouth. Xander would never understand why getting to know me is a bad idea. I'm broken and selfish. I've already let this new friendship go on longer than I should've, and while I know how everything is going to end, I just don't care enough about the consequences. *You care, Cee. If you didn't you wouldn't even think about it.* I force Lila's voice away and sigh.

"You can't think of an excuse, huh?" His smile pulls up on one side, and I know he's just kidding, but I can't stop from blushing.

A laugh bubbles in my throat. It's a foreign feeling, but it feels good, and I let it out. "Not a good one."

He licks his lip ring, and it turns sideways. "Then I'll pick you up at six."

I nod instead of arguing my way out of it. One dinner with his family isn't going to change anything, and I'll still be the same come Monday morning. It'll be better than sitting through another Sunday night family dinner in the Caraway household anyway. Caleb might be pissed that he has to go through it without me, and I won't hear the end of it for a week, but I know he'll survive. At least Mom can still look him in the eyes. She hasn't looked at me in months.

Xander doesn't let go of my hand when we turn the corner

to my street. He slips my tote bag off his shoulder and hands it to me. He was nice enough not to question the blanket sticking out the top, and that's what I think draws me to Xander. He doesn't ask questions, and if he did, I'm sure he'd be okay if I didn't answer them.

I let go of his hand when we reach the edge of my lawn. Mom's Mercedes is missing from the driveway. Thankfully, she's probably out shopping. I peer through the window at Caleb watching racing on TV and sling my arm around Xander in an awkward, one-armed hug. I need him to leave before my brother realizes I'm home. Caleb is nosey and overprotective and won't let things go, especially when it comes to who I hang out with. He'll pester me with a million annoying questions, and I just don't want him in my business. I really don't want anyone in my business, but especially Caleb.

"Call me if you want," I say turning away.

I climb the steps to our modernized Craftsman-style house and hear my cell phone ring when my fingers touch the door handle. I peek behind me at Xander, but he's already gone, and then I dig to the bottom of my tote bag to pull out my phone.

I smile seeing the number and say, "'Lo," while cradling my cell between my neck and shoulder as I open the door.

"Just wanted to call you." He chuckles into the phone, and my heart flutters for the first time in over a year, and I hate it and love it all at once. Why is this happening now and with Xander? I can't feel this way. It's not fair. I shouldn't get to be happy. I shouldn't get to like someone anymore, not when Lila can't. Who will I get to confide in now? Who will hug me when things turn bad?

I hover in the door. *You won't have to worry about any of that.*

"Coco?" Xander asks.

I shake the thoughts from my head. "I meant when you get home." I kick the door shut behind me. Caleb glances up but then turns his attention back to the flat screen.

"I couldn't wait."

I smile again on the way to my room. Flopping on my bed, I grab my ear buds from my nightstand and lean back, just listening to Xander's voice until he lets me know he's back at his car. He hangs up with a promise to call again later, and I hug my pillow, trying to calm the excitement Xander stirs in me.

My heart stops when my gaze falls on the marked up calendar hanging on my door. *What are you thinking, Coco? This isn't right and you know it. You're running out of time.*

Chapter 4

fifty-one days

I HEAD DOWNSTAIRS to eat breakfast around eight-thirty, which is extremely early for me on a Sunday, but I couldn't sleep. I kept thinking about how much Lila would've loved Xander and how she would tell me to make the most of the time I have left.

Mom's alone in the kitchen, sipping her usual two pots of coffee with extra cream, watching the news on the TV stationed on the breakfast bar.

I reach around her and pull my favorite square ceramic bowl from the cabinet and pad across the cool tile to the fridge to get my cereal from on top of it.

I sit on a barstool, fixing my breakfast, and glance up to see Mom blatantly staring at me. She sets her half full cup of coffee in the sink and pulls another mug from the cabinet before pouring more coffee. If it were my turn to do the dishes, I'd mention that she just had a cup, but there's no point in arguing now. It's too early.

She taps her long, French manicured nails on the granite counter, glancing between me and the TV. "I don't spend hundreds of dollars on makeup each month for you not to wear it," she says, narrowing her heavily shadowed eyes.

"I just woke up." *Not again.* She's in one of her moods this morning, probably because Dad's out of town yet again, making sales plans or whatever for Digital Signage Today, the tech company he co-owns with his long time friend, Chuck Deeds.

"And that matters to me, why? You don't see me strolling out of my room without my face, do you?"

Before the accident, I could come downstairs in a bikini and moisturizer for all she cared. She thought I was beautiful with or without makeup and loved when her friends always said how much we looked alike.

Having metal plates and screws surgically implanted in my cheeks, rhinoplasty, and what I like to describe as a face lift when the doctors had to stitch up a gaping wound on my forehead along with removing twenty-six pieces of debris from my skin, will change how a person looks. I don't know what my mom expected, that I'd come out of a car that had been crushed between a guardrail and a truck, and look exactly like I did before? Knowing her, she probably did expect it, and it was probably the only thing she prayed for. Who cares that Lila died and my body was burned and broken? As long as my face still resembled hers, the world wouldn't come to an end.

"I didn't realize you were wearing makeup," I mutter against my better judgment. "I just thought you had a terrible night with the way your eyes look puffy with bruises under them."

She bares her overly whitened teeth at me, slamming her fists on the granite counter top. "You will not speak to me like that. I'm your mother."

I push the barstool back, shrieking it across the tiles, and head to the stairs. "Then I won't speak to you at all!" I pound my bare feet as loud as I can on the carpet.

On mornings like this, I'm happy to scratch another day off my calendar. *Thank God, only fifty-one left.*

***

Xander rings my doorbell at six sharp, and I rush to leave before Mom or Caleb has the chance to figure out that I'm skipping Sunday night family dinner. I left a note on the fridge telling them both not to wait and that I'm going to a friend's to eat.

Xander's wearing a pair of black and white board shorts with a white t-shirt. His damp, dark hair makes his green eyes stand out like glittering emeralds. He smirks, showing off his one dimple, and takes my hand.

We walk in silence until we reach the corner and Xander says, "I have to warn you. My family is...excited."

The corners of my lips curve up. This is the first warning I've received of someone's family being excited. I've heard crazy, weird, demented, and even cool—but excited? Never. "Please, don't say they're excited about me."

He laughs, his hand tugging mine as his shoulders shake. "Okay, I won't."

Maybe this wasn't a good idea. What if his family is disappointed? What if they can see through my fake smile and my forced small talk? What if they see right through my makeup to the ugly scars I hide? *Shut up. They're going to love you.* The thought isn't my voice but Lila's. She said the same thing to me when Cameron Hartman invited me to his house for dinner a couple weeks after my sixteenth birthday. And she was right. They loved me so much that when Cameron and I broke up, his mom called me crying, telling me that we could work things out.

"Are you nervous?"

Yes. "Not really."

"Good. You shouldn't be."

When we pass the cemetery, I catch myself heading toward the entrance but play it off by picking a daisy from the plants along the wrought iron fence. Xander raises an eyebrow when I hand the flower to him, and then he sticks it behind my ear.

The farther we walk away from the cemetery, the more nervous I become. I knew Xander lived near the cemetery, but I had no clue he lived in this direction. I haven't been this way since—since—Lila.

Play it cool. Don't make a scene.

Slowing down, I drag my feet forward. The edges of my vision darken, my palms sweating and my heart racing. Even my knees threaten to give out on me if I force myself to walk forward. I'd say butterflies were fluttering in my stomach, but the feeling is much worse, like a tornado touching down, twisting my stomach in knots. I gasp shallow breaths to fight against the nausea rolling through me.

The world spins as panic seeps into my bones. I have no choice but to plant myself right in the middle of the sidewalk, a panic attack threatening to be the death of me. My anxiety is worse now than my first car ride after my accident, and I'm tempted to push to my feet and run as fast as I can in the other direction. I can't even focus on the street that waits ahead of us.

"Whoa, what's wrong?" Xander kneels next to me and pulls my arm away from my face.

"Just give me a minute. I'll be okay," I mumble, squeezing my eyes shut.

"Let me help you. My street is two over."

"I said give me a minute." I don't mean to snap, and I feel terrible for doing so, but the world is spinning like crazy, and I'm fighting not to throw up from anxiety.

I peek through my lashes at Valley View Road, forcing the memories to stay locked up where they belong. But the street name obliterates the lock, and everything pours into my mind. Valley View Road was the last place I saw my best friend alive.

We were on our way to what was supposed to be the Best Party Ever held at Michael Thompson's mansion at the very top of Valley View Road, which Lila declared as a fitting street name because halfway up, we could see the sparkle of city lights glowing for miles.

We were laughing and singing along to the radio, me behind the wheel and Lila in the passenger's seat, applying glittery gold eyeshadow, using the visor mirror. She was nearly bouncing in her seat because Michael was supposed to ask her to prom that night even though it was still a couple months away.

Lila flipped the visor back up. "Do I look total glam or what?"

I turned my head to look at her. Glitter had spilled from her eyelids and onto her cheeks. She looked beautiful, like a fairy, and I remember how dazzling the glitter looked, glinting off the white light shining in through the window.

We didn't see the truck coming.

I'll never forget the sound of metal against metal, the crack of the windshield shattering, the ear-piercing noise as my side window exploded in the collision. But none of that compared to the shrill noise of my own scream, louder than Lila's, or how she released a tiny laugh when the car finally stopped shaking.

Pain swelled in every part of me, and my vision blurred and tinted everything red. Lila laughed through her sobs, and she clutched my hand, sending pain into my chest and stomach.

Our eyes met and she slowly blinked at me. Her chest heaved, and she whimpered, bringing her hand to my face. There was so much blood. I couldn't tell who it was coming from, but just the sight of it made me want to throw up.

Not even a second later, black smoke billowed in through the vents in a dark haze. I could no longer see the glitter sparkling on Lila's face.

Lila coughed, and it sounded like her lungs were coming up through her throat. "Are we going to die?" she whispered.

I wanted to tell her I was thinking the same thing. "I'm scared." Every inch of me hurt, and it was getting hotter by the second. I never thought about dying until that moment, and it seemed so easy. I just wanted the pain to stop.

Lila squeezed my hand, and I wished I could see her clearly. "Promise me you won't die," she whispered.

"Only if you promise me the same thing. I don't want to live without you."

"Promise."

I didn't expect that to be the last thing I'd hear Lila say, but it was. I don't remember much after that, just the wail of the sirens and people talking about us like we were dead. I thought it was cruel at the time, because I knew I was still alive, and I thought Lila was, too. I didn't find out that she broke her promise until well after her funeral—when my parents thought it wouldn't affect my recovery—when they thought I could handle it. They were wrong.

"I think I should take you home." Xander's voice cuts through my memory.

I flatten my palms against the sidewalk, pushing to my feet. "And disappoint your family? I'm okay, really." I force myself to smile at him.

"You sure? They'll understand."

"I'm fine. I was just a little light headed from skipping lunch." The lie comes so smoothly, even I almost believe it.

"Then I better get you to my house, stat."

Xander flips me over his shoulder and breaks into a jog. We're turning on his street before I realize that we've passed Valley View Road, and I was too busy laughing and clinging on, that I didn't even have time to think about the accident again.

He sets me on my feet in front of a two-story, brown stucco house with huge flowerbeds in place of what would be a front lawn. The Mini Cooper is parked in the driveway next to an SUV, and it looks tiny in comparison. An old Ranger sits next to the curb on the street and behind it a newer Corolla is parked. I bet there's even more cars in the garage, and it looks like the Romano's have their own little car dealership.

A blond woman in a bright orange sundress with purple bikini straps peeking from under the sleeves hovers in the doorway and beams me the biggest smile I've ever seen. It's like her eyes and nose have moved up to give her mouth extra room.

She opens her arms, and before I have time to prepare myself, she rushes at me and swings her arms around my shoulders in the tightest hug ever. If that's what a real hug feels like, I don't know why so many people enjoy them. I think she may have cracked a rib or something.

She pulls away, holding my hands, and continues to smile. I have no choice but to smile back to save her from a moment of awkwardness.

"You're prettier than Xander described, Coco. Are you hungry? Want something to drink? Make yourself at home." Xander's mom doesn't even take a breath between sentences, and she's throwing so much at me at once, I totally forget to thank her for having me over.

She drags me inside and into the kitchen with Xander close on my heels. "Christian's grilling hamburgers." Spinning around to face me, she slaps her hand over her forehead. "Oh, shoot. I forgot to ask Xander what you like to eat. Are you okay with hamburgers? Or are you a vegetarian? I can make you whatever you like."

I shift my eyes to Xander who shrugs. "Hamburgers sound great. And thank you for having me over, Mrs. Romano."

"Call me Holly, please. We're an informal bunch, if you haven't noticed." I hadn't really noticed.

I don't really know how to respond, so I just nod.

Xander twines his fingers with mine. "Brave enough to meet the rest of my family? 'Cause if you're scared, we can hide in my room."

"Bring 'em on," I say, earning another ridiculously huge grin from Holly.

Xander leads me through the family room to a glass sliding door and into the backyard. My flip flops snap against the wet cement and drops of water speckle my face when I step onto the patio. Two guys, that look just like older versions of Xander, splash around in a pool, while two girls, which I assume are his sisters, sunbathe in white lounge chairs, wearing huge sunglasses and two-piece bikinis.

A man wearing a Hawaiian-print shirt and khaki shorts mans the grill. His hair is the same color as Xander's, but long enough to be braided down his back. Xander lets go of my hand and strolls up behind his father, patting him on the shoulder.

"Dad, this is Coco," Xander says, motioning to me.

Christian turns around with a spatula in his hand and waves it. "It's good to see Xander making friends already."

Before I have a chance to answer, Xander's siblings join us, and I can finally put faces to the names. Justin is the shortest of the brothers with blond hair like his mom and green eyes the same color as Xander's. Bradley is a little taller, with the same color hair as both Xander and his dad. He has full sleeve tattoos on both arms that go up to his shoulders. They're fascinating with a portrayal of hell on one arm and the other heaven. His sisters, Tonya and Elaina, look just like Holly with blond hair and blue eyes and the same huge smiles. Elaina is the shorter of the two, with thinner lips and higher cheek bones, and both girls are gorgeous.

Xander slides his arm around my waist. "Everyone, this is Coco. Please, don't scare her off. She just got here."

They all laugh, and I smile. It's strange being around people so comfortable and easy-going. I imagine this is what a normal family is like with the joking and laughing, and altogether family feel. Nothing like mine.

Holly comes out with paper plates and a stack of red plastic cups my mom would scoff at if she were here. And I'm glad she's not, because I'd never be invited over again. Xander pulls me through his family and to a large picnic bench stationed under a pop-up awning next to the pool. It only takes a second for the others to join us and before I know it, the hamburgers are eaten and everyone is laughing.

"So tell me, is Coco a nickname?" Christian asks, scooping vanilla ice cream into a few bowls.

"I wish. My mom's obsessed with Coco Chanel."

"Who?" Justin asks.

"Seriously?" Tonya says. "Gabrielle 'Coco' Chanel is a legend. Was one of the biggest fashion and beauty icons ever."

"Well, I like it," he says, scooping a heap of vanilla ice

cream in his mouth.

"Me, too," Xander whispers, making me blush. He'd be the first. Even Caleb hates my name as much as me. It's why he and Lila changed it to Cee.

My cell phone vibrates in my pocket, and I glance at the screen to see Mom calling. Xander looks at my phone before I shove it back in my pocket without answering it.

He leans over, brushing his lips against my ear. "I should probably get you home, huh?"

I nod even though I never want to leave. For the first time in forever, I'm actually happy, and I don't want it to end.

"I don't want you to leave, either," he adds. "But I don't want to risk your mom hating me before she even meets me."

I say my goodbyes and promise I'll be back for dinner soon. Xander carries me on his back the whole way to my house so that he doesn't even notice I'm squeezing my eyes shut and silently praying as he passes The Worst Street Ever. He kisses me on the cheek at my door, hovering next to me until I hug him once more. I watch as he strolls down my driveway, leaving me alone to face my own family. I end up sitting on my steps for another two hours before Caleb finally drags me inside.

Chapter 5

forty-seven days

"ARE YOU AVOIDING me?" Caleb hovers in the bathroom door as I finish my makeup. "Is this about Sunday? Mom's still pissed you missed family night dinner, you know."

I dust my eyelids with my favorite matte brown eyeshadow. "Like I care."

He crosses his arms over his chest. "Cee—"

I flip around to look at him, cutting him off. "Don't you dare try to make me feel guilty. There was no way I was eating dinner with her. She's a lunatic."

He scrunches his eyebrows. "You could've at least told me where you were going."

I release a breath, biting back the anger threatening to ruin my peaceful morning. "Whatever."

Day three hundred and five to go was the day Caleb went from being my friend to being my overprotective brother. I was allowed to go back to school to turn in all the assignments I had missed during my healing period and also to take my finals so I wouldn't be held back a grade.

He walked with me to school that day, shadowing my every move. It was hot and humid, and I was pouring sweat under my hoodie, but I refused to take it off because I didn't want people to stare at the burns that peeped out from my camisole.

Aiden Stone and Jose Gonzales greeted Caleb at the gate, giving him the usual fist bump hello. I felt vulnerable and naked as Aiden gave me a once, twice, third time over before glancing at my brother. "I've never seen you here before," he said to me, licking his lips. "You dating lower classmen now, Caleb?"

My brother stiffened next to me. "Dude, you know my sister Coco."

Aiden and Jose both stared at me for a minute, piecing together whatever they were missing. I wanted to turn around and walk away forever that moment. I was prepared for the whispers about Lila, and about me, the girl with the dead best friend. I was even prepared for the obvious stares and hurtful remarks. But I wasn't prepared to have people not recognize me, to not know who I was.

"Damn," Jose whispered under his breath. He took a step closer, and I shuddered when his clammy hand brushed the hair out of my eyes. "I like the new face. It's hot."

I jerked away from him and crossed my arms over my chest. It was the first time I was no longer seen as Caleb's twin. I was new meat on the market, free for any guy to put his grubby hands on.

Before, Caleb would've laughed it off, said that his friends were idiots, but this time he didn't. His hands balled into fists, and he clocked Jose in the nose. Blood dripped onto Jose's lips and down his chin, and he just stood there in stunned silence.

"Don't talk to my sister like that. It's not cool."

After that, most guys at my school didn't talk to me at all. I don't know if it was because of Caleb's friends hitting on me or the fact that they commented on how different I looked—I never asked him—but something shifted in our relationship that day and it wasn't for the better.

"Don't act like that," Caleb says, bringing me back to the present.

I push past him and beeline for the door. "I will act like this until you realize she's not the one needing defending. I am. From *her*."

I slam the door and bolt down the steps. Tears burn my eyes as I crash into Xander, who's standing in the middle of my walkway.

"What are you doing here?" I ask.

He steadies me. "I wanted to walk you to school."

"Oh." I turn my face away to hide my tears. This was supposed to be my great escape, and I wasn't expecting him to be at my door this early in the morning.

"You okay?" he asks, without forcing me to look at him. He just gathers me into his arms and holds me against him.

As he rubs soothing circles on my back, I blink away the tears. He doesn't push me to answer his question or even ask me what's wrong, and I'm glad for it. Some things I have to deal with on my own. My family is one of them. The last thing I want to do is burden him with my problems.

I look up into his eyes and can see the burning questions, but still, he doesn't push. The words stick to the tip of my tongue and all I answer with is, "I hate my family."

***

Yessica and Bridget discuss their weekend plans while picking at the tray of chili-cheese fries set in the middle of the table.

I search through the crowd for Xander, expecting him to waltz toward our table any minute. He told me between first and second period that he'd see me at lunch, and I'm getting anxious that maybe he found someone better to sit with now.

Bridget snaps her fingers in front of my face. "What's your malfunction? You've been people watching for at least fifteen minutes. Who you lookin' for?"

It takes me a second to hear her. "Oh, uh, Xander. He said he'd sit with us today."

Her lips narrow. "Something going on between you two?"

"We're just friends."

She frowns. "I saw him leaving campus with Becca and Grace on my way to the cafeteria."

My heart sinks into my stomach. Why would Xander leave with Becca and Grace? We have a closed campus. It's not like there are any food places in walking distance, and the parking lot is locked until sixth period. Xander didn't even drive today. So the only thing I can think of is he's ditching with two of the prettiest cheerleaders.

You shouldn't care so much. Nothing can happen with Xander. You only have forty-seven days to go. The thought is a whisper in the back of my mind, and I push it away.

I shake my head and decide to change the subject. "Doing anything fun this weekend?" If I don't get my mind off Xander, I'll drive myself crazy. Just because I met his family doesn't mean that we're suddenly more than friends. He hasn't even kissed me, well, except for on the cheek, and that doesn't mean anything.

Bridget raises an eyebrow. "Weren't you listening when we were talking about finding an awesome party or ten?"

"I need to shop for prom, too. Only a month and a half to go," Yessica adds. "I refuse to not have an amazing dress in time."

The bell rings, saving me from having to listen to Bridget and Yessica go on and on about the amazing weekend they'll have when I'm stuck with my family at home.

I grab my backpack off the ground and swing it over my shoulder. Instead of heading straight for Ceramics like I usually do, I take the long way and hang outside Xander's Economics class.

I stay until the warning bell rings before reluctantly leaving. I consider ditching for all of two seconds, changing my mind because there's no one to ditch with me. It's not as fun doing it alone.

The first time I had ever ditched was during freshman year. Lila's birthday had landed on a Wednesday, and she pouted the entire way to school because neither of our parents would let us stay home to celebrate.

My mom dropped us off a block away from school because

we had decided we were too cool to be seen getting a ride, and Caleb stayed in the car, arguing that it was better than taking the bus or walking.

The moment my mom pulled away, Lila grabbed my hands and smiled. "Let's ditch." Her eyes lined with excitement, and I thought if I said no, she'd burst into tears. I wasn't going to do that to her on her birthday.

I smiled and nodded. "We could go to the movies."

"We could do that anytime. I have another idea. Don't worry it's the Best Plan Ever!"

My jaw dropped when Lila dragged me to Tattoo Mania, acting like it was my birthday surprise instead of hers. She wagged her eyebrows and dug her hot pink wallet from the front pocket of her backpack.

"We're getting pierced!" she declared.

I laughed, not because of how ridiculous her plan was—I was fourteen and she was now fifteen, and the sign said you had to be eighteen without a parent's permission—but because of how excited she was. You'd almost have thought she'd been asked to prom by Jared.

I decided not to mention the age requirement, since I was pretty sure at least Lila could pass for being older, and instead asked, "Belly rings?"

"Well, duh!"

The door chimed as she pulled me inside. I was blasted with cold, sterile air. The walls were covered in all sorts of pictures of tattoos you could get, and my eyes lingered on a 3D butterfly before my gaze fell on the glass case of faux-diamond jewelry that could be pierced anywhere on my body.

The guy behind the counter had too many piercings to count, and the only part of him that wasn't tattooed that I could see was his face.

Lila sauntered forward and leaned in front of him, pressing her boobs together with her arms. She wrapped her index finger with her hair and looked him dead in the eyes. "You have time for two naval piercings?" she asked, reading over everything the tattoo parlor had to offer.

The guy's eyes shifted to her chest and then he winked at me. I gave him my best smile, sticking out my chest as far as I could without looking stupid. I lifted up my shirt to just below my bra and asked, "Wouldn't one look totally sexy on me?"

Lila's eyes widened for a second. "Totally sexy, babe."

The guy, who told us his name was Devon, had us sign waivers and didn't even ask to see our IDs. Thirty minutes later, our belly buttons glittered with fake pink diamonds, and we both had Devon's number, just in case we wanted to call him.

After that, ditching at least one class a month became our ritual and a full day if it was a special occasion. And we did visit Devon one more time, during the summer before junior year when we got matching butterflies on our hips in white. No one except Lila knew about the tattoo. It was always our little secret.

I fiddle with my belly ring through my hoodie before Mrs. Grayson waves me in as the final bell rings. I toss my backpack under the table and stare at my lopsided coil pot for a whole five minutes before I raise my hand and ask to be excused to the nurse.

The nurse's office is small and decorated with cartoon pictures of smiling kids of all colors, one even an alien green, holding hands, showing off their unity. The waiting area has two plastic chairs and a desk, and off to the right is the room with the paper covered bed that some kids occasionally nap on even when they're not sick.

Ms. Dawson steps from the quiet room, and my mouth drops open when Xander steps out behind her with an ice pack covering his right eye. We lock gazes, and he frowns.

Ms. Dawson signs a late slip for Xander and slides her pen behind her ear. "I haven't seen you in a while, Coco. What can I do for you?"

She shoos Xander out the door, and I spin to follow. "I had a headache, but it's gone," I call over my shoulder as the door shuts behind me.

Grabbing his free hand, I pull him around the corner by the bathrooms, holding my index finger over my lips. I check to make sure the coast is clear and motion for him to follow me. We walk in silence behind the math building until I spot the gaping hole in the fence Lila liked to use to get off campus without having to climb any fences.

I squeeze my way through first and pull the fence wider so Xander can fit. We cut through a lemon grove and end up on Shadow Lane, a block from school.

"I think I hate your family, too," Xander blurts, catching me off guard.

A million reasons why he would say that flash through my mind, but nothing seems plausible. He's never met my mom. I shove my hands in my pockets and shift on my feet. Xander's staring at me like he's expecting me to know why he now hates my family, and I don't return his gaze.

He slides his fingers under my chin and coaxes me to look at him. "Has he ever hit you? I swear to God, if he has, I'll kill him."

My jaw cracks as I open and close my mouth, trying to find the words to answer him. "Are you talking about Caleb? He's the one who punched you?"

Xander's eyes narrow. "Has he ever hit you?"

"What? No. Why would you think that?"

"He just seems like he has anger problems."

"So he did punch you." I don't ask because I can see the answer heating his cheeks. I dig my fingernails into my palms and silently count to five. It's not like I can't believe that Caleb is capable of hitting someone, I just didn't think he'd hit Xander. God, he must've seen us together this morning. This is like the Jose situation all over again, but Xander was undeserving.

I grab his hands, squeezing them. "I'm so, so, so sorry. We had a fight this morning, and he's probably trying to get back at me."

"He wants me to stay away from you," he mutters, kicking at the ground. "He had these two girls lead me to the groves under the impression that he just wanted to introduce himself to me. He then said that he couldn't deal if you got your heart broken again, and when I said I didn't intend on it, he punched me and told me to stay away from you."

I grab my chest, suddenly winded by his words. My hands tremble, and I squeeze his fingers to stop the shudders beginning deep in my stomach. Caleb wasn't referring to a boy when he told Xander about my broken heart. He was talking about Lila.

"He has no right. He has no right to be in my business," I say, mostly to myself.

Xander pulls me against him, and I feel the wall around my heart begin to crumble. He kisses my forehead, and I lean into him, pressing my face against his chest, breathing in his warm scent.

"I won't break your heart," he whispers. He doesn't say it as a promise but as a fact. And I believe him. He'll never have the chance to break my heart, because I know his heart will be the one to get broken.

I open my mouth to tell him this, half hoping that he'll leave me to the fate of my decision. I half hope that he won't care or that maybe he'll try to talk me out of it. But the words stay buried in my throat because he kisses me. His hands slide to my hips as he pulls me closer, and his tongue parts my lips.

I melt into him, tasting mint, and feel the metal of his lip ring brush against my bottom lip. He kisses me softly, his lips moving in sync with mine. His hands stay on my sides, never wandering, unlike the other boys I've kissed. It's the sweetest kiss I've ever experienced.

He pulls away, pressing his forehead to mine, our noses touching, and gazes at me like he can see underneath my makeup and scars and see the fragile girl I've become.

His warm breath tickles my lips and we just stand together, staring at each other. I want to tell him about Lila, about the accident and my scars. About the way Mom treats me and all the things that terrify me. I also want to tell him about the promise I can't break and how much it hurts obsessively counting down the days until they finally run out.

But I don't say anything.

I just cling to him like he's the only thing I have to hold onto, the only thing that can save me from my dark thoughts and never-ending nightmares. I never thought I'd really miss anything from this world because the one thing I do miss isn't even here. But standing here in Xander's arms, looking into his bright green eyes, I know I'll miss him. I just hope he understands.

Chapter 6

forty-two days

CALEB'S BEEN AVOIDING me since I found out that he punched Xander in the face. He waited until I left the house this morning to even come out of his room. He's a smart guy when he wants to be, because when I see him, I'm going to knock him upside the head and tell him to stay out of my life. This was the break I was looking for, a way for him to hate me so he doesn't miss me when I'm gone.

Xander sits with me under a large oak tree in the corner of the track field away from the crowd of hungry students and loud whispers. He leans against the tree, and I rest my back on his chest with our fingers twined together. It's almost like we're the only ones left in the world and nothing can come between us, except for the permanent marker slashes on my calendar.

"Why can't it always be like this?" I twist around to look at him. His eye is no longer swollen, but it's still shadowed with a bruise. It's nothing compared to Jose's, the first time Caleb defended me, and I'm guessing he held back a little. But not enough for me to forgive him.

Xander kisses my nose. "It can." The last few days have been so easy without having to deal with Caleb or even Mom. I lock myself in my room when I'm forced to be home, but I mostly hang out with Xander.

Everything feels so right this very moment. It's the same feeling I get on Saturday afternoons in the cemetery, except it's less empty. The hole in my heart isn't as painful.

I want Xander to promise me it will always be like this. That we can be together, apart from everything, without a worry in the world. But I can't ask that of him. It wouldn't be right. Not when broken promises can change everything in seconds.

I tip my head back, resting it on his shoulder, and look at the stars of sunshine penetrating through the leaves. Xander's breath is warm on my neck, and he brushes his lips against my jaw. My scars burn under my clothes and makeup, screaming that I'm leaving myself vulnerable, and I can't ignore them.

Leaning forward on my knees, I squeeze my eyes shut until the phantom pain washes away, and it's just me and Xander, the stillness of the field, the low whoosh of our breathing, and the tiny voice in the back of my mind, whispering that Xander's right. None of this has to end.

***

Tonight's family dinner was unavoidable. Dad arrived this afternoon from New York—maybe San Francisco—I'm not sure these days because he always seems to be everywhere but here. And that's why family dinner is a must, even though Dad looks exhausted and ready to doze off before Mom has even set the lasagna on the table.

Dad sips a cup of coffee, leaning on one of his elbows for support. "Anything new?"

He asks the same question any time we're all sitting together. Most of the time it's followed by silence, but occasionally one of us will speak up and say, "Yeah, you missed a lot." And tonight's one of those nights.

"Well, let's see," Mom says, setting down her fork without even touching her dinner. "I got a phone call from Mrs. Fitzpatrick informing me that our daughter skipped the second half of her day last Thursday. Oh, and she stood us up on Sunday night dinner twice in a row, not to mention that she's decided she can talk back to me."

My glass of water falls from my hand, and I manage to catch it before it spills across the table.

"You know, she didn't even tell us where she went or at least apologize for making me worry. I thought something terrible happened to her. I just don't know what to do with her anymore, Henry." She's talking about the night I went to Xander's for dinner.

It takes everything in me to not scream. Mom has reached a new low, acting like she actually cares when what she really wants is to see me suffer. She never asked me where I was and hasn't even looked at me since that Sunday morning.

"I'm sure Coco can explain, Charlotte." Dad brings his eyes to mine.

Caleb clears his throat, and he shifts his eyes away from me, almost pitifully. I expect him to stand up for me, to say that Mom is being unreasonable, but instead, he says, "It's the new guy at school. I heard he moved here to get out of a gang."

My mouth drops open.

Dad glances between Caleb and Mom and then settles his gaze back on me. "Is that true?"

I slam my palms on the table. "Of course not!"

"Then how did he get all those scars?" Caleb asks.

The words stick in my throat because I don't know what to say. I don't even know how Xander got his scars. I never saw a reason to ask.

Mom folds her arms across her chest. "Well?"

I drag my hands down my face, distorting the three people waiting for me to respond. "Does it really matter?" By the look on Mom's face, I know it does. I also know that anything I say will be useless because she's already made up her mind about Xander, and there will be nothing I can say to change it. "If you must know, I haven't asked." Mom's eyes widen and Dad sighs. Caleb just stares at me like I've lost my mind.

"And why not?" Mom's voice is cold enough to freeze hell.

"Because it's not important." My voice cracks and tears burn my eyes.

"The hell it isn't," Caleb quips, and it takes everything in me not to lunge across the table and shake some sense into him.

I push my chair back. "You're such a jerk! I *hate* you!"

Before anyone has time to stop me, I yank my hoodie and bag off the entryway table before opening the front door. In moments like this, I wish it were me who had died first instead of Lila.

***

The sun vanishes, dipping into the horizon, before I even make it to the cemetery. It supposedly closes at sunset, but the gate is wide open so I stroll down the road to the back section.

Without the sun, the cemetery exudes a morbid atmosphere. All I can think about is curling up on my side next to Lila to join her in eternal sleep. It's so tempting to forget my calendar and counting down the days until I can finally just go. It's not like I'd be breaking my promise, because I did try. I tried to be the perfect daughter and the perfect sister. I tried to move on and continue living, but no matter what, I always end up here with the one person in the world who understood me, who could overlook my flaws and stood by my side no matter what.

I met Lila in the third grade when Dad reconnected with his old buddy and decided to start a business. I hated leaving my old school and my friends and cried the entire car ride to John P. Anderson Elementary. I never even heard of the guy who founded the school and wished it were named after someone more familiar, like a dead president or a rock star—anyone besides some guy that meant nothing to me.

You would think that school officials would be nice to the new kids, let the new twins be in the same class, but some annoying school psychologist insisted that it was healthier to separate us so we could grow into our own identities. Lame, I know.

Mom walked me to the door of Mrs. Parks' classroom

while Dad took care of Caleb. I begged Mom not to make me go inside, said if she made me, I'd die from a heart attack. She just laughed and patted my head before opening the door wide.

Mrs. Parks greeted me with a huge smile, and I remember how happy I thought she looked. She showed way more gum than teeth, and her eyes squinted, disappearing under her wrinkled skin. She guided me to a desk in the front row, and I sunk low in my seat to hide from all the other kids I knew were staring at the back of my head.

"Class, this is Coco Caraway. Now I need a volunteer to show her around at recess." No one raised their hand, and I tried to act like it was no big deal, like I wouldn't cry the second I was alone. It's not like I would've given up recess at my old school to show some dorky girl in pigtails around.

"I guess I'll have to just pick someone," she muttered under her breath. "Sofia Flores? Will you please show Coco around?"

I didn't want to look and see who Sofia Flores was, so I just sank lower in my seat. I assumed she nodded, because a second later, Mrs. Parks started talking about the weather, which was part of our science hour.

When the bell rang for recess, I didn't get up to leave. I was hoping Mrs. Parks would understand and let me hang out inside for the rest of the day.

A girl with brown hair, almost the same color as mine, stood in front of my desk. Her hands were on her hips, and she stared at me like I had a booger or something hanging from my nose.

"I like your shoes," she said and kicked the toe of my pink

and white checked Vans with her black and purple ones.

I smiled under the bangs I let fall onto my face. "I like yours, too."

She flipped her hair over her shoulder. "Well, you comin'?"

I pushed out of my seat and smiled. "Yeah. Thanks for showing me around, Sofia."

The girl laughed. "Sofia was out of here before the bell finished ringing." She looped her arm in mine. "I'm Lila."

Tears rim my eyes when I think about how lucky I was that Lila decided we should be friends because we both had good taste in shoes. If she were still here, she'd remark that Xander was a perfect match for me because of our shoes. It's kind of funny, but I thought the same thing.

Footsteps sound out, pulling me from my memory of Lila. I expect that the groundskeeper finally discovered me and is about to tell me to get out, that I have no business hanging out in a cemetery after dark, but when I look up, I see Dad working his way around the headstones, heading right for me.

He doesn't say anything when he plops down next to me, folding his legs over each other until he's sitting cross-legged in front of me. I want to joke that he looks funny doing so in a suit, but I'm not really in a joking mood.

He pats my knee, his way of showing that he loves me without saying it. He's never been a big talker, especially about feelings, and his presence alone helps ease the ache in my chest.

"I'm sorry for ruining dinner." I keep my eyes trained on Lila's grave.

He grunts, reaching to grab my hand. "Kiddo, you didn't

ruin dinner. It tasted just fine to me."

I laugh, but it comes out sounding more like a sob. "How'd you know where to find me?" The last time Mom made an effort to come searching for me, this was the fifth place she decided to look. That was when she still cared about me, still loved me, right before I announced I wasn't going to get anymore plastic surgery.

"I had a hunch," he says, shrugging. "Plus, I was out the door not more than a minute after you."

"You do realize that something's going to get broken now," I say.

Dad laughs. The deep rumble in his throat shakes his shoulders. "Oh, your mom will get over it."

I try to smile, but I can't. "Like she got over me? She yelled at me, you know. For leaving my room without makeup. That's why I didn't tell her about going to Xander's house for dinner."

His eyes widen for a split second and his fingers curl. I expect him to jump up and rush home to yell at Mom—I want him to—but instead he only sighs. "That's because she can't leave her room without makeup because she'll scare the neighbors."

I laugh even though I know he doesn't mean it. I see the way he looks at Mom, and I can tell he still thinks she's beautiful. He's only saying it to make me feel better.

"And don't you dare tell her I said that," he adds with a grin.

I look at him, a smile curling on my lips. "And if I do?"

He gasps, covering his hand over his heart. "You

wouldn't!"

"I'll have to think about it."

"Suit yourself. I thought you liked all the furniture in one piece." He leans on his hands, taking a little too long to get to his feet, before tugging me to mine. He slings his arm over my shoulder. "You know, she'll break the bowls first."

I can't stop the grin from taking over my face. Dad and I always joke about Mom breaking things when she is angry even though it only happened once and by accident. We never let her live it down.

I follow Dad through the cemetery. Even though he isn't home often, he still knows more about me than Mom ever will. And for that, I'm going to hate writing his letter the most.

Chapter 7

forty-one days

I SIT AT the bar next to Dad, eating my favorite cereal out of my square bowl while he sips his coffee, black, nothing fancy like Mom. Caleb headed out the door twenty minutes ago, and Mom soon after, explaining to Dad that she had errands to run, but she'll be back by dinner. She didn't even glance at me.

When I woke up, there was a little sticky note on my vanity mirror, announcing that today was father-daughter ditch day, and no moms or brothers were to be included. It brought a smile to my face the way he circled and crossed out their names and ended it with an exaggerated smiley face.

A light knock sounds on the door but neither of us attempts to answer it. I'm not decent enough to answer the door because I'm still in my pajamas and without makeup.

A couple minutes later, the doorbell rings.

Again, we ignore it.

It rings again.

I sigh, pushing away from the bar and my breakfast. "I guess I'll scare them away."

Padding through the living room and into the entryway, I shuffle to the door and lean forward to look through the peephole. I stumble back when I see Xander on the other side. Now there's definitely not a chance I'm going to answer. Not like this.

The bell rings again in three quick successions. Dad comes up behind me and places his hands on my shoulders. "I thought you were going to scare them away?"

My eyes shift between the door and Dad. "It's...Xander. I can't open it. He'll see me." My voice is just above a whisper so he doesn't hear me through the door and think I'm avoiding him. Yeah, I kind of am, but he doesn't need to know that. "Tell him I'm sick, or better yet, I'm sleeping."

I dash back into the living room and into the hallway, peeking around the corner when Dad opens the door.

"What can I do for you?" Dad asks, leaning on the door frame.

Xander steps back and shoves his hands in his pockets, caught off guard. "I'm here to walk your daughter to school," he says. He glances past Dad and into the entryway.

"You don't have a car?"

Oh, jeez.

Xander's eyes widen. "Well, um, well, yeah. But I thought—"

Dad chuckles. "I'm just yanking your chain, kid."

"I almost thought I was at the wrong house. So is Coco

here?" Xander asks, blowing out a breath.

Dad leans on his heels and crosses his arms. "Now that I think about it, you may have the wrong house."

I want to smack Dad in the arm as I watch Xander shift uncomfortably on his feet. He's going to scare him off if he doesn't stop messing with him.

"At least you do this morning. Coco and I are playing hooky, and I'm sure as heck not gonna let you see her in her pajamas. Not until she's twenty-five at least. You can come back later when she's decent."

Xander's lips twist to the side, and he nods.

When he turns to leave, Dad calls out, "Hey, kid? Nice lip ring. You think if I got me one of those, it'd up my cool factor?"

Xander smiles. "Totally, sir."

***

You'd think Dad was preparing to have lunch with a movie star or someone, minus all the glitz and glam. He shuffles around the kitchen, whistling the theme song to Indiana Jones, while pulling out everything he can think of to put on sandwiches.

I don't know what makes me more nervous—the fact that Dad is rushing around the kitchen more excited than I am as he prepares lunch for three, or the fact that Xander should be here any minute without a clue of what he's gotten himself into.

I pick up the bag of marshmallows Dad flings on the counter. "Seriously, Dad? No one puts marshmallows on a sandwich."

"And have you ever seen Mr. Rock Star eat a sandwich?"

I narrow my eyes. "Dad, I swear if you call him that I'm—"

"Relax, kiddo. Your teenage-girlness is showing."

"Well, your wannabe-cool-guyness is showing."

He sticks out his bottom lip. "You just wait. One of these days I'm gonna come home all tatted out with shiny bling to match. Then who will you call a wannabe?"

I laugh, a full on hyena-style bark of a laugh. I can't help it. Dad's cool in a dorky kind of way. It's hard to even explain. He didn't even think twice about Xander's appearance or his black eye. Dad's the opposite of Mom, and I never knew what attracted them to each other. Mom is high strung and Dad's mellow. I guess they balance each other out, but I don't know how Dad handles it.

The doorbell rings, and I race through the living room before Dad has a chance to offer to answer it. Flinging the door open, I welcome Xander with my brightest smile.

I don't let him in right away, though. Instead, I step onto the porch and close the door behind me. "Remember when you warned me that your parents were excited to meet me? Take their excitement and times it by ten and you have my dad."

He chuckles, the comforting sound rolling over me, sending a shiver down my spine. "I take back what I said the other day. I don't hate your entire family."

Bending down, he brushes his lips against mine. If Dad wasn't on the other side of the door anticipating Xander's arrival, I might be tempted to drag Xander up to my room. I break free and lock my fingers with his before guiding him inside.

Dad pokes his head in from the kitchen doorway. "So, you found the right house this time?" He winks and then chuckles to himself. "Good thing, because lunch is ready."

I lead Xander into the kitchen, and his eyes widen at the crazy sandwich-making selection Dad lines up on the counter-top like a never-ending buffet. There's a ton of different kinds of breads and rolls, meats, and toppings a normal person wouldn't even consider putting on a sandwich. I hand a plate to Xander and motion for him to dig in. I don't know if he was just being polite or has the same strange taste in toppings as my dad, because he piles his wheat roll with everything Dad had to offer, including the marshmallows.

Dad pokes my side, and I almost drop my plate. "Told you."

We end up in the living room with our plates on our laps and the TV blasting Dad's favorite Oldies music channel. Mom would have a hissy fit if she saw us eating in a No Food Zone, wearing our shoes on the carpet, and using Christmas-patterned paper plates Dad discovered in the very back of the pantry.

When we're finished eating, Dad excuses himself, pretending he has something important to do, even though I know he doesn't, and I find myself leading Xander out front to the rickety swing set where Lila and I spent a lot of time just hanging out.

It was where we first swore off boys in the eighth grade, because Travis Walsh asked Alisha Cummings to a school dance instead of me. It was where we drank beer for the first time when Caleb stole a can from Dad's stash before he stopped drinking the stuff, and it was where Lila told me she thought she was pregnant, and we swore off boys again until she got her period three days later. It was also the place where we made plans for our future, deciding that we were going to wait a year before going to college, and instead figure out a way to go to Europe—not backpack—but stay in fancy hotels, eating the best cuisines, and maybe even meet our future husbands because neither of us could resist an accent.

Xander stands in front of me, and I rock back and forth on the swing, watching Mr. Delany mow his lawn next door. I can feel Xander's eyes on me, and I look up and smile. He smiles back, showing off his dimple through the shadow of stubble only growing on one side of his face.

He rests his hands on my shoulders, pulling me closer, and my feet skid across the dry grass until my legs rest between his. "I missed you at school today."

My chest tightens. I haven't heard those words in a long time, and I'm not sure how to take them. I feel myself shutting down, like that little word triggered my guard to shoot back up. *You're going to hurt him.* The thought creeps its way into my mind, and I push it away as quickly as it came.

I slide my hands around his waist. "It was only a couple hours."

He tilts my chin up so he can see my face. "I know. It's just—I don't know how to explain it—like everything is better. I feel like I know nothing and everything about you." He pauses and twists his lip ring to the side between his lips. "And I sound really cheesy, don't I?"

He's expecting me to say yes, but I don't. I gaze down at our shoes, thinking of my theory about them. "You know I decided that I liked you because we had the same shoes? Crazy right?" I consider adding it's also because our bodies match, how we never talk about our scars, and also how when I'm with him, everything seems quieter, less painful. Like I'm a different person and not the broken shell of one that I've become.

When I think about our similarities, I think about mine and Caleb's differences. Maybe that's why we're two strangers living under the same roof now. Same with Mom. I've always chosen my friends because of what we had in common, and I never had to do that with my family because we were always alike in one way or another up until last year. Caleb was my twin, just a more masculine version of me, and now, we don't even look related except for our eyes and hair color, but it isn't enough. The accident stole not only Lila from me, but it stole my twin from me, my mother, and a huge chunk of my identity. I don't even know who I am besides the scars and the makeup, and my ability to still keep a promise.

Xander pulls me to my feet and kisses my temple, moving to my cheek, and then ever so softly, kisses my lips. His breath caresses my lips when he says, "We're all a little crazy."

We stand together, our faces an inch apart for what seems like forever. I imagine what it would be like to melt into him, to seep beneath his scars and discover the story behind them. I wonder what he was like before whatever happened that did this to him—if he's angry because of it, if he's a different person, if he lost a part of himself.

I brush my fingers along his face, tracing the edges of his scars that travel down his forehead and around his eye and nose. I feel the tight, bunched skin on his cheek, and work my way to his neck, stopping when his T-shirt prevents me from going any farther.

He's frozen under my touch, his fingers resting on my lower back. I bring my other hand up to the other side of his face, rubbing my fingers along his stubble, a prickly difference compared to his smooth, shiny scars. He sucks in a breath, closing his eyes, just letting my fingers explore every groove of his face.

"You are supposed to be spending time with your father."

I jerk my head up to Mom standing next to her car with her arms weighed down with bags from her favorite department store, including one from the makeup counter.

I tug out of Xander's arms. "He said he had some work to do."

Xander meanders forward, extending his hand. "Can I help you carry your bags, Mrs. Caraway?"

Mom steps back, swinging the bags out of his reach and gives him the once over. "No, thank you." Her voice is so cold I expect to visibly see her breath fog from her lips.

I stroll over to Xander and take his hand. "Come on." I tug him back.

Mom sets the bags on the ground and places a hand on her hip. "Where do you think you're going? I did not give you permission to go anywhere."

"I don't need your permission," I snap. Anger rolls through me. Mom used to never act like this. She never gave a damn about any boy I dated as long as she knew I was careful. She'd remind me daily about the birth control she had me get when I was sixteen and that was that. She was always hands off. "The rules are that we can go anywhere we want as long as we don't break the law or miss curfew. Do you even know where Caleb is? Would you even ask?"

Mom snatches my arm and locks her fingers around my wrist. Her French manicured nails dig into my skin. "I don't have to answer any of your questions. I'm giving you ten seconds to get in the house right now. I will not allow you to be around someone like him." She turns to Xander. "It would be in your best interest to leave and stay away from my daughter. I will not allow a boy like you to have a bad influence on her. She's been through enough."

My mouth falls open and heat travels up my neck and into my cheeks. I can accept my mom being horrible to me but not to Xander. He's done nothing to deserve the hatred emanating from her.

Xander glances from me to my mom, and then to the house, like he's hoping my dad will come out at any second to intervene. "I'm sorry if you feel that way, Mrs. Caraway, but I think you've gotten the wrong impression of me."

I squeeze his hand. I hope he realizes that he's not helping the situation by trying to convince Mom to give him a chance. She's already made up her mind because of what Caleb had said. She'd hate him regardless just because of the way he looks. It's why she hates me now. She's bitter and vain and shallow.

"Excuse me? I know your kind, and you'll say anything to

manipulate the situation."

"Mom!" I shake out of her grip. "Xander's not manipulating anyone."

She narrows her eyes. "This isn't a discussion. Now get inside."

I don't move.

She reaches her arm out to grab me, and Xander pulls me away before she can touch me. Her eyes practically bulge from her head when he starts tugging me down the driveway. I freeze when he clicks off the alarm on his Mini Cooper. Opening the door, he looks at me expectantly, but I can't move.

"You are forbidden from seeing him!" Mom yells.

Xander nudges my shoulder. "Please, come with me." He pleads with his eyes, and I want to get in the car and drive away with him. I want it so much that I step forward an inch, but then panic seeps into my stomach and the edges of my vision shadow over.

"I promise you'll be okay. I won't let anything happen," he says.

He looks so sincere about it. I almost believe him and get in, except it's the worst kind of promise a person can make. He has no control over anything that happens to me once I get in the car.

I shake my head and pull away. "You should just go."

His face falls, and my heart feels like it's about to shatter at any second. He shakes his head, disappointment clouding his eyes. A second later, he gets in and drives away, leaving me alone and feeling completely empty on the sidewalk.

***

I take deep breaths. There's no way around it. Valley View Road is nestled amid tract homes a block away. My hands tremble, and I clench them at my sides, staring at the street that haunts my nightmares. If I had the courage, I would charge forward, ignoring the whisper of Lila's voice, and head straight to Xander's house to tell him I'm sorry for being too afraid, for not going with him, for not telling him why I'm like this. I'd show him my scars, my vulnerability, and let him in on my secret promise. I'd explain that I'll only end up breaking his heart, disappointing him more than when I refused to go with him. Maybe that's what he needs—to be disappointed in me so he'll let go so I can.

I'm broken, and people don't like damaged goods. I tried to fix myself, put all my pieces back together, but they didn't fit. Too many were missing. I'd be lying if I said I wanted help. It's pointless to have a stranger tell me that time can heal everything, because I've given it time, and time only seems to make it worse.

I lose myself to my panic, flashing back to the accident.

After the noise of the wreck finally subsided, I remember how relieved I was when I heard the sirens. I sat as still as possible, trying not to think about the pain or the blood painting everything in its sticky, red color.

I clutched Lila's hand without saying a word. I couldn't. My chest hurt. I could feel the intensity of the heat crawling onto my stomach, and I didn't even fight against it. We were trapped together in a car that was supposed to be twice the size it was, stuck between the guardrail and the other vehicle.

There's a hole in my memory from when a Good Samaritan I never met pulled me from the broken window before the flames consumed me to hearing the paramedics yell back and forth to each other. I must've passed out, and somewhere in that time is when Lila died, and I didn't even know it. The doctors told me there was nothing I could've done. She bled too much, inside and out, and her organs just stopped working. I still think the doctors were wrong. If I was able to stay awake, I could've begged her not to leave me, threatened her even, but because I couldn't, she didn't, and now I'm without her.

"You lost or something?" a man asks from his porch, pulling me out of my memories.

I shake my head, breathing hard. Turning on the balls of my feet, I head back in the direction of the last place I want to be right now. I hate myself for letting a stupid street stop me from going to Xander. I hate how the tears sear down my cheeks and how every step takes me farther away from him. And I hate how much he makes me regret making my promise, and also how I just want my forty-one days to be up. Because after that, there will be nothing left to hate.

Chapter 8

thirty-eight days

THE LAST TWO days of school have been excruciating. I only saw Xander for a few minutes on Thursday, and then Friday, I didn't see him at all. A million thoughts whirl through my mind. I stroll down Fire Mountain Road in the direction of the cemetery, trying to process everything.

I shouldn't be so hurt. Not only was Mom a nightmare, but I was a coward. It didn't help that Xander looked at me like I'd broken his heart, and I couldn't even summon a measly apology for how horrible Mom acted. I bet he thinks I'm no different than her, since I couldn't even find the courage to tell him anything except asking him to leave.

I have no idea how I'm going to fix this or even if I want to. It's probably better that Xander distances himself from me now, since—

I sigh when I reach Lila's grave. "What should I do, Lila?" I ask, plopping down on the grass. Pulling a pair of scissors from my tote bag, I slowly trim the grass around her stone. "It feels almost too late to apologize."

I can almost hear her saying, "It's never too late to apologize, Cee. Just suck it up, send a text, and if he doesn't accept it, then to hell with him."

Those are the exact words she told me the day before of our sophomore homecoming dance when I had turned Cameron Hartman down because I was still stuck on Scott, but I didn't want to go alone since Lila had a date.

The last thing that I wanted was to end up as a third wheel to Lila and Gabe Aguilar, her own rebound from Jared. We were sitting in my room with Lila curled up on my bed with her chin resting on her knees while she painted her toenails the same color blue as her dress. I sat at my vanity table, looking through the few celebrity pictures I had printed off in hopes that Lila could recreate one of their hairstyles on me, which she couldn't, and we laughed about it for days when she got the comb stuck in my hair when she attempted to tease it.

"Suck it up, Cee. I don't want to have to break Gabe's heart," she said. Her nose crinkled as she peered up at me.

"He's just a Rebound Boy, remember?" I said with a laugh.

She rolled her eyes before she slid off the bed and crossed the room. "Here, I'll do it."

I protested, but she snatched my phone away and tapped the screen a few times before she set it down in front of me. We both waited the excruciating thirty seconds it took for Cameron to reply.

When my phone vibrated, I swiped it off my vanity out of

fear, and Lila caught it with a laugh. She squealed and held it up. "You're going to homecoming with Cameron!" She waved my phone around so I didn't even have a chance to read the screen. She didn't even let me reply and did it herself.

I'll never forget how embarrassed I was that she used a dozen purple hearts after she replied, *Can't wait!*

Pushing the thoughts away, I pull my phone from my tote bag and set it among the pile of grass I trimmed from Lila's grave, like having my cell close enough will somehow magically summon Lila to reply for me.

Instead of texting Xander, though, I pull out my notepad and begin to write.

Lila,

I don't know what has gotten into me. Every time I think about Xander, I can't help not thinking about anything else. He makes it so easy to forget what a jerk Caleb is or how unbearable Mom is. But then I go and ruin it. I don't know how much more I can take. It's like the world doesn't want me to even find an ounce of happiness in my remaining days. It's like it doesn't care what happens to me. Maybe I shouldn't drag things out anymore. Thirty-eight days seems like forever. Maybe it's better if I forget everyone. I don't think anyone would care anyway. I just, I don't want to leave things like this, you know? You were always the lucky one. I miss you. Bye for now.

I twist the letter around the daffodils Dad had picked up at the grocery store last night and rubber band it in place before I shove it in the underground vase. I'd give anything to get a response from Lila, to have her snatch my phone away and embarrass me with Xander. But I'm alone now.

My phone lights up, sending my heart racing, but it isn't a text from Xander like I had hoped. It's one from Dad asking if I'd be home for lunch.

Me: *Depends.*

Dad: *Mom and Caleb went to Rita's.*

Me: *Give me an hour, K?*

Dad: *I checked my pockets, I'm all out.*

I roll my eyes, holding my cell in my hands. Switching between messages, I pull up the last conversation I had with Xander. He had told me he couldn't wait to see me.

After a moment of hesitation, I find my nerve and quickly text, *I'm sorry.*

My phone lights up like he's going to respond, but then nothing happens.

He never responds.

***

On day three hundred and fifty, when I was finally settled at home and out of the hospital, my phone was bombarded with hundreds of texts. I had never received so many from different people, that I was sure someone had given out my number to the world, or at least to my school.

The only person who would ever text me a hundred times was Lila, and even then, it was always silly stuff like how she'd bet me five dollars she could get Caleb to make us lunch or how cute the hottie coming our way was, because with Lila, the only time we really needed to text was if we were having a private conversation because we were always together.

The first text message I had read was from Renee Mills, a girl who threw awesome parties and who Lila and I would occasionally hang out with, but we were never more than acquaintances. Renee had sent me a text that was so long that I almost didn't read it after the first line, where she declared how much she missed Lila.

I was angry—not because she had missed Lila—I was pretty sure the universe had missed Lila, but because not once had she mentioned that she had missed me. I hadn't been in school in weeks, and I was feeling absolutely miserable, that if she had mentioned anything other than how sad she was or how much she missed Lila, I might've been okay. I might've responded. Instead, I immediately deleted the text and her number, along with the dozens of others all sent my way.

Because when it came to me, I was the lucky one. I was the survivor, the miracle girl. I got to live and breathe and grow old all while Lila was just gone. No one cared that I lost my best friend, only that she was lost. No one even really welcomed me back. How could they miss me when Lila was the one gone forever?

Maybe they were right. Maybe you can't really miss someone who isn't truly gone. But I feel gone already. But I doubt I'll ever be missed.

"Hey, kiddo," Dad says, drawing my attention from the blank screen of my phone. "You expecting a call from Hollywood or something?"

I shake my head, my hair flying against my cheeks. "No, the lottery."

He laughs.

I don't. Because I'm pretty sure the chances of getting a call from the lottery or Hollywood are better than getting a text from Xander.

It's been hours, and he still hasn't responded. I don't think he ever will.

Leaving Dad in the living room, I head to my bedroom and close the door to face my calendar. I scoop up a sharpie from my desk and cross off today's date. *Only thirty-eight to go.*

Chapter 9

thirty-six days

XANDER WASN'T WAITING for me at my door this morning like I had hoped, even though I knew he wouldn't. Dad offered to walk with me to school, probably feeling guilty over the way Mom treated his new best friend, but I turned him down. If I can't be with Xander, I'd just rather be alone.

Everyone at school was already in vacation mode, with the long weekend just days away, and it seemed like half of my classmates decided to start it early because more than the usual amount of desks were empty.

I expected to bump into Xander at lunch, hoping I could tell him I was sorry and only trying to respect Mom's wishes, but he never showed up. I texted him a few more times, receiving no response, and I can't blame him for not talking to me. I wouldn't want to either after the way my mom treated him.

Finally, after sitting alone in my room for over an hour, I decide to call him from my house phone because I'm afraid he won't answer if I try from my cell.

The line rings a few times, and I prepare myself to leave a message when a high-pitched, feminine voice answers. "This is Xander's phone."

I'm tempted to hang up, but instead, I say, "Hi, Elaina. Can I speak with Xander, please? It's important."

I hear an intake of breath and expect her to tell me no when Mom's voice bellows through the line. "If you don't get off the phone right now, you're grounded."

I sigh, creating static. "Never mind, Elaina," I say because I can hear her soft voice muffled through the phone, like she's talking to someone she doesn't want me to hear.

I hang up without waiting for a response and pad across my room to head downstairs when I find Caleb lurking on the other side of my door. He nudges my shoulder until I let him in, and then he shuts the door behind him.

Just seeing his arrogant face gets under my skin. "Get out of my room."

He crosses his arms and doesn't move. "We need to talk."

"I have nothing to say to you."

"I have something to say to you."

"I don't want to hear it."

He sighs, moving forward to sit on the edge of my bed. I stand with my hands on my hips, impatiently tapping my foot. If I didn't think he'd fight back, I'd try to smother him with my lavender-scented pillow.

"Come on, Cee. We used to be friends."

"Until you started acting like my dumbass brother."

He chuckles. "I *am* your dumbass brother."

I glare. "Who is trying to make my life miserable."

"That's not fair. I'm just trying to look out for you."

I point to the door. "Get out."

The last thing Caleb is doing is looking out for me. If anything, he's trying everything in his power to see that I can't live my remaining days the way I want to. For the first time in who knows how long, I've found a little piece of sunshine on my never-ending rainy days, and he wants it to go away, leaving me cold and alone.

He pats the bed next to him. "Not until you hear me out."

"I'll hear you, but I'm not going to promise to listen."

He sighs and pats the bed again, and I reluctantly shuffle to the opposite side and plop down. I snatch my pillow up and cradle it against my chest just in case I do feel like smothering him.

"I don't want you to see Xander anymore."

He says it so seriously, so demanding, I lean forward and smack him upside the head with the pillow. "Get out before I end up in prison for murder."

He leans away when I try to hit him again, this time, with my open palm.

Grabbing my hands, he squeezes them between his until I stop struggling. "Let me tell you why. You need to understand that I'm not asking this for no reason."

"You have one minute."

"Do you know what it was like for me getting a phone call from Dad, telling me that you had been in a car wreck and that they weren't even sure you'd live through the night?"

I press my lips together at the pain stabbing my insides. We've gone over a year without talking about it, and now all of a sudden he wants to? This is crap. Complete crap. When I needed someone to talk to, he wasn't there to listen. He avoided me until the day he offered to take me to visit Lila's grave, but before that, it was like I'd not only lost one best friend but two.

I squeeze my eyes shut, rubbing circles on my temples. "Couldn't have been worse than being in the accident."

He drops my hands. "It was like someone punched me in the stomach over and over again. I almost lost it because I almost lost you. And that wasn't even the worst of it."

My anger dwindles. "What was?" My voice cracks as I ask.

"How I almost lost you all over again when they told you Lila wasn't in recovery but gone. It was like watching someone rip your heart out and smash it on the ground. I was sure you wouldn't survive that. I didn't think I could."

"I almost didn't." *I haven't.*

"And that's what scares the hell out of me. You looked so empty and sad, like you could break any second. You still do sometimes. Like the other night when Mom got all crazy. If Dad wasn't here, I didn't think you'd ever come home."

I tuck my hand under my armpits so he doesn't see how badly I'm shaking. "You did that to me." I can barely form the words.

Tears line Caleb's eyes, and he runs his hand across his face, wiping them away before they can fall. "I'm sorry for that. I'm so, so sorry. I just—I just want to protect you."

"Why from Xander?"

"Because I'm afraid he'll hurt you."

"But *you're* hurting me. Mom's hurting me. Xander makes being alive a little more bearable."

His lip trembles, and I can see how my words kick him while he's already feeling down. "That's what bothers me, Cee. What if he decides to leave you? Or something happens? You're already only hanging by a thread, and I don't want some guy to be the reason it breaks. I can't stand by and watch your heart shatter all over again."

I twist my lips to the side. Caleb has it backwards. Xander's not the one who'll push me over the edge. You can't be pushed if you're willing to jump.

"Xander won't break my heart." Because I'm not even sure he'll ever talk to me again anyway. This argument might end up being pointless.

"How do you know that?"

"I just do. Now trust that I can take care of myself."

He doesn't look convinced, but he nods. He sits on the edge of my bed, staring at his hands. "I miss her, too," he says without looking up. "More than you know."

He glances at me, and my mouth falls open because for the first time, I can almost feel his pain. He looks tired and defeated, and I don't know why I never thought about this before. When I look into his eyes, I see something I've never noticed. I see love. I see his love for my best friend, and all this time I've been so concerned with my own loss that I didn't recognize his. It wasn't always just me and Lila. Caleb spent a lot of time with us, too.

Every summer up until last year, Dad and Mom would rent a beach cottage in the northern part of San Diego, and every year since the third grade, Lila always came along as my plus one.

The summer before high school, Dad decided it would be a great idea to go during mine and Caleb's birthday, and for our present he paid for a week's worth of surf lessons for the three of us.

I'll never forget how excited I was, practicing getting up on the board in the warm sand, the way Surfer Babe Bobby, our instructor who was only two years older than me, showed us. We each had a foam long board, which were heavier than you'd think when you had to lug it four blocks from the surf shop, trying not to take out pedestrians and the side mirrors of cars parked along the street, that we had positioned in a row on the sand.

Lila wore her famous white bikini that made her look super tan in comparison to me and showed just enough of her butt to be sexy without being too revealing. I wore my favorite pale pink bikini with matching cotton shorts, because my assets were on my chest, so I liked to keep the attention where it was deserved.

I remember the way Lila and Caleb joked around, and the way he snuck glances every time she positioned herself to stand. It never even dawned on me that he liked her like that, because I was even checking her out that day.

"If a shark is swimming my way, would you jump in front

of me and let it snack on you?" she asked, tossing her dark hair over her shoulder.

He rubbed his chin and took his time answering. "What would I get out of it besides a missing limb?"

"I'll love you forever," she said in her sexy voice. "And ever and ever."

Caleb smiled. "You better."

She laughed. "And ever and ever and ever."

Surfer Babe Bobby chuckled at the two of them, then winked at me and whispered, "I'd do it for you for a kiss."

After that, I spent a lot less time learning to surf and a lot more time getting to know my surf instructor. Caleb and Lila spent a lot of time together that trip, and I should've suspected that it was more than just friendly flirtation. At least for Caleb. I guess I just brushed it off because the next week when we got home, it was just like it was before we left. Lila and I glued at the hip, and Caleb trailing behind us.

I scoot across the bed and rest my hand on Caleb's shoulder. "Did you ever tell her how you felt?" I ask, knowing he didn't because Lila would've told me.

He pinches the bridge of his nose like it's bothering him. "I waited too long. I never got the chance."

"I'm sorry," I whisper, feeling close to my brother for the first time in what feels like forever. "I wish you would've told me sooner."

"It never felt like the right time."

"You know, I think you and Lila would've been perfect together," I say. I don't say it because he's my brother, but because I believe it. And it brings tears to my eyes. Because Lila will never get to know, and Caleb will always regret not telling her.

He doesn't respond. All he does is hold my hand and wait for me to pull myself together.

But even though I pretend to hold myself together, I'm already torn apart.

Chapter 10

thirty-five days

I SKIP DINNER after another disheartening day at school. Xander finally showed his face, but he didn't talk much over Yessica and Bridget. And when the bell rang for fourth period, he said he had to use the bathroom and left with a polite good-bye. I hate how he's pulling away. I hate how I don't want him to.

I stare at my cell phone, thinking it might be broken. I still haven't gotten a response from Xander, and I'm starting to think that my mom canceled my phone or something. It would explain why Xander hasn't responded and why he's been distant at school. I'm anxious with the thought.

He doesn't seem like the type to just stop talking to some-one. *How do you know? You don't even know him that well.* Pushing the nagging thought from my mind, I decide to text him one last time. If he doesn't respond, then I'll force myself to ask him about it at school. At least then I'll know whether or not I'll have to write him a letter.

I click open my messages.

Me: *Please, stop avoiding me.*

I don't even have a chance to set my phone down before it chimes, alerting me of a message.

Xander: *Okay. Meet me?*

My stomach sinks. He was avoiding me.

Me: *Where?*

Xander: *On the corner of Hillcrest and Sunset.*

I glance at the time. It's well past my curfew, but I slip on my Converses, yank my black hoodie over my head, and shove my phone into my pocket.

I pad out of my room and downstairs, making my way through the dark house. I disable the alarm and stroll right on out, knowing that my parents and Caleb are asleep. After clicking the door closed, I stand on my porch for a few minutes, considering going back inside. Meeting Xander before midnight is a little insane for me on a school night, and I don't know how much good can come out of it.

But I need to see him, to talk to him. When I'm around him, it's like nothing in the world matters except the feeling of his strong hands holding onto me, keeping me together. I want so badly to apologize and make this work, because I don't know if I can handle any more what-ifs. I have enough of those haunting me as it is.

When I turn onto the sidewalk, I tug my hood up and shove my hands into my pockets. At this time of night, I force myself to walk with purpose instead of allowing my annoying fears to take over. I should be fearless by now, without a care about what happens to me, but I've already lost enough control of my life. At least with my end, I know I'll have complete control.

I reach Hillcrest and pass by Yessica's house on my way to Sunset. Light shines from her room, and I wonder what she's doing. I wonder if I knocked on her window if she'd look at me like I was crazy. Instead, I keep going until I see Xander leaning his back against his Mini Cooper.

My heart picks up pace, and I resist running to him and flinging my arms around him. He tucks his hands into his pockets as he watches me walk to him. His lips don't glide into his usual lopsided smile. He looks tired and sad more than anything, like I'm the last person he wants to see, even though he was the one who wanted me to meet him.

Goosebumps crawl up my arms under my hoodie in the chilly air, making the tremble in my hands even worse.

Without wasting time on informal greetings, I jump right in and say, "I'm so sorry about my mom. She's a bitch."

He nods his head. "It's not the first time someone hated me based on assumptions because of the way I look."

The breath whooshes out of me. Not because he thinks Mom doesn't want me to be with him because of the way he looks, which I know is part of the reason, but because he's dealt with it before. I know people are heartless and cruel. If I didn't, I wouldn't be hiding under so much makeup and concealing clothes, but I absolutely hate how easily he accepts it. Because I never could.

I stare at him for a minute, my teeth chattering. I feel so cold inside and out. "T-that's n-not it."

The corners of his lips turn up, and he steps closer and pulls my hands from my pockets, blowing his warm breath onto them. "You're cold. Come on, I'll start the car."

I pull my arms away and shove my hands back into my pockets. "I'll survive." *And if I don't, it's not like it matters.*

Ignoring me, he strolls around the car and opens the driver's door, bending inside to stick the key into the ignition. "Please, get in. I promise I won't drive anywhere." He folds the seat forward. "Look, we can even sit in the back."

My chest tightens while shadows threaten the edges of my vision. I feel like if I get into the car now, I'll die. I know I'm contradicting myself; it's just I don't want to die like this. I know exactly how I'm planning on going, and it's not in a car. I can't go through that again.

My breath comes shallow as I fight against the fear crawling across my skin. *Just get in. Just get in. Just. Get. In.* I chant the words over and over, commanding myself to do it.

I slip my leg in first and duck so I don't hit my head on the roof. The leather seat freezes the sliver of skin showing on my lower back, but the warm air from the heater takes the chill away. I close the door, and Xander grabs my hand and squeezes my fingers.

My eyes stay glued to the door. I lean forward so I'm prepared to jump out if the scream burning in my throat doesn't subside.

"It's okay. I'm here. I'm not going to let anything happen

to you."

His fingers glide under my chin, and he turns my head so I'm facing him. I focus on his bright green eyes until the edges of my vision blur, and then I release a tiny breath, letting my panic melt away in a shudder.

"It's okay," he whispers over and over again, holding me against him while I rest my head against his shoulder.

When my breathing starts to even out, I say, "I think I'm okay now."

He kisses my forehead. "You say it like you didn't think you would be."

"I didn't. It's just—it's just, I had a bad experience with a car."

He stares at me expectantly, and for a split second I consider telling him.

"My grandma got into a pretty bad wreck last year," I lie.

He nods sympathetically. "I can understand why you're afraid."

I suppress the guilt threatening to bring me to tears. He knows nothing about my past, and I want to keep it that way because it's hard to deal with the pitying stares and empty words people say when they don't understand that it only makes me feel worse.

I decide to change the subject. "I didn't think you were ever going to talk to me again, you know. It really hurt. You just need to understand, my mom, she—"

"I thought that maybe she was right. That I'm not good enough for you. Look at me," he says, waving his hand over his face.

"Xander..."

He's always seemed so confident and sure of himself; I had no idea he'd think that he's undeserving of anything, especially me. What he doesn't know is I think he's too good for me. That maybe I really don't deserve to have him around because I'll just hurt him in the end.

I open my mouth to tell him this, but the words refuse to come. So I kiss him. I kiss him desperately, locking my hands around his neck, shifting my legs over his so I'm on his lap. His fingers press into my lower back, and his lips part, his tongue tasting of spearmint gum. My body tingles everywhere, and I imagine what it would feel like with his skin against mine; what it would feel like to have his hands touch the burn marks across my chest and the thick, puckered lines trailing around my stomach and up my sides.

My breath catches when his fingers find the bare skin on my lower back, and I freeze. I want him to touch me. I want it so much that tears burn on the backs of my eyelids, but the thought of him discovering the ugly marks scares the crap out of me. No one has ever touched them before besides me and the doctors who left them behind.

He pulls away, searching my eyes.

I fake a smile. "I couldn't resist," I whisper. "It was the only way I could think of to show you that you were wrong. You're perfect for me."

Chapter 11

thirty-four days

THE DASHBOARD CLOCK flashes twelve-thirty. Xander holds my hand as music fills the silence between us. It's not awkward or uncomfortable, and just being next to him is enough for me. His thumb traces circles on the back of my hand, and my eyes begin to feel heavy, but I'm not ready to go home and go to sleep. Even though it's officially another day, I want this moment to last.

I turn toward him, knocking my knees against his. "Being with you is totally worth being grounded." I don't know why I say it, especially if I'm not even sure if it's true, because I don't want to spend my last days confined to my room with the person I hate most in the world.

"Maybe I can talk to your dad."

I shake my head. "It won't work. He's leaving again tomorrow night until next week. When he's gone, my mom has total control."

His brows furrow so low, they cover half his eyes. "I can't believe she hates me so much because of the way I look."

A knot forms in the pit of my stomach. "It's not that...well not completely."

His eyes bore into mine. "Then what?"

I pull in a long breath and exhale until my chest begins to hurt. It's so hard bringing the words to my tongue without spitting them out in a stream of incoherent babble. It's more than just the scars. It's how he got them. It's something I don't care about and don't really want to know, because for me, it doesn't change anything. It doesn't change Xander and how he makes me feel. Well, maybe just a little. What if it's something as terrible as what Caleb told Mom? What if he refuses to talk about it?

The way he's looking at me—with his bottom lip sucked in, his lip ring sideways, and a small line between his brows—I know there's no way around it. He wouldn't believe me if I told him it isn't important.

"There are a lot of rumors," I start, "about you. And Caleb told my mom the one he's heard. She totally flipped out, and my dad tried to calm her down and everything, but she wouldn't hear it. I tried to stand up for you, but the thing is— the thing is, I didn't know what to say."

He smiles, surprising me.

"You think this is funny?"

His fingers play with my sleeve. "Is this your way of asking me how I got my scars?"

My eyes widen. "What? No! I'm just telling you what happened. It doesn't matter to me."

"It was a stupid accident. Totally my fault. When I was eleven, my brothers let me tag along with them to this beach party held by one of their friends. There was this huge fire pit everyone was sitting around, you know, drinking, hanging out."

My stomach churns, all the different scenarios of how he was burned flying through my mind.

"And then this guy, Chase McAdams, announced he was going to really get the party started, and he jumped over the fire. I thought he was the shit, like Superman or something, and then I thought to myself, I can do that, too. The problem was that Chase was a good two feet taller than I was, and I wasn't expecting to trip on the loose sand. The last thing I remember is some girl screaming her head off, and I woke up in the hospital looking like this." He sweeps his hand over his body. "But a lot worse."

Tears burn in the corners of my eyes, and I feel horrible. "There was nothing the doctors could do?" I shift my eyes away because the question sounds harsh as it comes out of my mouth. But I couldn't stop myself.

The doctors, my mom, everyone who came to visit me tried to talk me into fixing myself, like I was some hideous crea-ture that no one would be able to look at if I didn't. But I re-fused after the reconstructive surgery I already had. Not because I was afraid of the pain or the risk of it, but because the scars are a constant reminder of what I've been through. And really, a part of me died with Lila, and even if the doctors could've transformed me into what I used to look like, I didn't want it. I still don't. I don't want to be that girl anymore.

Xander sighs, and I look at him. "Sure there was, but my parents didn't have the money. My mom was working on her doctorate, and my dad couldn't get more than substitute teaching jobs at the time. Taking care of five kids costs a lot."

I don't know what to say, so I just nod. He didn't choose to accept his scars, he was forced.

He brushes his fingers across my cheek. "Please, don't cry. As you saw, my parents have worked things out. They even told me that if I wanted to get plastic surgery, I could. But I decided against it. I'm already used to the way I look. This may sound crazy, but I kind of like it now."

I lean closer and kiss his cheek, the scarred one. "I like it, too." And I really do. I couldn't imagine him being any different.

He laughs. "Well, that's new."

"I'm serious. I think it's because—" I catch myself before I say, *because we're the same.* "It makes you unique. You know, adds some mystery. You should hear all the things people say."

He runs a hand through his hair. "Let me guess. Plane crash, rescuing a baby from a burning building, a bomb, gang initiation?"

"You know?"

"I made them all up. I learned a long time ago that if you make up awesome enough stories, people will think the scars are cool. If you don't, then you're just made fun of."

I wish I could make up some cool story to cover up for what really happened, but everyone knows the story. It's just not talked about anymore. I'm glad for that now, though. I hate when people remind me how terrible it was. How Lila was so young and had so much going for her, and me, the poor girl who lost her best friend.

I ended up asking Lila's mom if I could disable her social media pages because of it, and she let me on day three hundred and fifty three to go, right before she told me she and Lila's dad were moving to Texas. She promised her decision wasn't because of me; she said they just needed a little change. But I know that wasn't true. It was too hard to stay when I was the one still around and not her daughter.

The dashboard clock glares at me, and even though I would spend the entire night talking to Xander, I can't. I press my face into his shoulder, breathing in the traces of cologne clinging to his shirt, like if I breathe in deep enough, I could keep his scent with me through the night.

"I should probably get you home," he whispers into my hair.

He slides across the leather and out the door, and I panic when he thrusts open the driver's door and gets in. I'm out of the car in seconds, stepping back until I brush against some hedges in a stranger's front yard.

"Nope, not happening. I'm going to walk."

He raises his eyebrows, shutting off the engine. "I know. I was just turning off my car so I could walk with you."

Xander kisses me softly in front of Mr. Delany's house. I cling to his shoulders, not letting him pull away, and he laughs into my mouth, kissing me once more.

I wait until he disappears into the shadows before quietly making my way inside and up to my room. I flounce on my bed and bury my face in the pillow. It feels like I just drank a gallon of Dad's black coffee, my hands shaky and my body ready to bounce off the walls. My calendar glares at me in the blue light created from my alarm clock, and I turn over, trying not to think about the fact that I didn't cross yesterday or today off. *I'll do it when I wake up.*

I flip over again and reach for the box I keep on my nightstand. I haven't opened it in months, and I'm not sure if I should open it now. But I do it anyway. I need to lose myself in my memories of Lila.

The summer before eighth grade, my parents bought both me and Caleb digital cameras for our birthdays. It was the most expensive thing they'd ever bought just for me, and the same day, I decided I was going to be a professional photographer. Not surprisingly, Lila announced she was going to be a model; not just any model, but my model, and occasionally Caleb's if he promised to give her a copy of every picture.

The first couple pictures I snapped were of Lila twirling in the middle of my front yard with one of Mom's sun hats and a pair of her huge sunglasses she used to wear over her regular glasses before she got contacts.

I must've taken at least a hundred pictures, most of them blurry because I thought being a professional photographer only consisted of having a working index finger and a pretty subject, which I had, and I didn't bother learning any of the settings. But I didn't care because we were laughing so hard at Lila's signature pose of puckered lips, a raised eyebrow, and a hand glued to her hip.

"It's perfect. You look total glam," I said, showing her the photo on the tiny screen.

"I love it!" she said, touching the screen, leaving behind her fingerprint.

She took the camera from me, squeezing her cheek against mine, and snapped a picture of the both of us.

"Now this is super total glam," she said. She dashed away and into my house before I even had a chance to look. I followed after her and found her leaning over Dad's shoulder as he hooked the camera up to his computer.

Lila waved her hand over her shoulder. "Don't look yet. It's a surprise!"

I plopped on the couch and folded my legs under me. A few minutes later, she dropped a glossy printout of our picture on my lap with the words *Best Day Ever* typed across the top in bold, purple font.

It was the start of capturing every moment, so I could always remember them. And it wasn't just the good memories either. In the box is what Lila always referred to as my photo diary. Because with every picture I've ever taken, I wrote a caption on the back. A quick note explaining what was going on.

I scoop up a stack of photos and stare at the top one. It's one of the bad memories. Across the back in messy scrawl is *Worst Breakup Ever, Part Two.*

In the photo, I sit on the carpet in the corner of my room, my knees folded up to my chest with my arms clutching my legs. My hair covers part of my face, like a tangle of dark shadows, and my eyes are closed with mascara smudges painted down my cheeks.

At the time, I thought my life was over, like nothing that happened could be worse than when Cameron Hartman broke up with me in the middle of the quad during lunch for everyone to see. The only reason I let Lila take the picture was because she said that every memory mattered, repeating the same thing I told her when I took a picture of *Worst Breakup Ever, Part One.*

I set the picture aside and find the one I want to look at, the one of Lila and me sitting on a sheet in the front yard, smiling bigger than Mrs. Parks with her odd tooth to gum ratio, with the caption, *Best Memory Ever,* on the back. Nothing special happened that day, but it was one of the few pictures that Lila and I agreed that we both looked hot. And it really is one of the best memories I have of her. Because that day, I thought we'd be best friends forever.

***

Xander slides onto the bench next to me, slinging his arm over my shoulders. Bridget raises a single eyebrow and looks between the two of us, and I guess if I were her, I'd have been surprised, too, considering we barely said two words to each other the last week in front of my friends.

Bridget swirls her finger at us. "Did I miss something?"

I shrug. "It kind of just happened. Don't make a big deal, all right?"

"But it is!" Yessica says, her voice rising to a level I'm sure only dogs can hear. "You've been Ms. Untouchable forever. Caleb's going to shit bricks. I remember what he did to Jose last year."

My fingers curl into fists, my nails biting into my palms.

"And Levi! Don't forget about Levi," Bridget adds through a mouthful of fries. "All he wanted was to hang out with you at winter formal."

Yessica smacks her in the arm. "Knock it off. I think Xander can handle Caleb."

Xander smiles. "You're right, I can."

He squeezes my hand under the table. The gesture keeps me from getting up and storming off. I know Caleb won't hit Xander again, not after our talk, but I didn't even know about Levi. I thought I had said something wrong when he started to ignore me, and then I just forgot. I had no idea it was because of Caleb.

Bridget rolls her eyes. "Well, if it turns out you can't, I still need a date to prom. You're going, aren't you?"

Xander glances at me, and I keep my eyes trained on the half eaten turkey sandwich in front of me. I haven't thought about prom because I knew I wouldn't be going. It's the weekend after day one.

He bumps my shoulder. "You want to go?"

I brush back my hair that's fallen in my face. "No."

My friends gape at me like I've gone crazy, and it dawns on me what's just happened. Xander wasn't asking if I just wanted to go to prom, he was asking if I wanted to go with him, and I just rejected him in front of my friends.

My cheeks heat. "Prom's just not my thing," I add, begging Xander with my eyes to understand that it's not him, but a whole lot of other crap. Even if I wanted to go I wouldn't because I'd have to wear a dress, and long-sleeved, turtleneck dresses haven't been in season, like, ever. At prom, you accessorize with fancy fake jewelry not with scars. And it's definitely not the night I want to show people the real me.

He kisses my cheek. "That's cool. We could do something else."

I'm tempted to tell him to go with Bridget. I'm sure she'd guarantee he'd have a good time, but the thought makes my right eye twitch a little.

"My offer still stands," she quips, batting her eyelashes, which doesn't make her look as cute as she thinks. It looks like one of her false lashes is poking her in the eye.

I try to brush her off, but I notice her sparkly pink toenails brushing against Xander's jeans under the table and his legs inching toward mine.

I do the only thing I can think of—I kick her in the shin.

"Ouch! What the heck?" She bends over, showing off an excessive amount of cleavage from her low cut sweater.

I smile, but I'm sure I look like I'm baring my teeth. "Xander doesn't want your dirty feet on him."

Yessica barks a laugh and slaps her hand over her mouth. Xander's shoulders shake as he laughs silently. Bridget could kill someone with the look she's giving me, but then her lips split into a smile, not a fake one either. It's the kind of smile that has guys following her everywhere she goes, at least, when she allows it.

"Damn, someone grew some cajones over night," Yessica says.

"Totally." Bridget winks at me. "I like the new you. Way better than the quiet, boring Cee that's been sitting across from me since September."

Her words sink into my mind. The new me. She likes the new me. I know she's referring to how I've been acting since I came back to school because I never talked to her before then. She didn't know the old me, and that's another reason I sit here. These girls didn't notice my change because they had nothing to compare it to before.

Even though Bridget meant it in a good way, it bothers me. I've been through too many changes to count, and I'm tired of changing. Tomorrow when I wake up, I need everything to be the same.

Chapter 12

thirty-one days

I FINISH WRITING my letter to Lila and shove it into the front pocket of my hoodie. It feels like forever since last Saturday, and there aren't enough pages in the world for me to tell her everything, so I keep it short and simple.

I head downstairs to grab my makeup bag from my backpack that I left leaning against the wall in the entryway when I realized Dad was leaving again, for Los Angeles this time. It's not like LA is far, it's only an hour away, but it felt like he was leaving the country.

Mom leans her elbows on the counter when I walk past her. My backpack sits where I left it, and I unzip the front pocket and reach in and grab...nothing. My zebra print bag isn't where I left it.

Turning my backpack inside out, I drop everything on the floor and then toss the bag at the wall. Panic slides up my back, cold and painful, and a scream builds in my throat. *This isn't happening. This isn't happening. This isn't happening.* I chant the words over and over. Maybe it's in the bathroom.

I pad across the carpet and down the hall to the bathroom where I hate to get ready in the morning because Caleb is a bathroom hog. I doubt my bag is in there, but I have to look.

I search in the drawers and under the sink, praying that Dad put it away without thinking, but it's not there either.

Mom stands in the doorway. "Do you honestly think I'm stupid?"

My heart races in overdrive.

"I told you that if you saw him again, you'd be grounded."

I clench my teeth, breathing in quick breaths through my nose. "He goes to my school! I can't avoid him!"

She laughs. It's a cold, heartless sound, nothing like I remember it to be. "I know you snuck out the other night. I heard you leave."

My face falls, and she sees it immediately, smiling smugly. There's no way to lie my way out of this, and Dad's not around to overrule her stupid decision.

"Why did you take my makeup?" I know she did. I can see it in her eyes.

"Because it will guarantee that you won't just leave again."

"But I wasn't going to see him. It's Saturday. You know where I go on Saturdays." My voice is no louder than a whisper. "Please, just give it back. I swear I'll come straight home."

"Did you not hear me? You're grounded."

"But Lila—"

"Won't be going anywhere. You should cut back on your

visits anyway. I spoke to Dr. Fitzgerald a while back. You know, it's not healthy for you to spend so much time at the cemetery."

"She's my best friend!" I swipe at my cheeks as the tears trickle down.

"*Was.* Lila's gone, Coco. When are you going to get that? You have to let her go. People are going to think you're crazy."

"Like how you let it go? Like you let me go?" I smack the counter top, and Mom flinches. "You're still hanging on to the daughter you always wanted, like I'm magically going to wake up one morning and be exactly who I was. But that's never going to happen. Your daughter, your beautiful daughter who looked like you, she's dead. She died in the car accident. Don't you get it? Lila's not the only one who died."

Pushing past her, I dash up the stairs and into my bedroom. I catch my reflection in the mirror and snap my eyes closed when I see the ugly stranger with puffy eyes, a runny nose, and covered in scars, staring at me from the mirror. She looks sad and alone, and a little crazy with the way her eyes shift around wildly.

Hate and disgust seep into my every pore, and I scoop the bottle of Ginger Flannigan perfume Dad bought for me a couple of weeks ago and throw it at the mirror. It explodes in a glittering waterfall of glass, spraying across my carpet.

My chest heaves, deep, guttural sobs threatening to knock me off my feet. I clutch my bedpost as the room spins out of control. Everything swirls around and around, and I feel like I'm being sucked into a vortex.

I force my legs to work and stumble through the glass to

get to where my shoes are near the door, ignoring as shards pierce the bottoms of my bare feet. Dusting the glass from my heels, I shove my feet into my shoes without untying them and turn quickly to head to my dresser for the rest of my stuff. I trip on discarded clothes on my floor and fall to my knees in the glass. I don't even flinch as blood drips down my fingers and onto the carpet.

Sucking in a shuddering breath, I get up and grab my cell phone and sunglasses off my dresser, and then I tuck the box from my nightstand under my arm.

Pain swells in my body, and it feels like my scars have all split open to take me down before I can leave. I run down the stairs and out the door, clutching onto the only thing I have left of Lila, like it's the only thing that keeps my world from shattering.

***

I press my face into the soft grass around Lila's grave, digging my bloody fingers in as far as they can go, as I sob. Unbearable pain consumes me, and I think of how easy it would be just to die right here, right now, with Lila by my side.

My shoulders shake as my stomach convulses, and I cough and spit through my tears. "I-I'm so pissed off at you right now. You promised me, Lila. We freaking made a promise. We were supposed to live together or die together. How could you leave me? How could you?" I pound my fists into the grass. "We had plans. We were supposed to go to prom together and Europe. Did you forget? Did you think about me at all? You promised me you wouldn't die."

I push up on my elbows and flip the lid off the box, scattering the pictures across her grave. My digital camera thumps to the grass. "You know I haven't taken a single picture this year? I can't. I don't want the memories without you."

I wipe my nose on my sleeve and stare at the pictures. There are thousands of moments captured by each image, and I can't stand even thinking that this is all I have left. Stupid pictures with stupid captions. And I hate it.

The sound of my phone ringing reverberates over the sound of my ragged breathing, and I swipe my finger across the screen without taking the time to wipe my eyes to see who's calling because Dad owes me a phone call today.

I clear my throat. "D-Dad? You have to come home." My voice cracks, and I sniffle.

"What's wrong?"

My heart sinks, and I almost hang up at the sound of Xander's voice. He wasn't supposed to call me until tonight. I told him I was busy.

The sobs rake my chest so fiercely, just the sound of his voice sets me off all over again. "I-I need you."

"Where are you? I'm getting in my car right now."

I swallow hard. If I tell him where I am, he'll come, and then he'll see me. The real me. The broken and scarred girl that can't even stand to look at herself in the mirror.

"Tell me where you are," he says again as I hear the Mini's engine start.

I release a shuddering breath. "In the cemetery. The back section."

I curl up on my side and shut my eyes, praying the weight of my sadness will crush me before he can see me like this. If I pray hard enough, maybe someone will finally listen and see what a mess they made of everything. But like always, no one hears me. No one cares.

I don't hear Xander pull up over my never-ending tears, and before I realize what's happening, his arms slide under my knees and back, pulling me onto his lap.

"Oh, God. You're hurt."

I press my face into his chest. "I'm fine. It's just glass."

"Let me take you back to my house." He tenses feeling the tremble rolling through my body.

"Just hold me," I beg. And he does. He rocks me back and forth in his arms until the tears dry, leaving behind sticky trails on my cheeks.

With his arms around me, I feel so safe, like nothing else can go wrong. But if I believed that, I'd just be lying to myself. This year has been nothing but wrong. One day after another of horrible days that pushes me closer and closer to the day when I can finally let go.

"I'm sorry," I whisper, hugging his neck.

"There's nothing to be sorry about."

"But there is. And it's okay if you hate me, because it wouldn't be the first time." *Because I hate myself.* "Remember the other night in the car? I lied to you."

"So my scars do matter?" he asks.

I laugh through my sobs. I can't help it. It's so ridiculous that he assumes I lied about the one thing I was honest about.

He tugs off my sunglasses and looks into my eyes. He studies me, and I watch as his eyes trail lower to the scars slashing across my face, the scars I've spent so long hiding from the world.

"It wasn't my grandma who was in the car accident," I say after a minute. "It was me. And her." I point at Lila's grave with all our memories scattered across it.

He doesn't say anything. I stiffen, preparing myself for when he tosses me off him and leaves me here to think about how I screwed everything up. But he doesn't. He hugs me tighter and kisses my hair.

"She was my best friend in the entire world, and she died because of me. I wasn't paying attention, and I didn't see the car. I was supposed to die, too."

He pets my hair, cradling me against him. "Is this her?" he asks, picking up one of the photos from the grass. "She looks like she's a great friend."

He doesn't reference her in past tense, and it makes me feel a little better, because she is a great friend, the best, even if she isn't around anymore.

He collects a couple more pictures and flips through them, pausing to study one of me and Lila at the train station. I don't even have to read the back to know that the inscription says, *Lucky Number Seven.*

The photo was taken a month before the accident, on a cool Monday afternoon by a woman wearing the most ridiculous hat I had ever seen. It looked like a doll-sized top hat with these long peacock feathers glued to the back. It was pinned to the top of her head, slightly covering her forehead, and her hair was pulled back in a bun so severe, it looked like it pulled her wrinkles back in a temporary face lift.

Lila's eyes were squinting, and her smile was huge because she couldn't stop laughing. "That's an amazing hat," she said through her smile to the woman, and the woman chuckled and snapped the picture.

The train had pulled into the station seconds before, and we hopped on as soon as we had our picture taken, walking through the cars to the front where a sheriff always sat before occasionally going around to check tickets.

We sat down in the seats that had a table, Lila in the seat next to the aisle, and me by the window. We never sat across from one another—it was easier to whisper to each other that way.

I pulled out a pair of dice from my purse and set them on the table. "It's your turn to roll," I said, pushing the dice to her.

We never had a destination in mind, and once we rode the train until there weren't any more stops without having to get off and switch trains, so we created a game, roll the dice and get off at the stop that coincided with the number.

Lila cupped the dice in her hands, shaking them, and then held her hands open to me. "Blow us some luck, babe," she said, and I blew into her hands.

She tossed the dice. One fell off the table, and she bent over and looked at it. "It's a three. What's the other one?"

"A four," I said, knocking the die back and forth between my fingers.

She nudged my shoulder with hers. "Lucky number seven, Cee. It's going to be an awesome day. I can feel it."

I laughed. "How does it feel?"

She smiled. "Better than kissing Jared."

I bit my lip because if Lila thought anything was better than kissing Jared, it would be in one of our Best Ever categories.

And it was.

Stop number seven was near Mount Bernal Community College, and we strolled on campus and somehow managed to find the cafeteria, where we sat down at a table with these really hot guys laughing and joking around without even asking.

They totally believed we were in college, too, and the guy I'd nicknamed DM, for dark and mysterious, invited us to a house party that Friday night, which turned out to be the first and only college party I'd ever been to. It was the first and last for Lila. Looking back, I'm glad the dice landed on Lucky Number Seven, because if it hadn't, going to a college party would've been another thing Lila would've never done.

I wipe a tear from my eye, and I trace my finger over the photo. "You would've loved her."

Xander smiles softly, setting me back on the grass to scoop up the scattered photos. He stacks them in the box and twines the cord of my digital camera around his wrist.

I rest my head on my knees. "Can you take a picture?"

I haven't used my camera in over a year, and I'm not even sure the batteries work. Xander tilts his head to the side and frowns.

I slide my sunglasses back over my eyes. "Please. Even bad memories are important."

I don't move or pose, and I don't smile as he brings the camera up to his eyes and aims it at me. The flash goes off, and he looks at the screen, and I swear I see his eyes shining in the sun. But he blinks and they're back to normal. He tosses me the camera, and I stare at the stranger sitting next to Lila's grave with dirty, bloody hands holding herself together.

When I print it later, I already know the caption will say, *Xander Meets Lila: Day Thirty-One.*

Chapter 13

twenty-seven days

MY CLASSMATES RUSH around me while I sit in the middle of the busy quad instead of bee-lining straight for the nearest exit.

Pressing my phone to my ear, I say, "You can't just come home for the night? You were supposed to be here yesterday." Even though Mom returned my makeup to me for school, I still can't stand being around her, especially without Dad.

Dad releases a breath through the line. "I'm sorry, kiddo. Meetings got pushed back. Even if I left now, I'd hit traffic and who knows how long it'll take. Just hang on a few more days."

Tears prickle in my eyes. "I don't think I can."

"Oh, come on, Coco. This is hard on your mom, too. I know these last few months have been crazy, but I'll be home again soon enough. Just stay low until I am. Your mom's not purposely trying to ruin your life. You snuck out."

"Because she—"

"Kiddo, can I call you back? I have to take another phone call." It's like he doesn't hear what I say but does it even matter? Dad's never here. Sometimes, it feels like he doesn't want to be either.

On day two hundred and seventy-five to go, Dad had to go to New York, which was his first extended trip away from me since the accident, and I cried while sitting on the edge of my parents' bed while he packed. Three weeks was an incredibly long time for him to be away, and I told him that at least a dozen times.

"It'll go by in no time," he said as he zipped up his extra large suitcase. He pulled it from the bed and set it next to an empty carry-on he'd take to be able to bring something back for all of us. It made Mom less annoyed when he returned bearing surprises.

"Is this because I've been fighting with Mom about—"

Dad wouldn't even let me get the words out. "Of course not, kiddo. We both understand and respect your decision. Plus, I think you're still just as beautiful as you always were."

"Tell that to Mom," I said, trying my best not to glance at my reflection in the mirror above their dresser. It had taken me a long time to not want to break down and cry every time I passed anything shiny enough to see myself in.

Dad sighed and sat down next to me, hugging me against him. "She just worries about you. You've been through so much."

He was right. I had. It was enough to make me break down and cry as hard as ever. He sat next to me, drawing soothing circles on my back until his phone rang. I could tell he needed to leave, that there was no point in begging him to stay, so I sucked in a deep breath and got myself under control.

He stood up and faced me. "I'll call every day. And who knows, this might be a good thing for you and your mom. You both could use some mother-daughter time. Tell Caleb to get lost and find his own thing to do."

I forced myself to smile. "Sure, Dad."

After he had left, Mom spent a good hour complaining about how miserable the next three weeks were going to be without Dad. It was one of the only times since my accident that I had agreed with her.

I thought maybe Dad might've been right, that I just need-ed time alone with Mom to remind her how close we used to be. But all it took was her grabbing her car keys and telling Caleb and me that we were going out for dinner at Alfonzo's Italian for us both to realize that we would never fall back into how things were.

She had screamed at me for a good ten minutes to get in the car and then gave up after I turned around and locked my-self in my room. That was the first time I had realized I'd prob-ably never eat at a restaurant with Mom again. I was right.

Warm hands slide over my eyes, pulling me from my thoughts, and I tilt my head up to see Xander smiling at me. A dimple peeks out on his shaven cheek and his lopsided smile is enough to make me push from the table to face him.

"Can I walk you home?" he asks, stealing my backpack away from me before slinging it over his shoulder.

I frown at his question, not because I don't want Xander to walk me home, but because home isn't the place I want to be anywhere near.

"Can we go somewhere else?" I ask, turning my gaze down to look at our matching shoes.

"I thought you were grounded," he says. He reaches out to link his fingers with mine.

"I am, but my mom's probably not even at home anyway. Even if she was..." I let my words trail off.

With only a slight bit of hesitation, Xander pulls me with him as he heads toward the gate that exits to the front of the school. A few students hang out on the lawn in front of the Mark T. Hopkins High concrete and metal sign, and Xander waves at Gavin and Finley, two kids from my Calculus class. I force myself to nod and smile as we pass by them toward the sidewalk.

Twenty minutes later, Xander opens the door of Coffee Addicts for me, and I stroll in before him, taking in the familiarity of the place. I haven't been here since before my accident, and it hasn't changed one bit except there is an additional cork board full of printed photos taken in the lounge area that anyone can add to.

"Want to find us a place to sit while I order?" Xander asks.

I nod as I pull my wallet from my backpack, but he doesn't take my money. "Something iced, caramely, and with whipped cream."

As he goes to order, I stroll to the only available place to sit, which is a loveseat that faces the cork boards full of stapled on photos. I try as hard as I can not to search through the photos, but I can't help it, because I see *Coffee Saves the Day* in the same spot that Lila had stapled it over two years ago.

Lila was never big on coffee. She always complained it left a gross taste in her mouth, so she always went for the fruity tea—passion fruit was her favorite. It was the day before winter break and the day of the semester's finals and neither of us had gotten any sleep the night before. Lila had spent the night at my house because her parents were both out of town, but also because we had both gotten into the habit of waiting for the last minute to study. Procrastination was the love of our school life, and no matter how much we loved it, we regretted ever falling for it.

"I fell asleep during the last presentation in Gold's class," Lila said, the imprint of her spiral notebook on her cheek. "I don't think I'm going to survive the rest of the day."

I laughed. "If we run fast enough, we can get to Coffee Addicts and be back in time for Mrs. Davidson's class."

Her eyes lit up at the thought. "Genius, babe! I think I'll even get a coffee with a million espresso shots."

"You'll stay awake through Christmas," I said as Lila pulled me toward the back of campus near the grove where we'd make our escape.

"Sleep is for suckers, anyway."

"I'm a sucker."

"Duh, so am I."

We had made it to Coffee Addicts in ten minutes, but it took us double the time to get back to school, because Lila insisted that she had to drink her extra large, triple shot caramel coffee the moment she picked it up off the counter and before she made it to the door. She'd asked the barista to take the picture at the counter and the next time we went, she stapled it right in the center of the cork board, moving and re-stapling other pictures that were in the way.

Xander plops down on the seat next to me, and I turn my eyes from the pictures. He holds out a caramel coffee freeze to me with caramel whipped cream. His knee bumps into mine as he rests a cup of passion fruit tea on his other leg.

"That was Lila's favorite," I mention to fill the sudden silence between us. It's not like it'd matter if we said anything at all, the music blares almost too loudly from the overhead speakers that it's hard to even hear myself talk.

"She had good taste," Xander says.

"The best."

Xander smiles at me, holding my gaze for an extra long moment before I force my eyes away from his to look back toward the picture of Lila and me on the board. A second later, I find myself standing up and crossing the small space before I rip the picture from the wall and then return to my place at Xander's side.

We spend the hour talking about all the crazy things we've done, and most of my stories include Lila, because I haven't done anything worth talking about in a long time. Xander on the other hand? He can talk for days, and I don't mind listening to every little thing he says.

"I'm so boring compared to you," I quip, bending the straw in my empty cup back and forth.

He smirks, not showing his teeth, before he reaches over and tucks strands of my hair behind my ear. "I doubt it."

"No, rea—"

Xander cuts off my words with a kiss so sweet that I smile into his lips as I shift closer, sliding my hands up his shoulders to his neck where my fingers brush against the curls of his black hair that feel softer than my hair.

Slowly, we break apart. He smiles at me, slightly tilting his head toward me and laces his fingers through mine. My heart flutters in a good way, and I suck my bottom lip between my teeth. The way he's looking at me, the way his bright green eyes seem to look right into me—it's enough to make me blush. No one's ever looked at me the way he's staring at me now, drinking me in like nothing else in the world is worth his attention.

Blush crawls up my neck to my cheeks, my skin warming with every passing second. And just when I think I'm about to melt into a puddle on the couch, he turns his gaze away, the intensity in his eyes shifting within a split second as he notices something out the window behind me.

My phone vibrates in my pocket a second later.

Mom: *Get outside.*

My hands shake, and I consider responding no or not responding at all. But fear grips at my chest, my heart racing as it slides into my stomach just imagining how she'd react. I wouldn't put it past her to come inside.

Sliding my phone back into my pocket, I shift my gaze to Xander. "I have to go."

"I'm sorry," he whispers, leaning closer. "Want me to walk

you out?"

I shake my head. "It's probably better if you don't."

I can feel the heat of Mom's stare as she glares at my back through the window. Then, my phone vibrates again. I don't look at it, though. Instead, I force myself to my feet, offer Xander a weak smile, and then head outside.

The door doesn't even shut before Mom says, "Do you not understand what the meaning of being grounded is, Coco?"

I push out a breath of air through my lips. "I'm sorry, I—"

"Get in the car," she says, holding open the back door to her Mercedes.

I don't move or say anything. She knows me better than to think that I'm going to get in the car, especially with her behind the wheel.

"Excuse me? Did you not hear me? Get in."

I lick my suddenly dry lips. "Mom."

"Now." She steps closer, locking her fingers around my wrist and yanks me forward.

It's the last move I expected her to do, and it catches me off guard. I stumble, catching myself with my free hand on the frame. If I wasn't holding onto the frame, I'm pretty sure she'd shove me in the back so that I'd fall in.

"Mom," I say again. "Stop. I'll walk."

She releases a frustrated breath. "I think you're doing this just to be difficult. I know you, Coco. You couldn't wait to get your license. You love driving."

I stiffen. Clearly, she knows nothing about me. "Not any-more."

"I don't get it. Why do you insist on always acting so miserable? You make it so no one wants to be around you. If Lila were alive she—"

"She's not, though!" My voice rises through the air, and a few people stare at us from the tables outside the coffee shop.

Angry tears burn in my eyes, and I tug away from Mom. The moment I do, I catch Xander's gaze through the window, and it's enough to send me spinning on my heels and running even though Mom screams at me, humiliating me for no other reason than she can.

A car door slams and tires squeal, but I don't look back. I'm sure she'll figure out a twisted way to punish me later.

Twenty-seven days, I think to myself. Just twenty-seven more.

Chapter 14

twenty-six days

MOM WAS GONE when I finally forced myself to go home. I spent another hour outside Lila's old house just three streets over from mine, pretending that she'd come home at any second to let me in her room. It was the same routine anytime either of us was angry with one of our parents, like we could avoid punishment if we were together.

On day one hundred and sixty, Mom was especially in a bitter mood when Grandma showed up at our door unannounced while Dad was on a business trip to Hong Kong. Grandma, who is Dad's mom, came in with the best hugs in existence and spent a good ten minutes telling me how well I've healed and how she thought I was turning into such a beautiful young woman.

"She'd heal even better if she'd use the two-hundred dollar cream I bought her," Mom said from the kitchen bar. "It's supposed to work magic on scars."

Grandma looked Mom dead-on and said, "Well, I think she's healing just fine."

"But the cream could help her look normal again."

Grandma blinked once, twice, three times before she turned her gaze to me. "She looks perfectly normal to me."

"I'm not buying her that makeup forever."

"Charlotte," Grandma said, reaching out to touch Mom's arm. "There isn't anything wrong with Cee or her scars."

Mom huffed. "Tell that to me when she comes home crying because someone made fun of her."

"You say that like I'm hideous. Maybe you should look at yourself!" I screamed. Mom was far from hideous, but I was so upset with her. It never failed that she used the possibility of others hurting my feelings to disguise her own.

"Coco, that's uncalled for," Mom said. "You—"

I shook my head and ran out the door without listening to what else she had to say. I ended up at Lila's house, sitting on the curb, even though my best friend and her family had been replaced by strangers with a screaming baby I could hear through their open window.

I'd have given anything to see Lila's room one more time, but like Lila, that was stolen from me, too.

I draw a big X through the dates on my calendar that I'd missed before slinging my backpack over my shoulder to head to the door.

When I get downstairs, Caleb sits at the bar, scooping scrambled eggs into his mouth. I've been hidden in my room since last Saturday, so I haven't even seen him much except for a passing glance. He's given me my space as well.

He glances at me with a pitiful expression when I slide onto the barstool next to him. He sets down his fork, leans on his elbows, and sighs.

"Mom went to LA yesterday in a hurry. What happened?"

"Nothing. We got in a fight."

"Another one? The last one looked pretty bad. Took me hours to clean up your room." After Xander had cleaned and bandaged me up from the shards of glass from my broken mirror, I had come home to a somewhat clean room that smelled heavily of fruity fragrance. It still clings to everything. I didn't realize it was him.

My eyes drop to the granite counter. "That was all me. Sorry you got stuck cleaning it up. At least nothing was broken yesterday."

"Are you okay?"

I open my hands and show him the scabs on my palms. "All better now."

He shakes his head. "No, I mean are you *okay*?" He presses two fingers to my chest. Not in a perverted way or anything, just touching the skin over my heart.

The gesture reminds me of day three hundred and forty-three. I was sitting on the swing set in the front yard, crying because I was still healing and the swing next to me was empty. Caleb shuffled down the steps and sat in Lila's swing before grabbing my hand.

He asked me, "Are you okay?" and I remember the question seeming like the stupidest question anyone had ever asked me.

I glanced at him, my lashes heavy from tears, and I shook my head. "I hurt, Cabey."

I hadn't called him by his childhood nickname in years, and I felt so young saying it, but I needed Cabey to be back—the boy who people always said was a handsome version of me. The boy who grew into a man the summer between eighth grade and freshman year, who still thought I was the coolest girl to hang out with.

"You want some meds?"

I rubbed a hand across my wet cheeks. "They won't work on my heart. It hurts so much, Cabey. I want it to stop already."

He looked at me with sad eyes, which made my chest hurt even worse. He didn't say anything, just sat there holding my hand like we did when we were five.

I rocked on the balls of my feet. "Do you think she's mad at me?"

He didn't ask for what. He already knew what I was thinking about. "You know Lila could never be mad at you."

I knew he was right. Something changed within Caleb the weeks after the accident. He stopped going to parties, stopped hanging out with his friends. It was like he gave up everything I couldn't—wouldn't do.

I blink the memory away and cover his hand with mine. "I don't know if I'll ever be."

I think he sees the truth in my eyes, because a tear slips onto his cheek and he rubs it away with the palm of his hand. His shoulders shake, and I slide my arm across his back, hooking my hand around his side, and pull him closer to me.

He wipes his nose on his sleeve. "Please, try. Please, try to be okay."

His words sting.

"I will," I lie. I'm over trying to be okay, because no matter what I do, it's never okay. Nothing is ever okay.

Chapter 15

twenty-three days

XANDER KNOCKS ON my front door around noon, dressed in a pair of red and black board shorts and a black T-shirt. His lip ring sparkles in the sunlight peeking through the trees, and I stand on my tiptoes to kiss him. Sliding his arms around my waist, he lifts me off the ground, and I wrap my legs around him.

Caleb clears his throat from behind us. Xander sets me back on my feet, and I lightly punch my brother in the shoulder. His lips press together in a line, but then he says, "Hey, man. I think we got off to a bad start."

Xander nods. "It's cool, dude. I have sisters, too."

They bump their fists together, a gesture I feel ridiculous even attempting. The three of us stand together, just staring back and forth, and I lace my fingers through Xander's.

"Ready?" I ask. I tug him down the steps and away from Caleb's scrutiny before Xander can even answer.

Stopping halfway down the walkway, he turns back to my brother. "You're welcome to come over, too."

Caleb shakes his head. "Thanks, but I have a date. Just don't keep her out all night, all right?"

I raise an eyebrow. "*You* have a date?"

Caleb smiles and walks back inside before I have a chance to ask who she is. My brother hasn't been out with a girl since, well, I don't even remember. It's been a long time, probably because of his secret feelings for Lila I never knew about. Whatever it was, I don't care now. I'm just glad he's getting out again. He deserves it.

Xander moves in front of me and bends his knees, and I hop on his back, wrapping my arms around his neck. I kiss the skin below his ear, and he shivers, turning his head to kiss my lips.

After a couple blocks, he sets me on my feet and we walk hand-in-hand until we reach Valley View, and my feet stop working, just like every time I see the street.

He stops and looks at me, his brows furrowing. "This is the street where it happened."

He doesn't ask me, like he already knows because of the way I'm acting, the way I acted the last few times I was standing in this exact spot with him.

He presses his forehead against mine so the only things I can see are his bright green eyes looking into mine. "Close your eyes," he says. His breath is warm against my lips, and I shut my eyes.

The ground falls away as he scoops me into his arms. My

dark hair blows across my face and everything shakes when he breaks into a jog. I count the heartbeats pounding in my head, keeping from thinking about where I am.

He slows down after a minute. "You can open your eyes now." I do and he smiles at me. "See? I knew you could do it."

I kiss his nose. "I couldn't do it without you."

"Nah, you could've. But my way was faster."

When I enter Xander's house, his family swarms around me, hugging and kissing my cheeks like it's been ages since we've seen each other. I wonder if he told them what happened to me, but they don't mention it and neither do I.

Christian mans the grill again, this time with a pile of barbeque sauce slathered chicken. I sit at the edge of the pool and dip my legs in the cool water. Xander's brothers splash around in the deep end, and I laugh when Justin does a cannon ball and a wave of water sloshes over me, soaking my rolled up jeans.

"Scared of a little water, Coco?" He swims closer, and I jump to my feet and run directly to Xander who's stepping through the slider with a towel slung over his shoulder. My fingers run over the shiny scars trailing down one side of his chest. His arms wrap around me, pressing my hands harder against him, and we just stand there for a minute.

He spins me back toward the pool, and Justin winks at me. Xander motions to the empty lounge chair between his sisters. "I suggest you sit over there unless you want to go swimming in your clothes," he says, tilting his head at his brothers.

I let go of his hand. "Maybe later," I say, making my way

to the lounge chair.

Plopping down, I watch Xander dive into the pool. He barely makes a splash and pops to the surface with his dark hair slicked against his forehead. He looks so sexy with the way water drips down his strong shoulders. I'm tempted to jump in after him.

"My brother really digs you," Tonya says, slipping her sunglasses to the tip of her nose.

I lean my head back on the warm plastic. "I like him a lot, too."

"Not many girls can see past the scars, you know," Elaina adds, flipping to her stomach, craning her neck to look at me.

I nod, swallowing the lump in my throat, because she's right. Last year, it would've taken some time to look past them, and it sucks to admit that to myself. Because Xander is the most caring, sweetest guy I've ever met. He's so selfless and strong, and a lot of things I wish I was—wish I had been.

"I know exactly what you mean," I whisper so quietly neither hears me.

Xander's dad waves his tongs, and Tonya swings her legs off the lounge chair. She offers her hand out to me, and I accept it, letting her drag me around the pool and to the same picnic bench we ate dinner at before. Elaina trails behind us, her flip flops snapping as she walks, and she slides in across from me.

The afternoon sun shines its warm rays on my skin, and I lift my head to the sky when a shadow crosses my face. Xander kisses my forehead, dripping chlorine water on my cheeks, and I laugh when he shakes his wet hair over me.

His arm hooks around my shoulders when he sits, and water seeps into my almost dry jeans. "What would it take to convince you to go swimming with me?"

"A wetsuit," I say. "Or the dark."

He bumps my shoulder with his and smiles. "I think I can pull one of those off."

Lunch with his family is so normal. It's kind of funny how Christian went into every little detail of his workweek, and then had his wife and all his kids do the same.

It reminds me of when Lila and I would talk about our days late at night on the phone. We spent every spare moment together, and when we didn't we told each other every detail so it felt like we did. And nothing was ever boring. We always had our own fun commentary to add.

Xander squeezes my hand. "You're up."

I'm taken aback, not expecting that I'd be included. Elaina just finished talking about her week as an intern at some PR company that works with the local blood bank, and how she spent hours coming up with slogans like, "Show the love, donate blood," and "Vampires aren't the only ones needing blood." I chuckled at the cheesiness of them, but I couldn't come up with a slogan to save my life.

I shift in my seat, my mind going completely blank. I'd never been fond of public speaking, and this feels pretty public with the seven people staring at me.

I clear my throat and say the first thing that pops in my head. "I got to hang out with this really sweet guy."

I kiss Xander's cheek, and his family starts smiling and

making embarrassing comments, causing his cheeks to burn a deep red. He looks so cute, embarrassed in front of his family, and I lace my fingers with his under the table.

Holly leans her head on Christian's shoulder. "Sounds like you had a great week."

I catch myself when I realize I don't smile, and I force my lips to fake it. Because hanging out with Xander is the only thing I can share without having his family look at me with pity. Everyone's having such a good time, just mentioning a day in my life will ruin everything.

I shrug. "It had its moments."

***

Xander tosses me a pair of black shorts and a band shirt. He's still shirtless, and I admire the lines of his hips that disappear into his toned stomach from his bed. He scoops a tiny black bag off his dresser and slides a camera from the pouch before aiming and snapping a picture of me.

I raise my hand a little too late. "What are you doing?"

"Capturing a memory," he says. "Now change." He smiles before he closes the door.

I rub his shirt between my fingers and bring it to my nose. It smells citrusy and delicious, and I'm tempted to tuck it into my bag and just keep on my navy blue, long-sleeved shirt instead.

I roll off the bed and stand in front of his closet mirror. Tugging my shirt over my head, I stare at myself for a long moment. Burn marks pepper the skin just below my shoulders. I try to remember the moment I got them, but I draw a blank.

My fingers run over the railroad track scars caused by the car door folding in. There are so many strange scars all over my stomach, it's like the doctors chose spots at random to cut open and sew back together along with the burns scattered over me, some above my knees, across my chest, one small mark on the inside of my arm. I look like a doll that has been carelessly stitched together after a child had torn it apart. Except pieces feel missing.

I unhook my bra and then slide Xander's shirt over my head before shimmying off my jeans and stepping into the shorts. I tug them below my hips to cover the patch of shiny skin above my knee, before I pad across the carpet barefoot and step into the hallway. Xander's talking with his dad, leaning against the wall, and his eyes light up when he sees me.

"So, why did I have to change?" I ask.

He strolls up to me and presses his lips to my hair. "Because it's dark."

I let him drag me outside, where the porch light has been shut off and the moon is a tiny sliver in the sky, lighting the ground just enough so I don't trip.

I shiver, wrapping my arms around my chest. "It's cold out here."

"Not for long."

Xander scoops me in his arms, rushes to the edge of the pool, and jumps. The water's warmer than I expected, and I open my eyes, staring at the blackness pressing in on me. I blow air through my mouth, seeing tiny sparks of light reflecting from the moon, and just float underwater until Xander pulls me to the surface.

I kick my legs as I grip onto his hands, and he pulls us to the shallow end where I can touch the bottom with my toes. His T-shirt clings to me and goosebumps prickle on my skin from the cool air. Steam wafts from the water, and I run my fingers across the top, trying to lock it in my hand.

My lips find Xander's, and the water splashes between us. His hands touch my skin just under the hem of my shirt, and I let him. I trail my fingers along the contours of his muscles on his back, and he shudders, pulling me closer and kissing me harder. My back bumps into the wall and I bring my legs up and around his hips, pressing into him.

His feather soft lips kiss my jaw and trail down my neck. His tongue glides across my collarbone, sending electricity through me. I nibble his earlobe, and his lips find mine again, and he sucks on my bottom lip, his lip ring cold against the heat of his breath.

I pull away gasping, my lips tingling. I rest my head on his shoulder, and his fingers stay locked around my waist. He watches my eyes as his hands trail to my stomach, and I lean back, stretching my arms over my head, letting my head touch the concrete. His gaze trains on my face, and I force myself to stay completely still as he brushes his fingers up my shirt, tracing around my belly button and over my belly ring until they brush along where I know one of my biggest scars is.

Shooting up, I fling my arms around him, knocking him back, and he pulls me under the water with him. I break the surface, coughing, before I swim to the stairs and sit on the top step, curling my legs to my chin.

Xander splashes his way to me and wraps his arm over my shoulder. My tears blend with the chlorine water dripping down my face, and I can feel my foundation washing off.

He cradles my chin, pulling my face closer until his lips find mine again. "I didn't mean to upset you," he says through kisses.

I shake my head, smacking my sopping hair against my cheeks. "You didn't. It's just—" I take a small breath. "I have scars, too."

Chapter 16

twenty days

"MOM'S NOT READY for her vacation to end, so we're going to spend the rest of the week in San Diego at the hotel we got married at," Dad says.

I frown. Not because Mom wants to spend more time away, but because she's making Dad do it with her. "Okay," I say into the phone.

"Is your brother there?"

"No, I think he stayed late at school."

"You sure you haven't killed him yet? I can go over how to hide the body." Dad chuckles at his own teasing.

"Dad."

"I'm kidding, kiddo. Sort of." He laughs again.

"I'm hanging up now. Have fun, Dad."

"Do everything I won't. Don't worry, I've been saving up bail money."

I laugh when he snorts another laugh into the phone.

"Love you, Dad."

"Love you, too, kiddo."

I hang up the phone and lean my elbows on the cool granite counter. The last few days without Mom have been nothing short of glorious. Caleb's been out of the house more often than he is home, hanging out with some mystery girl he hasn't told me about yet.

My phone vibrates on the counter with a text message from Xander.

Xander: *Can you sneak out?*

Me: *Yeah. The warden is on vacation.*

Xander: *I'm outside.*

Instead of telling him to come in, I slide from my chair and jog through the house to find him standing on the front porch. I consider inviting him in, but something holds me back imagining him in my room, having to explain the lingering smell of fragrance, my broken vanity mirror, and my excessively drawn on calendar. It also doesn't help that it's light, and I'm extra nervous of where being alone in my room could lead. Because it's where I want it to go despite knowing how badly it could end—how badly it will end.

Xander leans forward and kisses me the moment after I close the door. I smile into his lips, slowly pulling away, and then I meet his bright green eyes. His lip ring rests sideways on his bottom lip as he stares at me before taking my hand.

"So, up for a walk? I have something I want to show you."

"What is it?" I ask, smiling as he pulls me down the walkway.

"A surprise."

"I hate surprises."

"We'll see."

Lila would laugh if she heard us. The thought sparks another memory in me while I stroll with Xander.

The month of my sixteenth birthday was magical. Lila declared that we'd be celebrating every day one way or another, and if we wouldn't have gotten in trouble for skipping school, we might've ditched the last two weeks altogether.

Four days before my birthday, Mom decided we needed to go get mani/pedis before going to get our hair done. I remember how much I loved the cherry red polish because it matched the cherry red streaks peeking through the bottom side of my hair. The only thing that could've made the day better was if Lila had gone along. I didn't know it at the time, but she had skipped out on a beauty day to set up a surprise adventure for me.

When I got home from getting my hair done, I ran up to my room to call Lila. As I opened the door, my mouth fell open in shock, and I couldn't believe how many balloons filled my room. Hundreds shifted on the floor and rose above my knees when I kicked my way in, and in the center was a huge bouquet of Mylar balloons with our favorite Disney Princesses from our childhood, some bright yellow happy faces, pink ones meant for baby showers, a few black graduation balloons, and my absolute favorite, a mermaid the size of me with a dozen clear balloons that were supposed to be her bubbles.

Attached to the mermaid, who we later named Pearl, was a

small pink envelope. I broke the seal and pulled out a smiling picture of Lila holding a piece of paper with a note that said, *I know you hate surprises, but this will be the year I change your mind. Go to the place we met for your next clue. And hurry up.*

I ran all around our neighborhood that day, picking up clues and small gifts she left behind. By the time I finally finished the scavenger hunt to find Lila, she had already started eating the chocolate cake she had baked especially for me.

"I told you to hurry," she said, smiling as she offered out a forkful of chocolate frosting with sprinkles.

I laughed and plopped down next to her, giving her a huge hug that rocked us both back and forth. "You're the best."

She dramatically batted her eyelashes. "I know, babe. I had to top the concert you took me to for my birthday."

"Well, you did."

"Were you surprised?" she asked, bouncing in her seat with so much excitement that I was pretty sure she had stopped by Coffee Addicts before she came here.

"Most definitely." I bumped her shoulder with mine. "And you know what? I think I actually might like surprises now."

She beamed a brilliant smile that lit up brighter than the sixteen sparkler candles Mom put on mine and Caleb's cake for our actual birthday. But that cake never did compare to Lila's, even if hers was half eaten. Because for once, I didn't have to share with my brother.

I'll never forget how she looked, sitting on her favorite star-patterned blanket on the concrete stage of Green Meadows Park, chocolate smeared down her chin, her eyes bright with happiness, holding a piece a cake she stuck a candle into that we could never get to light because it was too breezy that day.

I wish I had my memory box with me now so I could sort through it to find the picture of *Best Surprise Ever*.

After that day, I still told Lila that I hated surprises, but that it was only because no other surprise could top hers. She said that we'd see about that. But we never got the chance. The only other surprise I ever got from Lila was the one that came after our accident.

And it definitely sealed my hatred of surprises.

"Okay, close your eyes," Xander says, pulling me from my thoughts.

I stop on the sidewalk and turn to face him with a smile. "Do I have to?"

He grins as he nods. "Unless you want me to do it for you."

With an exaggerated sigh, I close my eyes and hold out my arms as Xander stands behind me, pushing me forward by my shoulders. As much as I really want to peek through my closed lids, I don't. It helps that Xander whispers over and over again for me not to peek because we're almost there.

After an excruciatingly long few minutes of carefully walking, Xander pulls me to a stop. His hands release my shoulders before he takes my hand and pulls me a foot forward. I startle when his warm lips brush against my cheek, and he surprises me with a kiss. It's enough to make me open my eyes, but he's blocking my view.

He grins. "Sorry, I couldn't resist."

I stand on my tiptoes and meet his lips for a sweet kiss. "Was that the surprise?"

He laughs. "Would it change your mind about surprises if it was?"

I smile brighter, nodding my head. Surprise kisses from guys I have huge crushes on would be at the top of the list of things I enjoy. Lila would totally agree.

Kissing me once more, he slides his arm around my waist and moves out of the way so I see the view he's been blocking from me. His Mini Cooper sits in front of us, and I can't stop the frown from crossing my face. Xander holds up his finger before he drags me forward and pops the hatch to show off a genuine picnic basket, a huge flannel blanket, and a bouquet of sunflowers.

"What is all this?" I ask.

He lifts his phone up and snaps a picture of me standing with my mouth half open in surprise. The last thing I expected was for Xander to do something like this for me. I've gone out on dates before, to the movies, restaurants, and school dances, but I have never had someone put so much thought into a date like this.

"I—"

He twists his lips to the side. "You don't like picnics."

I blink my eyes a few times as I force myself to smile. "No, I love it. It's amazing."

"You don't look happy."

I step closer to him and slide my arms around his neck. "I am, I swear. It's just—" I take a deep breath. "I didn't know I would love surprises again."

I hate myself for how much I love it. I hate that in this moment, a moment I should be on top of the world and smiling, a moment I should be happy, that all I can think about is how much this small gesture devastates me. Not because it reminds me of Lila, but because it reminds me that once again, I'm undeserving of happiness. I'm undeserving of the life Lila left me alone in.

Chapter 17

seventeen days

I'M HOVERING OVER my bowl of cereal when I hear a peal of laughter come from upstairs. The familiar, feminine voice trickles down the stairs followed by Caleb's laugh. They both sound like they're having a great time.

Footsteps sound on the stairs, more high pitched laughter trickling to me, and in struts Bridget with Caleb clinging onto her hips. Her curly hair flies all over the place and smudged eyeliner streaks under her eyes. She dangles a pair of heels from her fingers that match her skimpy dress that shows off her smooth, muscular legs. I can't help staring at how pretty she looks, even though she's obviously just rolled out of my brother's bed.

Surprise makes me drop my spoon, and it clatters to the floor. The three of us stare at each other in silence, and then Bridget beams me a smile, tossing her hair over her shoulder.

"Hey!" she says a little too perkily this early in the morning. "Caleb said you were out with Xander."

I glance at Caleb, who keeps his eyes trained on my dropped spoon on the floor. I raise my eyebrows. "Last night." I can't help the way my voice sounds, half annoyed and slightly judgy, but only because I had no idea that Caleb's mystery girl was one of my two only friends at school, and neither of them cared enough to share the information with me.

She rubs Caleb's arm. "I guess you did tell me that yesterday."

I turn my back on them as awkwardness settles over me. Their relationship progressed fast. I didn't even know Caleb knew she existed, and now he's acting like a cute puppy trailing behind her.

Plopping down on the barstool next to me, she flicks my arm. "You're cool with this, right? You knew how much I liked him."

I shrug. It's not that I'm against Caleb being with Bridget—it just surprised the heck out of me. He's so quiet and laidback, and well, she's a high strung party girl. I guess if it makes him happy...

Caleb struts to the cabinet and pulls two bowls from the cupboard and pours the cereal and milk I left on the counter into them. "So, Cee. I was thinking since Mom and Dad are both gone, we could have a party tonight."

A party. This would be the first party we've ever thrown without Lila. Just the thought is enough to make me hesitate, and I think about the best party we had ever thrown.

On Halloween during junior year, Dad took Mom out of town for a Halloween Gala held by one of his clients. Mom dressed as an angel with the prettiest real, white feathered wings and a white, sequined gown and of course Dad was the devil in an all red tuxedo and horns Mom had a professional makeup artist adhere to his forehead. Lila and I were so jealous of how perfect my parents looked that we stole their costume ideas, except Lila wore a flouncy red dress with a cute horned headband, and I had sheer tulle wings with a gold sequin headband I wore across my forehead. And because we loved our costumes so much, we invited over a few dozen people the moment my parents left just to show off.

"Babe!" Lila called over the loud music blaring from the surround sound in my living room. "I'm going to corrupt you!"

A few cute guys from our class, including Cameron and Gabe, laughed while Lila raised her champagne glass to me, since plastic cups took away from the glamour of her costume.

It was one of the best Halloween parties ever, even if Lila didn't actually corrupt anyone. She did manage to make a devilish deal with my brother, though, and somehow convinced him to cleanup, which was her best idea ever, considering she threw Halloween confetti everywhere.

Bridget bounces in her chair, drawing my attention away from my thoughts. "A party would be totally awesome!"

I twist my lips to the side. How can I tell either of them no? "Only if you guarantee no one goes into my room."

Caleb hands a bowl of cereal to Bridget. "Deal."

***

After spending the late morning at the cemetery with Lila and the afternoon hiding away anything valuable Mom would kill us over if it were stolen or destroyed, I sit with Bridget in my room. It's strange that she actually saw Caleb's room before mine, but I haven't invited anyone but Xander over since the accident. It feels nice hanging out without having to worry about getting to class on time.

As I sit in front of the wall mirror I stole from my parents' bedroom since my vanity mirror is long gone, I finish applying the last coat of my concealer, a special formula made to cover tattoos, and brush on some setting powder. Bridget digs through my closet, tossing dresses onto my bed.

Caleb must've told her about my scars because she hasn't looked at them for long or mentioned them once since I've strolled out of the shower in just a towel and found her scouring through my wardrobe.

She holds up a navy blue dress with a sweetheart neckline. "How come I've never seen you in any of these? Your clothes are so amazing. I thought I was going to have to go home to change because I was under the impression you only owned jeans and hoodies." She laughs and holds the dress against her.

She slips out of the tank top and pajama bottoms she borrowed from me and into the dress. Spinning around, she stands behind me to glimpse at her reflection in the mirror. Bridget looks stunning in it, the way it hugs her curves in all the right places, and I remember the first time I wore the dress.

The same night as our junior winter formal dance, Renee Mills threw a party at her dad's penthouse apartment in the city to see if she could get the best of the best to show up there instead of the lame dance held at a small amusement park that consisted of a rickety rollercoaster, a log ride, and cheesy, unbeatable carnival games.

Lila wore the same dress in a deep plum, which looked amazing against her sun-kissed skin and dark chocolate eyes. Her hair waved over her shoulders, while mine was teased into a low ponytail with a headband the same color as my dress. We'd both spritzed ourselves in a new bottle of perfume Mom bought just for the occasion, and the floral scent swirled around us as we rode the elevator up to the twentieth floor.

"I wonder who's coming tonight," I said, watching the numbers light up with every floor we passed.

Lila locked her fingers around mine. "Who cares? It's going to be rockin' no matter what."

A goofy smile slid across my lips, and she blew me air kisses. The door chimed open, and we stepped into an elaborately decorated hallway with floor runners and gleaming metal and glass everywhere. There was only one door in the hallway, and it was the one we were heading to.

"Oh, my God! Is that Jared and Scott? What're they doing here?" She stopped in her tracks, and I almost tripped in my heels when she jerked me back.

I gaped at the two guys standing just inside the open door. "It doesn't matter who's here, remember?" I said and yanked her forward. "Plus, we're smokin' hot tonight. They're going to wish they never left."

We sauntered into the penthouse without even giving Scott or Jared a second glance. Within five minutes of being there, I felt big hands slide around my waist, and I turned to look into

Scott's eyes. He smiled lazily, like he'd already had a couple of shots, and brushed his lips against my temple.

"God, you look sexy, Cee," he whispered into my ear, and I shrugged him off.

"Miss me?" I said in my sugary, sweet voice.

"More than you know."

Lila locked her arm through mine and smiled at the boys who had left us for college. "Well, that's too bad, because she's my date tonight."

That was the last time I saw Scott and Jared. Caleb did tell me later that they both attended Lila's funeral and even tried to visit me in the hospital, but Mom didn't allow any visitors. Scott never even tried to call after I got out, and I guess he had his life to get back to and figured I was no longer a part of it.

"So, what are you wearing?" Bridget asks, pulling me from my memory, looking at my jeans and hoodie.

I look at my shoes. "This, I guess."

Her eyes widen. "No way! Not with all these great dresses you have." She holds up the black halter dress I wore to Dad's company-sponsored Christmas party two years ago and haven't worn since.

"Shows too much skin."

She drops it to the floor without arguing and heads back to my closet. She runs her fingers along my wardrobe and yanks out a pale blue dress I don't remember wearing.

She holds it up. "This is really cute."

The dress is made of some clingy material, with a high boat neck collar and quarter sleeves. It's an A-line cut that will hug every curve on my body and is actually pretty perfect because none of my scars will peep through as long as I keep my hair down. A price tag dangles from the sleeve, and Bridget glances at it.

"Holy crap. You spent three hundred dollars on a dress and haven't even worn it? You know, I'll gladly take the stuff you don't wear off your hands."

Holding the dress against me, I remember why I never wore it. Mom bought it for me when she went on a trip to New York with Dad for my cousin's wedding. I refused to wear it because it didn't show off enough skin, which is funny now that I think about it.

"I'll consider it," I say, heading to the bathroom to change. "It's not like I wear any of that stuff anymore."

An hour later, Xander shows up on my doorstep before the sun goes down, catching me in the middle of cooking dinner before the party starts. It's kind of a tradition, eating a big meal before a fun night. It was a way to make sure me, Lila, and Caleb wouldn't be knocked on our asses after a sip of alcohol, and it seemed to always work. It would take more than a cup of nasty beer before things got iffy.

Xander hovers in the doorway, just staring at me before he reaches into his pocket and pulls out his phone, snapping a picture. I stumble back, my hands flying over my face. I'm sure I look terrible, but I don't ask him to take another out of habit. It was the number one rule between me and Lila. No second chances after the button had been pushed, because the moment was over and trying to recreate the moment again was like trying to recreate a memory; it just doesn't stand up to the original.

Wringing my hands together, I stand nervously in front of Xander before I say, "Come on in. I made dinner." He smiles as he tugs me inside with him, and for the first time all day, panic seeps into my chest, sending my heart racing.

"You okay, Coco?" he asks as he slides his arms over my stiff shoulders.

I suck in deep breaths through my nose as Xander watches me in his peripheral vision. *It'll be fun. It'll be fun. It'll be fun.* The repetition of words does nothing to comfort the sinking feeling in my heart. "Yeah, it's just...it's been a while since I've done this."

"Had people over?"

I nod. "If you haven't noticed, I'm not exactly popular." Anymore.

"Well, I think it's going to be fun."

"Yeah..."

A flash of light startles me, and I turn and face Bridget. She takes a few pictures of us before calling Caleb to join her for a few of the two of them. Dancing around, she smiles and snaps picture after picture. The sudden gesture pulls at my heart.

I find it incredibly hard to smile at her excitement as she catches every moment, snapping pictures of us together, of the stranger I'm forced to live in. And I suddenly hate it. I don't want any more moments captured. Not because I look bad or anything, but because it forces me to see that life goes on even when I don't want it to.

"That's enough, Bridget," I say, pulling away from her to head to the kitchen. Only Xander follows.

It takes everything in me not to run and hide in my room, to ask Caleb to call this whole thing off, to go back to being the girl who lived every day like it was just one more toward her last. Thinking about everything makes it hard to breathe, to think, to do anything. I just can't accept that there's life after Lila. It isn't right.

Chapter 18

sixteen days

THE CLOCK GONGS twelve times from the hallway. I lean against the wall, watching the sea of strangers dance and laugh and talk. It took a dozen pleas from both Bridget and my brother to get me to come out of my room, and I finally relented when Xander sat down next to me on my bed, making me unintentionally feel guilty because he would stay with me whether I asked him or not.

Standing quietly, I watch everything from the outside, like I would if I was a ghost, wishing to be a part of it, but some stupid ethereal veil is separating me from the living.

I've never felt so alone in a room full of people that I know by name but haven't talked to in what feels like forever. I don't even know what I would say. Small talk seems so trivial, like a waste of words, breath, and energy.

Bridget and Caleb dance together, slowly grinding on each other in such an intimate way that I turn my eyes away, feeling like a perv for witnessing their private moment.

Xander glances at me every few seconds from across the room, where he's talking with Brett Gordon and Brynn Hallows. I regret telling him that he didn't need to stay with me the entire night, to have fun and make some new friends. It was something I used to tell Caleb to do when he tagged along with me to a party. And now, I feel like I should be taking my own advice, but it seems stupid. I shouldn't have to force myself to have fun.

"Don't look, but there's a hot guy staring you down."

I shake my head, my long brown hair slapping my cheeks, when Yessica leans against the wall next to me. She's wearing an ivory, eyelet lace dress with a deep V-neck cut that reveals her bronzer enhanced cleavage. Her nude heels are four inches tall, and she towers over me. She wags her perfectly shaped eyebrows, motioning toward Xander.

"Let's make him drool." Yessica grabs my hands and begins dancing around me. I just stand with her as she sweeps my arms back and forth, and I feel all sorts of awkward. "Come on, Coco. Don't make me dance by myself."

I slowly sway my hips, knowing I look ridiculous because the music is upbeat and peppy, everything I'm not at the moment. Yessica's hands lock onto my hips, and she guides my motions, matching the music, until I'm doing it on my own.

Turning her back to me, she dips to the floor and pops back up, sending her bleached blond hair in my face. I laugh, really laugh, and her ruby red lips part in a smile.

She leans in, her breath laced with a hint of beer. "He's totally drooling along with the rest of the guys in the room."

I glance over my shoulder, and my eyes meet with Xander's. He offers his adorable lopsided smile through his conversation with Brett and Brynn, his eyes never leaving mine.

"He's going to have some major competition after to-night," Yessica continues, flipping her hair back. "Which is good for the both of you. When Damien sees another guy try-ing to get my attention, he ups his game a million."

"So, that's how you do it?" I ask, losing myself in the beat of the music.

"You gotta keep a guy wondering. If he thinks he's losing you, he'll do everything he can to keep you. And if he doesn't, well, his loss."

I never thought I'd be listening to relationship advice from the girl who has set the record for most breakups with the same guy. Last I checked, Yessica and Damien had broken up three weeks ago, but I guess a lot happens in three weeks.

"Can I cut in?"

I drop Yessica's hands. "Sure."

"Not with her."

I bring my eyes up to Trent's before taking a step back. I've ignored him for the last few weeks after the jerk move he pulled on Xander when we first met. But now, as he smiles down at me, I'm pretty sure he hasn't noticed.

I shift my eyes to Yessica, who's already moved on to dance with Jamie Brooks, and don't get the chance to decline because Trent laces his fingers around mine and draws me close. He smells like cheap body spray and cigarettes, and I turn my head away to stare at the wall.

His breath heats my ear as he whispers, "You look super hot tonight." Before the accident, I'd have flirted right back. I'd have danced and had a good time. But now, knowing how he treats people like dirt, how he'd probably treat me horribly if he ever saw what I hide, I want him to just leave me alone.

I lick my lips, my mouth suddenly dry. "Thanks," is all I manage to say instead of telling him how I'm really feeling. But that's something that I haven't been able to do in so long. Everything stays bottled up, unable to escape no matter how hard I try.

Trent presses his chin into my shoulder, the gesture uncomfortable because of the sandpaper feel of his unshaven face against my neck. Tilting his head, he brushes his wet lips against the skin of my collar, and I stiffen. I step back to put some distance between us without making a scene, but his feet follow mine until the cool wall comes up behind me.

Jerking my head away, I plant my hands on his chest and push him back. "I'm seeing someone. Please, stop."

His hands lock onto my shoulders, and he looks down at me, grinning like an idiot. "I can't get over how sexy you are. Your new face really is better than the old one. Not that I'm saying you weren't hot before, but now you're smokin' hot."

I turn my head. "Trent, I said stop. I'm here with someone."

Trent brushes my dark hair behind my ear. "Then where is he?"

I dig my fingernails into his chest, fear slicing through me deeper than the pieces of glass and metal that gave me this face. "Does that matter? You're drunk and an idiot. I would never be with you even if I wasn't here with Xander."

Something flickers in his eyes for second before he smiles wider and leans down.

"Get back." The words fade into my ragged breathing and the pounding in my head. It feels like the oxygen leaves the room, suffocating me, edging my blurry vision. The world around me darkens as I slide into a vortex of a panic attack, helpless and terrified. I squeeze my eyes shut and try to disappear.

Pain rips me from the shadows. My head slams into the wall, and I slide to the floor, blinking through the starbursts blurring my vision as all hell breaks loose.

Fists fly, girls scream, and I just sit on the floor, clutching my knees to my chest. Xander punches Trent in the face and blood pours from his nose. Small red droplets scatter across the floor, and I think about how oddly beautiful they look against the cream-colored carpet.

Fights usually scare me to death. So much so that the first one I saw break out had me running in the opposite direction. In this moment, I wish Lila was here more than anything like that first fight.

"Babe! Wait up!" Lila called, chasing me across Sean Adkin's lawn.

She grabbed me by my long ponytail, and I jerked to a stop. Bending over, I clutched my stomach, feeling queasy as hell from the sight of some guy I didn't know spitting blood all over the place.

"Take me home. I want to go home." I gasped, sputtering through the tears ruining my mascara.

Lila pulled me into a hug, rubbing her hand over my back like a protective mother does to a frightened child. "Don't let a stupid fight ruin our night."

I squeezed my eyes shut. "I just don't get why people hurt each other."

Lila cupped my face, and I opened my eyes. "Because people aren't as smart as us. Don't know how to use their voices to get their point across. And unfortunately, some guys think Cara Hart is worth fighting over."

I laughed at her reasoning, and I find myself laughing now, because I can almost hear Lila saying, "Unfortunately, some guys think you're worth fighting over, too." She would never have said that to me, but I can't help thinking how funny it would've been if she did, especially because she'd have kicked Trent where it mattered for scaring me. She'd say, "I think you're worth fighting for, babe."

I stare through the circle of legs, watching Xander yell at Trent as he lies on the floor. Trent curls on his side, covering his bloody face, probably wishing that he'd never come. As I see the pain in his eyes, I know he doesn't think I was worth fighting over.

Caleb grabs Xander by the shoulders and yanks him back. "I think you got him for the both of us."

Paul, Trent's sidekick, steps out from the crowd, smiling like a deranged clown with some girl's hot pink lipstick smeared across his face and reaches down to help his friend up. He hands him a stolen towel from the bathroom and pushes him toward the door.

A shadow falls over me, and I use my hand as a visor to look up. Silhouetted in the harsh light from the chandelier, Xander just stares at me, a frown narrowing his lips. A red mark decorates his cheek and will probably bruise by morning from the one swing Trent got in. His shoulders slump forward, and he looks so tired and worn, I wonder if he regrets fighting for me. I wouldn't blame him. I'm not really worth fighting for. It's a wasted effort.

He kneels down next to me. "You okay?"

I don't answer. I don't know how. I just look into his sad eyes and wait for some response to form on my lips, but it never does. All I can do is dig my fingers into the skin of my palms.

His Adam's apple pops in his throat as he swallows. "Co-co?" he questions again.

I blink.

"Please, say something. Please, tell me you're okay."

Tears burn in the back of my throat, and my bottom lip trembles. How am I supposed to tell him I haven't been okay in a long time? That I'm so used to not being okay, I can't even tell whether or not I am. Everything just feels numb.

Xander pushes to his feet, and I expect him to leave. It's what I would do if I were him. He waves his hand, and Caleb appears next to him. My brother squats and absently plays with a tear on the collar of my dress I don't even remember getting. He touches the back of my head, probing the throbbing bump from when I hit the wall. I flinch from him but don't bat him away like I usually would when he acts like a medical professional, thinking that a first aid and CPR class automatically deems him an expert at taking care of my bumps and bruises.

He waves his index finger in front of my face, and I look at him like he's crazy. "Am I going to lose my head, Dr. Caraway?" My voice sounds so small and fragile, I'm not sure he hears me.

He smiles, tiny lines forming at the corners of his eyes. "I think you'll be all right with an icepack and some meds." He messes my hair and turns to Xander. "Take her upstairs. I'll be up in a minute."

When I was released from the hospital, I still had bandages wrapped around my torso because my wounds were still healing, but the doctors agreed that they could finish at home.

Mom refused to have anything to do with them, and it was nearly impossible for me to take care of myself. I remember she and Dad argued for hours over it. Mom wanted to hire a nurse, and Dad thought it was unnecessary because it was something they could take care of. So that left Caleb to take care of me when Dad was away.

I cried the very first time Dad went out of town for a few days because Mom told me I could do it myself. My eyes were still swollen from my latest surgery, and I could barely stand up without feeling like I was going to pass out.

I was lying on my back without my shirt, gripping the prescribed ointment in one hand and a mirror in the other. It hurt so much to look down, and the bandages were discoloring from whatever fluids still seeped from me.

I had just ripped off the tape holding the gauze on, and I was sputtering and sobbing my eyes out, contemplating on just letting it go another day.

Caleb knocked on my door, and I yelled for him to leave me alone. He ignored me and came into my room, hovering for a second by the door, just staring at me in all my disgusting glory.

I dropped the mirror and ointment and tried to stop the tears from flowing because they were burning my cheeks. "I'll just wait for Dad," I said, leaning back on my pillow.

Caleb shuffled forward and began to carefully pull off the dressing that clung to my skin because it should've been changed the day before. "He doesn't come back for two days. You'll have an infection by then."

I flinched as the cool air touched the skin under my bandages. "I'll be fine."

He frowned at me and said, "Maybe after another surgery when the doctors have to go and clean you out all over again."

I sighed and stared at the ceiling as Caleb quietly went to work, reading everything in the care packs the doctor had given us to make things a little easier. Having Caleb help me wasn't a huge deal. But what bothered me was that I couldn't take care of myself when Mom failed to perform her duties. That was the first time I realized I hated her, because she wasn't there for me when I needed her most.

After ten of the most awkward minutes of my life, my bandages were clean and my eyes were dry. Caleb smiled at me and rubbed his hand over my head, messing up my hair. He helped me get back into my shirt and even took the time to make me lunch and fill up my phone with the latest music I had missed.

I put my foot down when he offered to get me new sheets for my bed, but I was thankful when he did anyway. He claimed, "It'll be good practice for when I intern at a hospital when I'm premed in college."

His words surprised me at the time, because he always told me he wanted to be an engineer—to design and create the cars he'd always dreamed of having—and I was a little disappointed, because I was hoping that one day he'd design a car that couldn't kill.

After that, Caleb took it upon himself to make sure I was healing the way I should be. He even went to the extent of calling my doctor to make sure he was doing everything right. He filled the void Mom left when she decided she couldn't handle me anymore, and if he could've, he would've tried to fill the void Lila left behind, too.

***

I open my eyes to my pitch black room. Sounds of the party seep in through the walls, and laughter trickles in from the hallway. Turning on my side, I knock into a solid lump, taking up the spot next to me.

Reaching for my cell phone sitting on my nightstand, I touch the screen and let the soft backlight fill my room. Xander breathes softly, his face squished against my mattress since the pillow is under me. I gaze at him, watching him sleep in the light of my phone.

This is a moment I want—I need—to capture, because the way he looks, so peaceful and happy, is something that I never want to forget. I lean over and dig through my memory box on my nightstand and tug out my camera. The flash lights up my room, and Xander blinks awake. He holds his arms open, calling me to him, and I curl up against him. My cheek presses against his chest, the steady rise and fall of it soothing the thoughts swirling through my mind.

His lips brush the top of my head, and I turn my chin up to him, meeting his lips with mine. He kisses me so softly like a whisper, and I find my fingers tugging his shirt over his head.

With Xander in the dark room with me, the world doesn't feel so lonely. It doesn't feel as empty as it did only hours ago. Something about having his fingers trail down my body as I kiss him harder awakens me. I don't feel like my world is closing in on me or that I'm drowning while I'm still breathing. I feel utterly and blissfully alive.

He moans into my lips. I kiss him like it's the most important thing in the world, running my hands across his stomach, exploring every inch of him. His hands run through my hair, and then he slides them down my back to where my dress bunches around my thighs.

My breath quickens at the softness of his touch. I cling to his neck when he slips my dress up, and his hands travel up my legs and brush over the scars on my stomach, tracing them up to my collarbone. When his fingers brush over my lips, I shiver before he kisses me again.

I let him explore me, let his lips brush my shoulders and work their way to my stomach. He kisses every one of my scars, leaving my skin tingling all over and me out of breath until I can't handle it anymore, and I pull him to lie next to me.

His bare chest rests against my back while his arm hangs over my side, and we just lie together, listening to the sound of our breathing over the music and laughter echoing through the rest of the house.

Closing my eyes, I welcome sleep for the first time in a long time, because with Xander next to me, I know there won't be any nightmares plaguing my dreams tonight.

After a long, quiet moment, his lips brush my ear and he whispers, "I'm falling in love with you."

My heart stalls before kicking into overdrive, and I open my mouth to respond, but nothing comes out. Instead, I pretend I'm already asleep.

***

I help Caleb pick up the remnants of the party, dumping out empty bottles and cans into the sink. He steam cleaned the carpet, before deciding to move the rug a little further away from the couches to cover the blood stains he should've taken care of last night.

Xander dumps the empty bottles and cans into a garbage bag, stopping every few minutes to kiss me on the cheek. Bridget left about an hour ago, claiming she had plans. Plans that didn't involve cleanup, I'm guessing.

"Thanks for staying, man," Caleb says, strolling into the kitchen with more half drunken plastic cups and an empty bottle of wine that was taken from Mom's stash.

"Kind of owe you for the carpet," Xander says, bumping his shoulder into mine.

Caleb laughs. "No, dude. I totally owe *you* for that."

"So then we're even."

I smile, turning to the two boys I never thought would be laughing and joking around with each other. "You guys are so weird."

Xander kisses my cheek. "And you like weird."

I roll my eyes. "No, I just like you."

His lips twitch into a small smile, and Caleb chuckles from behind me. Xander stares at me so intensely, I have to look away for fear of him seeing what's on my mind, because the last thing he whispered to me last night plays over and over in my head.

I've only ever told one boy that I loved him, and he will forever be captioned as the culprit behind Worst Breakup Ever, Part Two.

Cameron and I got together the fall Scott went off to college. At the time, Lila nicknamed him Rebound Boy, because Scott had only been gone for two weeks, and I didn't argue. Cameron was pretty hot, and I couldn't resist his ocean blue eyes when he asked me to the homecoming dance, hearing that Scott and I had broken up.

Lila stopped teasing me about him being a rebound, because she had found her own Rebound Boy in Gabe Aguilar, for the same dance, only hours later. After that, the four of us went out together almost every night for a few months straight.

I thought I was in love with him. I really did. My stomach got butterflies every time I saw him, kissed him...and when I gave myself to him.

We were sitting on his bed, listening to *Forgotten Moments*, and he brushed my hair behind my ear and said, "I love you, babe."

My smile was bright enough to light up the room, because he said exactly what I was thinking, and I said it back. A week later, he told me he didn't love me anymore, and we said good-bye.

Lila hugged me while I cried, feeling so stupid for believing that I was in love, and I told her I'd never love again. And I didn't. Until last night. Because Xander knows who I really am, and he said he was falling in love with me anyway. He can look past everything that has ever happened to me and see underneath my scars.

Xander squeezes my hand, pulling me back from my thoughts. "I should probably get going."

I walk him to his car, and he hugs me until I pull away. I kiss him once on the lips and turn to go. He reaches for me, stopping me from leaving, and looks down at me, his eyebrows knitted over his green eyes.

My tongue sticks to the roof of my mouth, and it takes everything I have to tell him what's on my mind. "You can't fall in love with me, Xander."

His head tilts to the side, and his arms stiffen. "It's a little late for that."

I blink the tears from my eyes. "And I'm sorry. It's just, I—

I can't love you."

His face falls at the same time I feel my heart exploding into pieces in my chest. His fingers lock around my wrists, and he's the only thing holding me up. "Is it because you can't or because you won't? Can you honestly look me in the eyes and tell me you don't feel anything?"

I stare at the ground, at our matching shoes, and then slowly bring my eyes up to his. "I can't."

I watch as he gets into his car and drives away without looking back. Sobs heave my chest, and I drop to my knees, dragging my nails across the cement, looking for something to hold onto until the world stops spinning.

Go after him! Lila's voice echoes in my ears.

"I can't," I say out loud, because it's the only thing I can say.

Chapter 19

fourteen days

I CONTEMPLATED SKIPPING school again today like I did yesterday but forced myself to grin and bear it. I didn't see Xander and avoided my brother and friends just like I did at the beginning of the year. Now, I stare at the sun overhead, praying for cloud cover. The world shouldn't be so bright when I feel so dark. I want the night to come and switch off the sun so I can say goodbye to another day.

"Cheer up, sunshine," I imagine Lila telling me. I can picture her sitting next to me, right here on the grass by her grave because she's the one person I'd have turned to after the Xander Disaster. "The rain will go away."

I run my fingers along her name engraved on the headstone. It's strange, seeing her name beautifully scripted. She would've been jealous because she had the Sloppiest Cursive Ever. She would've hated it.

Whenever I was depressed, Lila would write me what was

equivalent to a love letter. She called it a Lila Letter. The first time she had ever given me one was the third day of freshman year.

I was never the most athletic person. I could manage a couple of push-ups, and that was pretty much it. It was track day in Gym, and Mr. Pete exclaimed that we were going to run the mile. He made it sound like we were going to Disneyland. And don't get me started on how important he made it sound, because we weren't running just any mile, but *the* mile.

I thought, *How hard could it be?* It was running a measly couple laps, and then I could spend the rest of the period sitting in the shade.

Everything started out better than I had hoped. I wasn't the last one struggling to keep up, and I didn't die from exhaustion when I crossed the starting line after the first lap. I was actually enjoying myself, how the wind blew through my hair and the sound of my feet pounding the dirt; I felt like I could run forever.

And then came the fall of my budding track stardom. I swerved to the outside of the track to pass up some kids that decided walking was more their style. I wish I would've done the same thing, because as I picked up speed on the long stretch, I slipped on a muddy patch of the dirt and skidded face first through it.

I just laid there in the mud with my cheek pressed into the ground because I was so embarrassed. I was mortified. After I finally caught my breath, I dug my fingers into the slimy mud and pushed to my feet. I ignored Mr. Pete when he called,

"Walk it off, Caraway. A little mud never hurt anyone."

I headed straight into the locker room and sat in a bathroom stall until Lila came knocking on the door about an hour later.

I opened the door with tears streaming down my face, and she handed me a wad of wet paper towels to wipe the dried mud off with.

"I wrote you a letter," she said as she unfolded a piece paper she tugged from her pocket.

I just stared at the scribbles. "I can't read it."

She laughed and snatched it from my hand. "Dearest Babe," she began, "I heard you got a little down and dirty today, and if I was there, I would've joined you. We could've made mud pies or wrestled or something. Whichever's hotter. Probably the latter, huh?" She smiled and looked up at me, her dark chocolate eyes shining in the fluorescent lighting. "Invite me next time, okay? We'll start a trend together while having the best skin in the entire school. And even if you're sad now, I want you to cheer up, sunshine. The rain will wash the mud away."

She took an exaggerated bow, like she'd recited a poem at an open mic night and blew me a kiss.

I rolled my eyes as I took the letter and shoved it in my locker. After that, any time we were having a bad day, we'd say, "Cheer up, sunshine," and it always worked. Until now. Because no matter how many times I say it, I feel like the rain has turned into a torrential downpour.

***

Bridget showed up at the door to whisk Caleb away at a quarter to six. I wish I would've asked him to stay with me, because he would've, but decided against it because he looked so happy, and I didn't want to take that away from him.

I haven't heard from Xander yet either, and I'm tempted to call him, but it would just make matters worse. He told me he was falling for me, and I gave him a half-assed answer that I'm sure has pretty much screwed up everything between us.

The house phone rings, and I don't bother to get up to answer it until Dad's voice booms from our old answering machine. I scramble to my feet and rush to get it before he hangs up.

"I'm here. I'm here," I say into the phone.

"Hey, kiddo," Dad says, "I thought you'd be out with Xander."

I sigh into the phone. "Not tonight. Something came up." *I broke his heart, Dad.*

"I'm sure it had to be important. Rock Star would never leave you hangin' otherwise."

I laugh despite the aching in my chest. My dad only spent like two hours with Xander, and he acts like they've known each other forever.

"Yeah, it was important." *Well, actually Dad, he's probably never going to speak to me again.*

"So, what's your brother up to?"

"He found himself a girlfriend."

"Do you know her?"

I adjust the phone against my ear. "Yeah, she's one of the

only friends I have at school. Her name's Bridget."

Dad breathes static in the line. "That's not going to cause you any problems is it?"

I shake my head even though he can't see me. "It's cool. You'll like her."

"I'm sure I will."

We're both silent for a few minutes, just breathing in the phone, before I finally say, "Sorry about pissing Mom off. It's just, she's been really intolerable. Did she tell you that she took my makeup away two Saturdays ago and then tried to pull me into the car at Coffee Addicts?" I didn't tell Dad last time because he sounded pretty happy to be headed on a spontaneous vacation with Mom.

Dad clears his throat. "I'm sorry, kiddo. I know what Saturdays mean to you. I'm sure she just forgot."

I don't respond. What's the point now?

"Your mom's having a hard time with me needing to be away all the time. She's taking it out on you when it should be my makeup she's taking away," he adds.

I can't help smiling, imagining my dad wearing a face full of makeup. He'd probably wear it just to make me smile. "Since you don't have any, you have to keep her until you come back."

Dad chuckles, and I press my ear harder to the phone, savoring the sound of his voice. "Deal. She planned on coming back to LA with me anyway through to next week. After this, I'll get a nice break and we can do something fun, okay? Just promise not to burn down the house or anything."

"Too late," I say with a laugh.

"Take care, kiddo. Put your brother in his place if you have to. Since you're four minutes and thirty-two seconds older, you're in charge until I get back."

"'Kay, Dad. Love you."

The line goes dead, and I set the receiver into its cradle. The house seems extra quiet now, and I grab my hoodie off the couch and yank it over my head and make my way to the door.

Sobs shake my shoulders when I see Xander hunched over on the steps. Blinking, I rub my eyes, expecting him to disappear any moment, but he doesn't. He's here. Really here.

He turns his head and looks at me. His red eyes look as if he hasn't slept in a while. I grip the door handle for support, my knees turning into Jell-O the longer he stares at me with his sad, vibrant green eyes.

He turns back around and rests his chin on his hands. "I don't want to lose you."

I slide down the door until I'm sitting on the ground. I can't find the right words to say to make this better, so I just clutch my ankles and stare at his back.

"I don't care if you don't think you can love me. It doesn't matter because I'm in love with you. And even if you refuse to say it back, I know how you feel about me. I can see it in your eyes."

"You're wrong." It hurts to say the words out loud, but I was stupid to take it this far. I was so concerned about making the best of the last days of my life, when I should've thought about what would happen to Xander after that. I never thought about it because I didn't think I'd have to.

"And you're a terrible liar."

He doesn't have to see my face to know he's right, and I feel all sorts of miserable for not giving in and admitting that. Meeting Xander was the best and worst thing to ever happen to me, all things considered, and that's why I haven't marked off my calendar in days, but counted them silently to myself.

He opens me completely to the things I want but don't deserve. He reminds me how messed up and broken I really am, and I hate it. I hate it because even though his just being here infuses me with a happiness I haven't felt in forever, it fades away the moment he's gone. I just feel so empty, and everything feels so temporary. I hate how I can't even find an ounce of something in myself to make living worth it. I'm just tired of living for others. I wanted nothing more than for Lila to live for me, but she didn't, so why should I continue to suffer, too?

"Why are you so stubborn? Why can't you just accept that this—" I wave my hand around, but he doesn't even glance at me. "Us, will end badly? I will never be able to give you everything you deserve, and you shouldn't accept anything less."

He drags his hand over his hair, and I see a small bald spot above his ear, one that's been covered by his curls. My hand reaches out, but he's too far for my fingers to brush against it, so I just fold my arms over my chest.

Pushing to his feet, he glares at me from under furrowed brows, and I cringe because I've never seen him so angry— angry at me.

"Neither should you," he mumbles. He shoves his hands in his pockets and rocks on his heels, looking up at the sky. "I want you to look me in the eyes and tell me to go. Tell me you never want to see me again." He brings his eyes to mine, and I feel so naked and vulnerable under his stare. "Tell me you don't love me—not that you *can't* but don't. And I'll go."

My gaze drops to my hands, and I stare at the chipped pink polish on my nails. It's all of a sudden the most fascinating thing I've ever seen, the way the color cracks down the middle of my thumb, showing the blue polish under it.

I don't look up until I hear Xander's footsteps on the walkway and then the slam of his car door. The Mini's engine sounds like a boom of thunder in the rain that refuses to go away.

I don't get up to go inside when his car disappears. I just sit and watch the sun crawl across the grass until it fades, leaving me alone in the dark.

***

I'm lying in the dark, wrapped in the knitted throw my grandma made for me when I was in the hospital, because she said that the hospital sheets were too white and I needed some color.

She sat at my bedside, clutching my cold hand for a week, only leaving to shower and change, and she was the only one who stood by my side when I refused any more surgeries.

She said, "It's okay to be scarred. Shows that you're strong enough to take on the world." She pulled down the collar of her shirt and revealed a clean, puckered scar in the middle of her chest. "Look at this sucker. Hurt like hell. But I gave death a run for his money, and you, baby, you sent him away crying."

I couldn't smile at the time, but I would've. My grandma always had a way with words. She'd find the smallest pinprick of light in the darkest moments, and I think it's where Dad got it from.

The living room light blinks on, and I rub the shadows from my eyes to see Caleb and Bridget staring at me like I've lost my mind. Caleb's holding take-out pizza, and Bridget has a bag of cupcakes from the shop down the road.

My brother strides forward and drops the box of pizza onto the coffee table. "I thought you'd be out with Xander."

I lean back on the armrest and cover my eyes with my hands because I feel like sinking into the couch and disappearing. Caleb's the last person I want to talk to about this.

He inhales a sharp breath, and I peek through my fingers as his hands curl into fists. "I knew it!" He punches the air and then struts to the wall and punches it too, leaving a small crater behind. "I'm going to kill him."

I try to stare at him with indifference, to show him everything's all right, but the way he looks at me with hatred so dark, I almost think it's aimed at me, turns the tears lining my eyes to full on gut-wrenching sobs. I choke and sputter and gasp and cry. And I cry some more. My hands shake and my bottom lip quivers, and then I just let go.

A loud wail escapes my lips, sounding so foreign and distant, but I know it's coming from me. Caleb kneels next to me, wrapping his arms around my shoulders. Bridget stands there with her mouth open, and then a spark lights in her eyes, and she's at my side too, wiping her fingers under my eyes and petting my hair. The gesture surprises me, and I begin to laugh through my tears because I thought she'd run for the nearest exit and bolt.

She coos in my ear, tells me boys are stupid while giving Caleb this I'm-just-saying-it-for-her-sake look, and then she pulls out her cell phone and begins squawking into it, her voice shrill and incoherent. She shoves it into her pocket and turns to my brother. "Go to the store and buy everything sweet and cold you can find and come straight back. If you make any detours or do anything stupid, I'll be the one doing the killing."

***

On day one hundred and twenty to go, I was sitting in my usual spot next to Lila's grave, listening to the sparrows chirp and watching the white puffs of clouds move across the sky in an invisible current. It was freezing and close to Christmas, and I came to give Lila a glitter-dusted poinsettia plant and a nostalgic Christmas card that said, "The holidays aren't the same without you/Wish you were here."

A woman, dressed in a burgundy dress that hung around her knees with a black fur coat draped over her shoulders, stood over a grave a couple rows down. She paced back and forth, yanking at the loose blond tendrils of hair that had fallen into her face. Her cheeks were smeared with black mascara, and her lips moved as she talked to herself.

After several minutes of pacing and muttering, she dropped to her knees and screamed. The shrill sound of her heartache sent the birds flying, and as soon as she stopped, it felt like the world stopped.

I held my breath, and it felt like the wind was holding its breath, too, because the trees stopped rustling and the cemetery became so quiet, like an invisible blanket covered us, separating us from the rest of the world, the living.

And then she wept.

She just stared at the headstone and silently cried. Her pain so deep, so raw, I could feel it curling around my own broken heart. It mocked me, and said, "You think you have it hard? Hah! You don't even know the meaning of hard."

She curled her fingers around the grass. "I take it back," she said. Her voice was low, but her grief was so intense, it was like she screamed all over again. "I know I said it was okay for you to leave me, that I'd be okay. But I take it back. I can't do this without you, Manny. I don't have the strength you have." She pressed her fingers together and looked up at the sky. "God, please. Oh, God, please, I'll do anything you ask, just bring him back. Take me instead."

Her voice reverberated to my bones, and I expected the sky to open and swallow her whole. I watched and waited as she prayed, begged. But nothing happened. Nothing changed. No matter how determined she sounded or how much she bargained, everything just remained as still and quiet as before.

That very minute I knew. I knew that the hush wasn't because someone was listening. It was quiet because no one was there. And why would they be? In the whole scheme of things, that woman and her broken heart and unheard prayers didn't matter. Nothing mattered.

I never saw that woman again. She just got in her car and

left without looking back. I didn't understand it at the time, and now, thinking back, I still don't get it. She loved Manny so much she was willing to offer her own life for his. But the problem with that—and I contemplated on telling her this, but bit my tongue instead—is even if some miracle occurred and she died instead, they still wouldn't be together. There's only one way for that to happen, and there's still no guarantee. But I'm willing to take my chance.

Chapter 20

thirteen days

BRIDGET TURNED MY unofficial breakup with Xander into a girl's night plus Caleb. Yessica and Bridget slept on either side of me, and sometime around three, Bridget snuck off to Caleb's room. She thought I was sleeping, and I let her, because honestly I wanted to mourn alone. Like always.

This isn't the first school night sleepover I've had. Starting freshman year, Lila and I would switch off days during the week and spend the night with each other. We'd do our homework and then stay up half the night talking. I miss those late night talks more than anything. While it was nice to have Yessica and Bridget to keep my mind off things, I couldn't talk through things with them. They'd have never understood.

I shimmy to the edge of the bed without disturbing Yessica. I'm tired of listening to her deep breathing, considering that I haven't slept at all. My makeup looks pretty much the same as yesterday with a little less mascara, so I slip on a pair of sunglasses and my shoes and head downstairs.

It's half past six and Caleb is still occupied in his room, so I write a short note, telling him that I'm ditching school and to call my cell if he needs me.

To my surprise, when I step on the porch, there's a vase of red tulips sitting in the middle of the walkway, looking vibrant in comparison to the cloudy sky. Stuck under the vase is a slip of paper, and I stare at it like it's the answer to my non-existent prayers.

Meet me at the train station.

I consider tossing the flowers and note in the garbage can waiting to be picked up at the curb. I shouldn't play these games anymore. Yesterday was painful to get through, and I need to keep my distance. But my curiosity wins the argument, and I leave the flowers where they are and stroll to the sidewalk. *You were going to ditch anyway,* Lila's voice says in my mind. *A train ride is better than walking.*

I used to hate walking. I hated it so much that I'd convinced Dad to drive me to Lila's house, which was only three streets over. When I got my license, it was like a dream come true. I had the freedom to go wherever I wanted no matter how far and was even planning to drive cross country one day.

For the Christmas of my junior year, my parents surprised me with a car. It was perfect. A glittering, midnight blue Miata with the shiniest rims I'd ever seen. I was so shocked that Mom picked out a two-seater convertible; I thought it was a joke until she handed me the keys and called me her Barbie Doll.

"And look, there's a seat for Ken, too," Mom said, waving

her hand at the passenger's seat.

Lila rolled her eyes. "You mean Skipper."

"But Ken is so dreamy," I said.

"I guess that makes me Ken then." Lila winked and got in.

We drove around town without a destination. The top was down, the music blasting, and it was the most liberating experience I had ever had. I dreamed about what it would be like to drive farther and farther. To just get out and go. But then those dreams turned into nightmares. Black, fiery nightmares. And I know I'll never leave this town. I don't want to.

The train station is empty when I arrive. The hustling commuter crowd has already left for work, leaving the platform eerily quiet.

Xander sits on a bench with his back to me. He leans his elbows on his knees, bowing his head into his hands. He's dressed in his usual black and is wearing a black baseball cap with his hair curling out from under it. The way he's just sitting there, hunched over, not moving a muscle, he almost looks frozen in time, like the ghost of the boy I rejected yesterday.

I pull my phone from my purse and use it to capture the moment forever. He's waiting for me, not sure if I'll show up but hoping I will. I know it's cruel to stand here and watch him like this, but I can't help it. I feel like the moment I open my mouth, it'll be over. I'll do or say something to mess things up, and then he'll no longer wait for me.

He stretches his legs out in front of him and pulls his phone from his pocket. He sighs, and I wonder how long he's been here. I wonder how much longer he'll wait. I'm tempted to see.

My chest tightens when he stands up because I expect him to leave, but he paces up and down the platform. He's wearing dark sunglasses, hiding his eyes from the world. Eyes that I wish I could see right now.

He turns around, and I stop myself from ducking behind the automated ticket booth. He freezes in his tracks and watches me watch him. We just stand there, staring at each other for what feels like forever.

And then I give in.

I close the twenty feet of distance and brace myself for a hug that doesn't come. Xander stares at me through his sunglasses. I wish he'd just take them off, but I don't bother to take mine off either. It's like the tinted plastic can somehow protect me, keep my secrets hidden away.

"I didn't think you'd show." His voice cracks, and he clears his throat.

I gently kick the toe of his Converse. "I almost didn't. I just ditched two days ago, you know." The old me would've glossed over the truth with a flirty smile. I would've shrugged my shoulders and said, "Of course I wouldn't leave you hangin'. It's not my style." The new, unfamiliar me is too tired to try.

His brows dip under his sunglasses. "I know, and I'm sorry. But I'm glad you're here. It's all that matters."

He shifts on his feet, and I wonder how we ended up with awkward babble and long pauses when just over a day ago we were lying in the dark of my bedroom, wrapped in each other's arms, exploring all the bad things life had done to us. I wonder how a little phrase could rebuild the wall Xander had finally broken through. But it wasn't the words he said, it was the emotion behind it, how he looked at me, how much I believed him.

It scared the crap out of me, like I was in my car heading straight for the lights of an oncoming vehicle, and that any moment his love would go up in smoke and flames and leave me empty and cold and broken. Or worse, it would leave him completely shattered.

A train pulls into the station. The rumble of the engine and the squeal of the brakes as it comes to a stop is a precious relief against the silence between us. My eyes trail to the doors where a lone woman steps off and click-clacks her way to the parking lot.

"Why am I here?" The words come out wrong, and it's like I've asked my own silent question out loud. "I mean, what are we doing here?"

His lips twist to the side, and he brushes his fingers over my hand until I let him take it. "We're leaving."

I open my mouth to ask where, but he's already dragging me onto the train. I don't resist. I let him tug me along until we're sitting at a table in an empty train car.

There's something comforting about being here. The way the ground vibrates under my feet when the train pulls out of the station and how the scenery flies by in a blur.

I haven't been on a train since Lucky Number Seven. But I thought about it. I even bought a ticket once. On day one hundred and ninety-six to go I decided I was going to leave it all behind. I thought maybe a change of scenery would help me forget everything, and I could just let go.

I packed a suitcase, withdrew my entire lifesavings, which was about two hundred dollars, and wrote Dad and Caleb a letter that apologized for not being able to stay around, that getting away from home was the only chance I felt I had left. I wanted them to get used to missing me, knowing I was somewhere out there trying to put my life back together, instead of mourning me because I had given up.

I was planning on running until I ran out of places to run away from. Until I could just disappear. I was going to change my name to something that matched the stranger I was living in. Because I didn't look like Coco anymore, and I was leaving her behind.

The platform was busier than it should've been for being a Sunday afternoon. Kids ran around screaming their little lungs off, having so much fun, so excited to be going on a train ride.

I perched on the top of my suitcase, gripping my one-way ticket in my trembling hands. The train was expected to roll in at any minute, and I was afraid someone at home would see my letter and drag me away before I could get on.

I swept my eyes back and forth through the crowd, expecting at any minute for Caleb to show and start screaming that I was an idiot. I felt like an idiot. I had no idea where I was going, only that I was going.

The idea seemed like a solid plan when Lila and I used to talk about it. Not knowing the destination was the fun of it, kind of like when we'd roll the dice. The destination wasn't some planned place, but wherever you stopped. The last place you ended was your destination.

I was watching the digital clock hanging from thin wires from the metal awning like the timer on a bomb counting down. An old woman stood next to me, watching the clock with the same intensity I was.

The train horn blared in the distance, and she looked down at me and smiled. "Needs to hurry up," she muttered.

I nodded and looked away, not really in the mood for small talk.

"Where you headed?" she asked.

I shrugged. I didn't have an answer.

"I tried that once. Thought I could just pack my things and see where life took me. You know where I ended up?"

I shrugged again. I didn't care. She could've said to the moon, and I would've just continued to stare at the clock.

"Right back where I started. You know why?"

I sighed, blowing my hair out of my face. "If you say because it was where you belonged, I'm going to sit over there." I pointed at the other end of the platform.

She laughed a deep, raspy number that sounded like a cross between a cough and a wheeze. "Are you kidding? Marble Hills was the last place I belonged. That's why I left in the first place." She wiped the tears that formed in the corner of her eyes from laughing. "I ended up back there because it was the last place I had to run to. You can only go so far before you end up back where you started."

I stared at her like she was crazy. There were a million places I could go that wouldn't take me right back here. "So you still live there?"

She laughed again, her wrinkled face turning a deep burgundy color, and I thought she was going to pass out any moment. "Hell no. The moment I stopped running and faced what I was running from, I was able to leave for good."

The train arrived a minute later. She shuffled away, and I watched her go. I didn't get on. I just picked up my suitcase and walked home to face what I was trying to run from. The problem with that was I was running from me.

Xander rests his hand on my knee, and I force my eyes away from the window, pulling myself from my thoughts. He's still wearing his sunglasses despite the lack of sun shining in the train car. I reach out to flip them up, and he grabs my hand and shakes his head.

I lean away, feeling completely rejected. I wish I would've sat in the aisle seat so I could get up and rush off at the next stop. "What're we doing? What do you expect to get out of this when I can't even talk to your face with you hiding under sunglasses?"

He lowers his head, pressing his lips to my ear. "I don't want you to talk," he whispers like it's a huge secret he's keeping from the empty seats.

"But—"

He presses his fingers to my lips. "Shhh. Do you hear that?"

I frown. "Hear what?"

"Shhh. Just listen."

I don't hear anything except for the sound of the train wheels sliding over the tracks. *Did I push Xander over the edge? Has he lost his mind?* I grab his hand and squeeze it lightly. "I don't hear anything. I think you need some sleep or something."

He raises an eyebrow. "Close your eyes."

I glare at him for a second before doing what he says.

He moves my hand to his chest, and his warm breath tickles my ear. "This is the sound of me and you just being together. No words. No messy feelings. Just you and me, together." His words are so soft it's like his voice whispers into my mind.

And then I hear it. The sound of our breathing in perfect sync with each other, the way his heartbeat drums against my palm, and my own heartbeat slows down to match his. It feels so right. I can't even remember what it felt like to be without him. I don't want to remember.

I open my eyes and see him smiling at me. He brings my hand to his mouth and brushes his lips against each of my fingers. Tingles shoot up my arm, and I shiver. My protective walls begin to crumble all over again, and my resolve melts away. I don't have the strength to build them up again. Not with him.

I give in and let him fold me into his arms. I bury my face in his neck, breathing in his spicy cologne, taking a little piece of him in me to carry around like a baby's blanket. He squeezes me tighter, and it's like he's tethering me to him. Like the moment he lets go, I'll float away and lose everything.

Icy fear seeps into me, burrowing deep into my mind, and my heart speeds up like it's running away from his. "Don't let go," I whisper. "I'm scared."

He kisses the top of my head. "You're not going to lose me. I'm here."

He sounds so certain that I believe him. But that's not what I'm afraid of. I'm afraid of what happens next. I'm afraid of what happens when this moment's over, and I have to return to my nightmarish reality.

"I know." It's all I can manage to say.

I pull away from him and trace my fingers along his sunglasses. He stiffens but doesn't attempt to stop me. I need to look into his eyes. I need to see that what he says is true, because if it is, it makes going home bearable.

I slide his sunglasses off, and my stomach twists seeing the fresh, purple bruise around his eye. I gently run my finger over his swollen eye, and he flinches and then relaxes. His smile fades into worry—no—something darker. Anger. But it's not at me.

All I can think about is Trent seeking out Xander and retaliating for his interference. For protecting me. "I'm going to kick Trent's ass," I growl, my shaky voice going shrill.

Xander shakes his head, dropping his stare to our twined fingers. "It wasn't Trent," he mumbles so quietly that I almost don't catch it.

My eyes widen, and it's like a thunder cloud swallows me. It's a darkness I haven't felt since, since—it's worse than when I accepted that Lila was gone.

The car accident was just that: an accident. Yeah, I feel it in my very soul everyday that part of me was responsible, but there was nothing I could do to prevent it. The other driver was in my lane. I don't even know why or what happened, but something had the guy on the wrong side of the road when I was coming. I felt cheated when I found out he died, too. Because I wanted to scream at him for shredding my life into pieces. But I never could. It was another thing I lost that day—the ability to blame someone else, which left the blame on me.

But this, what Caleb has done to Xander, wasn't an accident. It was planned. And it sparks a darkness within me so black, I feel like I'm being sucked into a void. It's like Caleb is trying to crush me all over again through Xander. It's like he doesn't think I deserve anything good anymore.

"When?" I ask.

"Last night."

Xander clutches my hand, but it's too late. Reality washes around me, pulling me farther away from him, away from myself until I'm lost, drowning in a sea of my own personal darkness.

Chapter 21

eleven days

WHEN I WAS in the hospital, I refused to speak for weeks. The doctors and nurses would ask me how I was feeling, and I'd glare at them because I thought it was the stupidest question to ask someone who had been through too many surgeries to remember.

I was angry. Angry that they wouldn't let me look in a mirror, angry that they wouldn't let Lila visit me. I was angry that they had taped my god-awful sophomore year school photo on the wall above my head. I just wanted to hurry up and heal so I could get back to living my life. I wanted to forget that I almost died, that I was a miracle with an army of angels watching my back, that I was a fighter, a survivor, and the bravest, strongest girl Nurse Stacy had ever had the pleasure to meet.

Everyone whispered to me, like a sudden loud noise would shatter me like the porcelain doll I'd become. I don't know if they thought it was comforting, the soft whispered words full of encouragement, or if it was just how people talked in the morbid environment I lived in. All I know is that it pissed me off to no end. Then one afternoon, I overheard Dr. Chavez, the psychiatrist the hospital had assigned to me to help deal with what happened, whispering to my parents in the hallway.

"Has she asked about her?" she asked. I couldn't see her, but I could picture her holding her stupid bedazzled pen to a clipboard, prepared to take notes.

"She hasn't said anything at all. Are you sure nothing happened to her vocal chords or something?" Mom asked. "My daughter wouldn't lie there in silence if nothing was wrong." I could feel the anger radiating from Mom as it seeped into my room. Every time she came to visit, she pestered the doctors about one thing or another that was different about me. I once heard her scream, "What kind of doctor are you? You need to fix my daughter. That girl in there is not my daughter. Fix her!"

"All the tests came back normal, Mrs. Caraway. Please, understand that Coco is suffering from post-traumatic stress disorder. She's detached from the situation as her way of coping. I've prescribed her a serotonin reuptake inhibitor and will continue to work with her for as long as it takes."

Dad cleared his throat. "How long do you think?"

"It could be months, sometimes years. It's too soon to predict, Mr. Caraway."

"Is there anything we can do?"

"I think it's time to tell her about her friend. The longer you two put it off, the longer it will take for her to heal."

Mom huffed. "She *is* healing."

"Physically, yes."

When Dr. Chavez brought up Lila, I remember feeling relieved because no one ever mentioned her around me. I was excited, thinking *finally*. I expected the doctor to come in and tell me Lila was just as beat up as I was, but that she was fine, and I could see her soon.

I licked my lips, which were cracked and scabbed and then said, "Listen to the doctor, Mom. I don't know why you won't let me visit Lila."

Utter silence greeted me and from the way the air suddenly felt heavy, like it was closing around me, I knew without having to be told. The air whooshed right out of me, and the pain in my chest was so intense, I was sure my heart had just exploded.

This can't be right. I'd have known. If something happened to my best friend in the entire world, I would have felt it, I thought.

Seconds later, my room flooded with so many people—doctors, nurses, my parents, and Caleb, who just leaned against the wall in the corner with tears shining in his eyes. I wanted to reach out to him and tell him not to cry, that this was some twisted joke to get a response out of me.

Sympathy hung on my audience's faces, and I wanted to sink into the bed and disappear. I wanted everyone to leave. They were just making it worse. They didn't have the right to be sad. Their silence was mocking me, like the world shattering around me was a show. Pure entertainment for the ones who hovered around me for weeks, just waiting. Waiting for me to get up and get back to my life.

Dad rushed to my side and grabbed my hand, careful not

to mess up the IV. "It's going to be okay, kiddo."

I'd never been angrier at Dad in my life. He knew that I thought those words were cheap and empty and a complete lie. He knew that nothing was okay and yet he said them anyway. And, he knew what I was thinking, because he took a step back and his eyes filled up with tears, and he began to cry.

I had never seen my dad cry. Ever. He didn't cry when Caleb broke three of his five fingers during a game of family football. He didn't cry at my grandpa's funeral when I was nine. Even when I woke up a couple days after the accident when Mom and Caleb were both bawling their eyes out, he just hovered over my bed and smiled at me and said, "My tear ducts are broken."

But when I was lying in that hospital bed, covered in my rainbow-colored knitted blanket with half the staff there as my "support team," feeling like someone dropped my heart in a blender and turned it on high, my dad crying confirmed my worst nightmare. That Lila had broken her promise and died without me.

Tears stung my healing cheeks as they trickled down my face. My stomach heaved, and I bit my tongue to stop myself from throwing up. The edges of my vision darkened through my blurry eyes, and it felt like I was watching my meltdown as a spectator in the crowd. I felt bad for the poor unfamiliar girl who had just found out her best friend had "gone to a better place," according to one of the nurses.

I wanted to ask him how he knew Lila was in a better place, and how could it be better without me. I wanted to argue with him, scream at him, tell him if it was the place I heard about, the one in the sky with white puffy clouds, the soft sound of harps, and angels just hanging out, then Lila was not in a better place because she was afraid of heights, once claimed to be allergic to classical music, and had an aversion to people with wings because she once had a nightmare that a mutated bird-man swooped down and was about to eat her alive. She always referred to the nightmare as *The Evil Angel Episode.*

Dad pulled himself together after a minute and turned to face my audience. "Get out. I need to talk to my daughter alone."

Everyone stood there and glanced between me and him. "Are you hard of hearing?" he exclaimed, pointing at the door. He even made Caleb and Mom leave.

He sat at the edge of my bed, his shoulders hunched and his eyes red and puffy, and he stared at me. He studied me for a minute and then leaned down and propped me against him.

"Dad." The words stuck in my dry mouth. "Why did this happen to me?"

He started crying again. "I wish I had the answer, kiddo."

I hurt all over, like my insides had been ripped out and shoved back in. "Is it true? Is she really gone?"

He sighed, releasing a haggard breath until nothing came out. "Y-yeah." His voice shook, and he looked like he was in more pain than I was.

I pressed my face into his shoulder. "Why?" I wasn't asking Dad the question. I don't know who I was asking. Maybe Lila, maybe God, maybe myself.

"I don't know," Dad whispered. "The Big Guy sometimes takes the best people too soon."

Anger crept into my mind because it wasn't right. I wish he didn't try to answer me. His words were less than comforting because I firmly believed that the best people deserved better than a short life. Lila didn't deserve to die. It seemed cruel that it could happen to my best friend. That I got to live and she didn't.

I lost my faith that day.

It seemed like such a joke to pray to someone who didn't listen. To have faith in someone capable of making the wrong decisions. Who put me through so much and didn't give me anything in return.

I laughed at the nurse who told me I'd be stronger because of it. I didn't feel stronger. I felt like I was hanging onto a thread that was unraveling with every passing minute. And I knew it would eventually break. That I would break.

***

Xander texted every few minutes since I got home from school. He'd been checking up on me because of the way I blew up on the train the other day. I was yelling so loudly at nothing that a patrolling sheriff asked me to get off at the next stop, and we had to wait for a different train to take us back home.

When I got home from the train, the house was empty and the beautiful tulips Xander got me were scattered across the lawn. Caleb hasn't come home since, and he either hid from me at school or skipped the last two days. Bridget wasn't around either.

A cold piece of pizza is halfway between my lips and my plate when I hear the front door squeak open. I jump to my feet and stomp into the living room to find Caleb hovering on the porch like he's considering leaving.

"How could you!" I scream. I run at him, my hands fisted at my sides, and he stumbles back trying to shut the door before I reach him.

I lunge at him as he reaches the bottom step, and we fall to the grass. He blocks his face with his hands, and I punch the grass next to his ear. "You said you'd trust me!"

He squints through his closed eyes. "I do trust you." His voice rumbles deep in his throat, and his face reddens.

"Then why'd you do it? He didn't do anything to you."

"He hurt you," he argues. "I couldn't stand to see you like that."

I narrow my eyes. Nothing he says will make up for what he did. "*I* hurt *me*. I hurt *him*. But did you even ask? No. You just assumed it was him."

"I don't care if you broke up with him. He should've listened to me in the first place. If he would've left you alone, none of this would've happened. I'd punch him again."

I push to my feet. I can't stand to look at him. "What is wrong with you, Caleb? You can't just go around hitting people for making me cry. It's like you want me to suffer. You don't think I deserve happiness, do you? You'd rather I sit in my room for the rest of my life. You probably wish I was the one dead."

"Are you kidding me!"

"You blame me for Lila's death. I know it. You're pissed off because you never got the chance to tell her how you felt. You feel like I cheated you of your happy ending. Well, you know what? I wish everyday that I'll wake up and be the one in that grave."

Caleb gets to his feet and grabs onto my shoulders. "Don't talk like that."

"I'm tired of pretending everything's okay. I thought you'd understand."

"I do—"

I press my hand over his mouth, cutting off his words. "You don't. While you're off having the best time of your life, I'm struggling to find some sort of happiness to keep me moving forward. And you're so damn insistent that I lose it the moment it's in my hands."

"Cee..."

I glare at him. "I don't want to hear it. You're so lucky I don't call Bridget."

His face falls.

"Hurts, don't it? It's crazy that after everything you've done to me, I still want you to be happy. But this—" I motion between us. "This is the last thing I want. I can't even look at you."

I bolt into the house and to my room where I shove as many clothes as I can fit into my backpack. I grab my memory box, makeup bag, and purse, and pound down the stairs.

Caleb blocks the front door. "Where you going?"

I turn on my heels and strut to the back door. "Away," I

call as I shut the door behind me.

***

Holly opens the door before the doorbell has a chance to finish ringing. She smiles before she frowns and motions me inside. The house seems abnormally quiet, and I don't see Xander or the rest of his family anywhere.

I hover in the entryway. "I'm sorry. I shouldn't have come here," I say, adjusting the strap on my backpack. It took a lot of convincing myself, but I managed to sprint across Valley View with my eyes closed. Anger pushed right through my fear and allowed me to get here.

Holly drapes her arm around my shoulders. "Don't be silly. You're always welcome here."

"I just—I just—" Tears swell in my eyes. "I had nowhere to go."

Holly holds me out and runs her gaze up and down me. "Did someone hurt you?"

I shake my head. "Not physically. I broke up with my brother."

She squeezes my arm. "I know how that goes. You know I broke up with my sister three times over the years?"

I smile for the first time in days. Holly reminds me of how my mom used to be. Lila spent so much time at my house because her parents always worked so late, Mom nicknamed us The Triplets. Lila even got her own pile of presents on Christmas.

I drop my backpack at my feet. "Did you ever get back together?"

She smiles sadly. "Wish I could tell you yes, hon. The last time was a doozy. I haven't talked to her in seven years."

I raise my eyebrows. "Wow."

"Doesn't mean I love her any less though. We just get along better when we're not involved."

I want to ask her why, but I don't want to pry. Or maybe I don't want to leave myself open for questions from her. Instead, I just nod my head and ask, "So where's everyone at?"

"Fabulous, Fun, Fancy, Family Fish Taco Night. It's kind of a tradition."

I twist my lips to the side. "Sounds...fantastic. Why aren't you there?"

"Got off late."

I kick my backpack. "I didn't mean to keep you from family night."

She links her arm with mine. "You didn't, hon. Come on. You're family, too."

I almost start crying like a baby because this is the first time in over a year where being included as a family member wasn't painful. I wish it was always this easy.

Chapter 22

ten days

BRIGHT SUNSHINE FLOODS Xander's room. I sit up, rub my eyes, and expect the dream to end. After a minute, I realize this is real—me sleeping in Xander's room—and a smile creeps onto my lips.

A tap draws my attention to the door, and Xander peeks his head in before stepping in. He greets me with a kiss on the forehead and then one on the lips. "Dad made breakfast. You should come join us."

I glance down at my sleep-twisted tank top and wrinkled pajama bottoms. "Can I get dressed and put my face on?"

He crinkles his eyebrows. "It's breakfast in the Romano house not fine dining at Le Kitchen."

"But—" I pause. *Mom would flip out*, I think to myself. "I don't want to scare your family."

"Have you seen me? If I don't scare them, nothing can." He grabs my hands and tugs me to my feet. "Now, come on."

I dig my toes into the carpet and twist toward his closet mirror. I look a wreck. Worse than usual. Besides my scars glaring at me since I took off my makeup to sleep, my cheek has pillow indents and my hair is a mess of tangles sticking out in every direction.

Before I have a chance to try to do something to make myself more presentable, Xander scoops me off my feet and swings me over his shoulder. He runs down the hall, and I flail my arms, smacking him in the back. He sets me back on my feet, and I turn to see everyone sitting at the dining table smiling at me.

"I'm not much of a morning person either," Tonya says, hovering over a steaming cup of coffee. "It's why I work the late shift at Federico's Tortilla de Casa."

Xander pulls out a chair for me, and I plop down next to Elaina. She bumps my shoulder with hers and hands me an empty plate. "Did you sleep all right? I know Xander's room isn't exactly girl friendly."

I want to tell her that it was the best sleep I've had in a long time, but instead I say, "Yup. It was fine," so I don't sound like an idiot.

I felt kind of guilty when Xander offered to sleep on the couch, but I'm glad he did, because it gave me a chance to cry in private. The weight of knowing that my family will never be the same presses down on me, extinguishing the tiny piece of life I've been clinging to. Being around Xander's family pulls my heart in a million directions. I'm happy and angry and miserable all at once.

I laugh and smile when it feels like I'm crying inside because I want this so much. I want to sit and be with my family without the arguments, the anger, the feeling that they keep me around because they have to. I want them to give me a reason to stay.

I think about how much easier it would be for them if I were gone. If Caleb was an only child and I was just...dead. I think about how at my funeral there won't be any tears. Only sighs of relief. And thinking about that relief. That bitter sweet relief. It's all I need to reassure myself that it's okay. It's okay to let them go because they've already let go of me.

"So, you want to go?" Holly asks.

I glance up from my half eaten breakfast. "I'm sorry, what?"

Justin and Bradley laugh in unison. "You definitely aren't a morning person," Bradley says.

Holly smacks his arm. "We're thinking of heading to the beach for the rest of the weekend. We'd love for you to join us."

My mouth goes dry, and I stare at the table, embarrassed. "I'm sorry. I can't. It's—I—" I'm not sure how to explain that my Saturdays belong to Lila, and the beach isn't exactly walking distance.

Xander touches my chin, turning my face to him. "We can still visit Lila today, and you and I can ride the train. Come on, please say yes."

His voice caresses my ears, and I find myself leaning toward him. "You don't have to come with me. I'm sure there are a million other things you'd rather do." My voice trembles because I want him to go with me. I just don't want him to feel like he has to. It's not like he knew her. To him, Lila is just a sad story told in front of a grave. He can't see her like I can.

"Actually we could all visit her if you'd allow it. And then we can all take the train together. I haven't been on one in years," Christian says.

My eyes tear up, and I swipe my palm over my face. I swallow the sob threatening to break free and whisper, "Lila would love to meet you."

***

I can't control the tears from spilling on my cheeks. Lila hasn't had this many visitors since her funeral, which Dad told me was so crowded, that almost the entire police force had to escort the line of cars that went on forever.

I pass around a couple of pictures of some of my favorite memories. I don't want them to know her as a grave. No one should be remembered like that.

"She was so beautiful," Holly says. "You guys look like you could be sisters."

I smile through my blurry eyes. *Not anymore.* "She was in a way."

Xander hugs me, kissing my forehead. I've never felt so happy at Lila's grave. But it's hard not to be. Even though Xander's family has never met her, it feels like they know her. They smile and laugh and hug and listen as I tell them the stories behind the pictures. They won't remember her as the poor dead girl, but the girl I knew and loved and wished I could've died for.

On day ninety-three to go, my school decided to have a one year memorial anniversary for Lila's death. I hated the thought of celebrating something that should've never happened. It was a way to remember the girl who died tragically, to celebrate the short life she did have.

I thought about not going. I really didn't want to. But Caleb said, "It's your job to tell these people about who Lila really was," and it was enough to convince me to drag my feet into the auditorium filled with almost the entire school.

I wanted to turn around the moment I had walked in. If it wasn't for Caleb gripping my arm, I would have. It pissed me off that the principal would allow freshmen to attend even though they didn't even know her. But who could resist a free pass from half a day's classes.

I walked with my gaze glued to the floor so I couldn't see all the smiling, excited faces. I sat down in the front row of the wooden bleachers with Caleb next to me and forced on a brave face.

Mrs. Davis strolled up to the podium and called everyone to attention. On the screen behind her, a projector beamed Lila's sophomore photo, and I had to grip Caleb's hand to keep from yelling out. Lila would've been mortified. Both of our sophomore photos were so bad, we skipped taking our junior ones, and now the school would always remember her as a girl frozen forever mid-laugh with squinty eyes.

And that wasn't even the worst of it.

The speakers overhead began to crackle and out poured some whiny, depressing country song. And it turned into another and another. My blood was boiling at that point because it was like the school had told the student government to throw something together, and they didn't even take the time to learn about Lila, to know what she liked and what she didn't. They didn't even come to me to see if I had any suggestions.

The music finally ended, and Mrs. Davis wiped her eyes like there was something to wipe away. "Lila Olivier was a great student."

I stood up, my hands balled into fists, and headed toward the door. I couldn't listen as she listed half truths and stuff that had been downright made up. If she had simply looked at Lila's GPA, she'd have known that Lila's grades weren't perfect. Mrs. Davis rambled about things Lila wouldn't have wanted to be remembered by. Lila would've thought it was a joke, too.

By the time I got to the door, Lila's remembrance had turned into a lesson about drunk driving and the damage it could have on a life. What was supposed to be about my best friend was now a fear-inducing speech. They took the opportunity to turn Lila into an educational tool, and I couldn't stand it.

I cracked the door open and hovered halfway out of the auditorium. "This is a load of crap!" I yelled. My voice echoed and the restless crowd drew absolutely silent. "What kind of person are you? You're sick for using Lila's death like this. You know there wasn't any alcohol involved!" I stormed out and spent the rest of the day locked in a bathroom stall, crying my eyes out.

Pulling away from my thoughts, I stick a dozen different

colored flowers Holly picked from her garden into the in-ground vase. I don't have a letter for her today, and it's okay, because everyone I wanted to tell her about is standing around me.

Holly slides her arms over mine and Xander's shoulders. "Thank you for sharing her with us. I know it wasn't easy."

I don't argue because it was hard. It was hard bringing the family I wish I was a part of here because I'm afraid that the next time we're here together, it won't be to visit Lila. It will be to visit me. And it terrifies me. Because this very moment, I don't know what to do.

"I miss her a lot." I touch Lila's engraved name before standing up. *Why is it so hard, Lila? Please, what should I do?*

You want to stay. Lila's voice echoes in my ears almost like she's standing next to me. I imagine her dark brown hair blowing in the breeze and how her eyes would squint when she smiled. It's been so long since I've allowed anyone in, allowed them to know about Lila, it's like her presence is stronger than ever. It's haunting me, but not in a way that scares me or depresses me. It's encouraging to hear her voice in my mind.

And she's right. Part of me wants to stay. But a more dominant part of me wants to go. *Leaving's easier.*

Chapter 23

nine days

FOAMY WAVES CRASH into my legs as I stand on the shore with the sun blazing overhead. The beach is packed with Californians ready to start summer early, ignoring the fact that the water is freezing.

My jeans are rolled up to my knees and sand clings to my calves. I haven't been to the beach since the summer before the accident. And I wish I had. It's so peaceful with the stretch of ocean and sky blending into each other, held together by invisible seams.

Xander presses his chest into my back, hooking his hands around my stomach. He gently pushes me forward until the water is knee high, soaking into my jeans.

He rests his chin on my shoulder. "It took me years to come back to the beach."

"How'd you do it?"

"I let go. I was tired of my fears keeping me from returning to a place I loved. From doing what I loved."

"You make it sound so easy."

"I wish I could tell you it was. The first time I came back, I panicked. Thought the sand was on fire. But then I realized that it was just memories of my accident and that I wasn't going to let it stop me."

I turn around to look at him. "What about bonfires?"

"Over that, too. It helps that I love roasting marshmallows." He says it like it's the simplest thing in the world. Like quitting something he loved wasn't an option. I wish it were that easy for me. I can't find the good anymore.

I lean my head on his chest. "I would give anything to be able to just let go. I'm so ashamed, you know."

He's silent for a moment before he says, "What did you love about driving?"

"That I didn't have to walk."

He laughs, bringing his lips to mine. "I thought you loved walking."

I shake my head, laughing into his lips. "I hate walking."

"Why don't you ride a bike?"

"I despise riding even more."

On day three hundred and twenty-two to go, Dad realized that there was no way I would be getting behind the wheel or into a car anytime soon. He said, "I feel guilty that you walk everywhere." I wanted to tell him that he was being ridiculous because I chose to walk and there wasn't much he could do. But he insisted there was. So an hour later, he knocked on my bedroom door and exclaimed, "I have the biggest surprise!" I almost expected that he discovered he could work miracles. I was kind of hoping he did.

He stuck his hand over my eyes, letting me peek through the cracks in his fingers until we made it downstairs, and then he closed his fingers, and I could tell we were heading into the garage.

I froze in the doorway. "If it's a car, you've wasted your money, Dad."

He chuckled and pushed me into the garage. "It's better."

I half expected a motorized scooter, maybe even a motorcycle, which would've been insane. Instead, he waved his hand away from my eyes, and I was face to face with a gleaming, chrome-colored bike. I just stared at the thing not really reacting, and Dad took it as a stunned silent expression. I didn't know how I felt about it at the time, but that quickly changed in a matter of hours.

I've never really been a bike person, and whoever said that you'd never forget riding a bike, lied. Yeah, I understood the mechanics and concept. I knew I had to balance and push the pedals, but when it came down to it, I was rusty from not riding a bike since I was little.

First of all, it didn't help that I was nervous and felt idiotic when Dad handed me a matching helmet that I could see my reflection in. Second, Dad's hovering made getting on ten times worse. I didn't really want to get on it for an audience, even if it was just Dad, but the fact he was so excited about his brilliant idea, I couldn't let him down.

I swung my leg over the bike and sat down. It reminded

me of the first time I had ever been on one, and my palms were sweating up a storm.

"Here goes nothing," I mumbled before I took off. I was a little wobbly at first, but then the ride began to smooth out, and I was doing it. I was riding a bike and just as excited about it as I was when I was a little girl.

Maybe Dad was right, I thought. Then came the pothole, and for some stupid reason, I didn't even attempt to avoid it, and I fell. I got up, dusted off my jeans, and turned to Dad. "Yeah, totally not worth it," I said. "Seems like too much effort to get somewhere a few minutes faster."

I left the bike in the middle of the street and ignored Dad's sad face as I headed back in the house. I didn't care if I never went anywhere again. My dreams of traveling were shattered when my travel companion abandoned me.

"Uh oh. I guess that means we'll be getting some alone time," Xander says, bringing me back to the present.

My brows scrunch. "Alone time isn't so bad."

"Definitely not."

"But why?"

"Family bike ride."

"Yeah, alone time it is."

He kisses my nose. "I'd have picked that, too."

A wave swells in front of us, and he scoops me up and runs back to shore before it swallows us. I laugh into his shoulder, and he drops to his knees and sets me on the wet sand. He leans over me, and I reach up to kiss his lips. His fingers lock onto my hoodie, and I let him tug it over my head. His lips trail down my neck and to my shoulder, and he brushes them along the scars peeking from my T-shirt.

I flinch away and press my hoodie against me. I'm embarrassed to be on a crowded beach, showing my flaws for the world to see.

"Don't be ashamed of your battle scars," he whispers, pulling my hoodie from my fingers.

"I'm not ashamed," I argue.

"Then why hide?"

"Can we not go there?"

He nods his head and falls next to me. We lie together and stare into the blue sky. The silence between us is thick, uncomfortable, and I hate not wanting to open up to him. It's like every time I want to let him in, I clam up.

I exhale, blowing my hair out of my face. "It's because I don't want people to know me by them."

"Like me?"

My mouth falls open, and I beg the world to spin in the opposite direction and rewind the last thirty seconds. I could kick myself, because even though I meant the words for me I didn't even think about Xander or how he feels about his own scars. I never asked, and I wish I did.

I'm not sure that anything I say now could make up for what I said because the truth is, Xander is known for his scars. But he's also known for a lot of other things. Like a bad boy, a hero, a survivor. Mine only tell one story. How I lost Lila.

I squeeze his hand. "That's not entirely true. Some know you as the guy who caught the attention of the untouchable or the crazy girl with the overprotective brother."

He chuckles. "I think you have that wrong. Your brother's crazy and overprotective. You're just you."

"You don't think I'm crazy?"

"Crazy people don't admit to being crazy."

"You didn't answer my question."

He brings my hand to his lips. "You're not crazy. You just have a few quirks. It's cute actually."

"It's so not cute. It's debilitating and horrible and aggravating and sucky."

"Sucky?"

"I couldn't think of a better word."

"I still think it's cute. Most girls wouldn't be cool with going on a date by foot. Or put up with my family for that matter. People think it's weird how close we are."

I dig my elbow into the sand and turn to him. "It's because they don't have what you have. I'd trade anything to have a family like yours."

"You don't have to trade anything. I'm pretty sure you had them the moment I mentioned you."

"It's not the same." I look past him at the stretch of beach.

"Things will change."

I nod, but not for the reasons he's thinking about. I know he's talking about after graduation and college. About the future I've given up on. And it hurts to think about. I never really thought about how life could be different. About just suffering through my pain. That's not a life I want.

But I'll always be the same, I say to myself.

***

I sit on the public balcony of the hotel, watching the sun dip into the ocean. Xander's family is still out doing whatever it is families do on mini-vacations.

Xander slumps into the chair across from me and slides a takeout bag to me. "Dinner," he mumbles.

My phone rings, and I tug it from my pocket. A smile creeps onto my lips, and I accept the call. "Hey Dad. What's up?"

"I just talked to your brother."

"That's good."

"He said you left."

"I did."

"Care to tell me where?"

"Does it matter?"

Dad sucks in a breath, and I can tell he's trying to keep his cool. "Of course it matters, kiddo. I wish you would've called me."

"Why? So you could tell me to go home and work it out with Caleb?" I take a breath to keep from yelling. Dad's not the one I'm pissed at. "I'm in Village Beach with Xander's family if you must know."

"Well, I'm glad you're okay. But I do think you should call Caleb. He's really hurt, you know."

I glare at my phone. "I'm done with him, Dad. I'm. Just. Done. I can't be around him anymore."

"He was only trying to be there for you."

"Whose side are you on? He hit Xander."

"Coco..."

My nails dig into the skin of my palm. "Don't. You don't know what it's like having to deal with him. Or Mom for that matter. You're never home."

"I'm sorry for that. I won't be traveling forever. I just have two more trips scheduled and then I'll be home for a while."

"But for how long? A month? Two? You're supposed to be here for me. Can't you see how much I need you home? I don't know how much more I can take."

Dad breathes into the phone for a long moment. "I'm always here for you," he says. He sounds worn and defeated, and I know I'm the reason for it.

Tears pool in my eyes because I want to believe him. But a couple phone calls a week doesn't mean he's here for me. I feel like he chooses to get away sometimes. Because he not only has to deal with my brother and mom, he has to deal with me, too. I'd go away if I were him.

"I know, Dad," I say. "It's just so hard."

"It's a good thing you're the strongest girl I know."

"I don't know about that. I don't feel strong. I feel like I'm on the verge of a midlife crisis."

He chuckles, and I sigh. "I'm sorry, kiddo. I didn't mean to laugh. You're just too young to have one of those."

I'm tempted to tell him that I'm on the verge of giving up on everything. But instead I say, "I know."

"Just try to enjoy your night at the beach, okay? We'll be driving home Tuesday, and then we can work things out."

I nod even though he can't see me. "I will."

The line drops, and I wipe the tears from my eyes. Xander gets up from his chair and wraps his arms around me. He just holds me, breathing into my hair, until I get myself under control.

I want Dad to be right about being able to work things out. I hate being so angry at Caleb. I wish I could just shut my eyes and rewind my life to the day of the accident. I'd stay home and Lila would be alive, and there wouldn't be anything that needed to be worked out. We'd all be happy again and act like a family. We'd be a family again.

The thing that bothers me the most is that I know if I tried, I probably could forgive Caleb. I'm just so tired of trying, of having to. And it bothers me that I'm the reason that everything is broken and foreign and different. It wasn't the accident that tore my family apart, made it unbearable to spend more than five minutes with them. It was me. It's always been me. And there's nothing I can do about it except...well, keep my promise.

Chapter 24

eight days

"ARE YOU SURE you're going to be okay?" Xander asks, holding me by my waist on my front porch. "You could stay with me as long as you want, you know. My parents get it. You wouldn't be the first person to crash at our house either."

I smile into his lips after a short kiss. "I wish, but I don't want to overstay my welcome. I don't think I'll murder Caleb at the moment, and my dad asked that I check up on things. Plus, I doubt Caleb will show his face until my parents get home tomorrow." This has been the longest I've gone without speaking to Caleb on purpose. I haven't seen him either. He's avoiding me like I'm avoiding him. I know this because I saw his car in the student lot at school today.

The only other time I can remember not speaking to Caleb was the summer after seventh grade when I went through a growth spurt and he didn't. It was the Fourth of July, and Lila and her parents joined my family at the beach to watch the fireworks over the ocean. Our moms packed the best picnic ever, and we managed to snag a fire pit in the perfect spot, close to the bathroom and the surf shop that had the cutest guy working the register, though he was probably already almost finished with high school at the time. That didn't stop Lila and me, though. Together, we were the most outgoing friends. Nothing held us back. Not like the world holds me back now.

That was also the summer Mom allowed me to wear my first bikini that she bought me for my thirteenth birthday just a week before. It didn't take Lila and me long to throw on our matching sheer covers and head into the surf shop to check out the different surf brand clothing. We had both been eyeing the mannequins in the window each wearing a turquoise and pink tank top with rhinestone logos. They were perfect to add to our summer style.

Lila, always the initiator, strolled straight up to the counter and asked for fitting rooms. We spent a good thirty minutes trying on a few dozen shirts and shorts, and all the while the boy at the counter watched us with an amused expression.

After finally sticking with the tank tops from the window, we made our way up to the register, and Lila pulled out her mermaid scale pattern wallet and handed the boy two twenties. In exchange, he gave her the change and a receipt with his phone number on it, which made us stay to talk about who-knows-what. I don't even remember now.

What I do remember is that Caleb got tired of waiting for us and came bustling in, slightly dripping, and he said, "Come on, Cee. I want to walk to the pier and Dad said you had to come with me."

I rolled my eyes. "Can't you see I'm busy?"

Caleb frowned, looked between me and Lila and then at the cashier, and said, "That guy's like twenty and you're thirteen."

He was definitely not twenty, but I was definitely still thirteen and both Lila and I had never been so mortified when our new surfer cutie was suddenly handing us our bag and backing away to do something with a display.

We never went to the pier with Caleb, and I didn't talk to him until the next day when he brought me a bag with a bracelet with a small mermaid charm because he thought I'd like it. The bracelet still sits in my jewelry box.

"Why don't I stay with you for a while, just to make sure everything's okay?" Xander asks, pulling me from my thoughts while rubbing his fingers under the hem of my sweater. His fingers play with the skin just above my jeans, sending tingles through me.

I try to think of a million reasons he should go, but none of them are persuasive enough to even convince me. Slowly, I nod my head before opening the door and allowing him to follow me inside.

Caleb's backpack sits on the floor near the door, but his car isn't here, so he must've stopped by before going out again. At least I know for certain he's probably out with Bridget or something.

Without waiting around a moment longer, I lead Xander to my room. The last time we were in it together was when he told me he loved me, and I consider just dropping my bags before hanging out in the living room.

I shut my door instead and pull my sweater over my head. "Summer's going to be brutal," I say as I turn my back on him to change into a camisole.

Warm hands slide over my hips a second before Xander kisses my shoulder. I spin in his arms, facing him, and meet him with another kiss, one long enough to steal the breath from both our lungs.

"You're beautiful, you know," he whispers, pulling me tighter against him. He brushes his lips on the nape of my neck. "And incredibly hot."

I laugh as his kisses tickle me, their feather softness lightly caressing all my exposed skin. I thought I'd be bothered by revealing myself to Xander. I thought I'd feel ugly and embarrassed, but with the way his eyes drink me in, the way he holds me tighter, ignites a flame within me bright enough to burn all my worries away.

In this moment, I can see what he sees in me, because I see it in him, too. With his lopsided grin and bright green eyes, the way his black hair curls around his ears, the muscles in his arms, the way his lip ring turns sideways when he's thinking, and how his whole face lights up when he sees me—all the little things that make Xander who he is on the outside—can't compare with how he makes me feel on the inside. With him, I don't feel like some stranger in my own skin. I don't feel like a dead girl walking. I feel so alive and vulnerable, so terrifyingly okay, that it's enough to cause a tear to slip on my cheek.

I gently push him to the bed before he notices. Because I don't want him to stop. I don't want him to let go of me or stop kissing me. I don't want to remember what it feels like without him holding me. I don't want to be reminded how quickly all this can be stolen away in seconds.

"I love you, Coco," Xander whispers as he lies on top of me. Those three little words pull me from the haze I've been trying to bury myself within.

I blink a few times, trying to get my mouth to work.

He leans down and brushes his lips against mine. "You don't have to say anything. I just wanted you to know."

My heart punches against my ribcage, threatening to spill out from my chest—but not in a world-ending way. My heart wants nothing more than to throw itself at Xander so he can protect it for me, so he can take care of it and cherish it. Because, unlike myself, he will proceed with care as I throw everything to the wind.

My fingers nudge the hem of his shirt, and I tug it over his head until our bare stomachs touch as he leans down on his elbows to kiss me again. His tongue slides into my mouth, gently slipping over my tongue, and I trace my fingers up and down his back, feeling the smoothness of his skin until I reach the edges of his scars on his side.

His own hands slide under my back until he feels the clasp of my bra, and I suck in my bottom lip while gazing into his eyes as he slowly unhooks it. We stay absolutely still for the longest, most intensely incredible moment of my life. He smiles, a fire lighting behind his bright green eyes and then he leans over and kisses me again.

His lips trail from my mouth to my neck and then graze over my collarbone. He gently kisses parts of me that I never thought I'd show anyone ever again. He kisses my scarred shoulder, causing me to gasp, and slowly pulls away to meet my gaze.

"We can stop," he whispers, linking one of his hands with mine while bringing my fingers to his lips.

I shake my head. "I want this. I want you. Just give me a second."

He kisses me once before he rolls next to me. I slide from the bed and grab my robe before sauntering from my room to Caleb's where I know he keeps a box of condoms in his dresser. I used to have some as well, but after the accident, I didn't think I'd be comfortable enough or brave enough to reveal my vulnerability to anyone ever again so I gave them to Caleb.

My heart races as I head back to my room and hesitate in the hallway. From the crack in my door, I watch Xander sit on the edge of my bed, fingers laced together, as he waits for me. His eyes meet mine for a second before they glance at the calendar hung on the back of my door and then back to me.

I quietly enter my room and cross over to him before sliding into his lap and kissing his cheek.

"What happens next week?" he asks mid kiss.

I shrug. "It's nothing. It's old."

He accepts my answer as I steal anymore questions with a kiss deep enough to make him flip me back over on the bed.

"You make me incredibly happy," he whispers through another kiss.

My heart falters for a beat and then I smile, a truly genuine smile. "You don't even know how happy you make me," I whisper.

And for the first time in over a year, I'm not faking it.

I'm just unsure how long it'll last.

If it can even last.

Chapter 25

seven days

XANDER LEFT AT midnight after begging me to go home with him when Caleb didn't show up. As much as I wanted to after the incredible night we had, I just couldn't get myself to leave. I didn't want to admit it to Xander, since he's the last person to care about Caleb at the moment, but I'm a little worried about him.

He didn't respond to my texts last night, and my phone died after I fell asleep on it talking with Xander until past two when Caleb still hadn't come home. And now, as I sit at the counter, looking at the early morning clock, I'm about to panic. Caleb isn't the one to hold things against me. I'm the one who can't let go of things.

Now, in this moment, I have a bad feeling. It's a terrible, fear-inducing feeling that leaves the room hazy and my stomach twisting. All of my terrible memories creep up on me at once, and my whole body feels like it wants to shut down.

The landline rings from the counter, startling me, and I nearly fall out of my barstool. Instead of letting it go to the answering machine like I usually do, I pick it up and hold the receiver to my ear with a shaking hand.

"Hello?" I whisper like a monster will suddenly jump through the line.

"Cee! Why aren't you picking up your cell phone?"

I release a long breath as Bridget's voice erupts through the line. "I'm sorry. It's on the charger. What's wrong?"

"Caleb's been jumped by Trent!" she screams. "We were leaving Midnight Bakery on Foothill when he was attacked."

I cling onto the counter before I fall onto the floor. A million horrible thoughts swirl through my mind, threatening to consume me altogether. "Is he okay?" I finally manage to ask.

"Would I b-be calling you if he w-was?"

It's hard to understand Bridget through her hysterics. But one thing is quite clear. Caleb is hurt or worse. It can't be, though. Caleb can't be...dead. Right? Just the idea sends me over the edge into a dark place that is nearly impossible to pull myself from.

I clutch the phone, my back pressed to the cool tile. My breath comes heavy, nearly painful. "He's not..." I can't finish the sentence. It's horrible to even imagine.

"Oh, God, no. He's hurt really badly though. You have to get down here."

"Where?"

"University Medical Center."

My teeth chatter as fear swells in my ribcage, threatening to crush my heart. "It's too far. It'd take me like five hours to get there."

"I don't care if you have to run. You need to get here *now*."

I let out a long breath. "I'll be there soon."

***

Xander pulls into my driveway and jumps out of his car the moment he puts it into park. He rushes to me, sliding his arms around my shoulders, and holds me as I shake and blubber into his chest.

"I'm so scared," I cry, digging my fingers into his back.

He buries his face into my neck. "Caleb's going to be okay."

I cry harder, ashamed that I'm not as afraid for him as I'm afraid of the car ride. "I can't do this."

"You can. I know you're strong enough. I'll keep you safe."

I stop myself from arguing, because who can really keep someone safe in a metal box that has the ability to kill you in a split second? Instead, I nod and let him guide me to his car. I plop into the seat, and Xander reaches over and buckles my seatbelt when my hands tremble so much that I can't even latch the darn thing. He kisses my forehead and shuts the door before I can make it out of the seat again.

The car closes in around me, and I feel utterly trapped like I did when my Miata crushed in on me. Panic rises in my chest, and I grip onto the dashboard and hang my head between my legs.

Xander's in the driver's seat in a matter of seconds, rubbing his hand along my back. "We'll be there in twenty minutes tops," he says as he starts the car.

I jerk in my seat as he reverses. "I need to get out!" I slam my head on the dashboard as I try to sit up to open the door.

Xander grabs my hands in his free hand for a moment. "Just keep your eyes on me."

I bring my eyes to his, and he smiles. He shifts his gaze to the road, but I never take mine off his. The tightening in my chest loosens, and I suck in a breath, settling my nerves.

I concentrate on the curve of his cheekbone, the shadow of stubble on his chin, and the way his lip ring glitters in the sunlight drifting in through the window. The way the glow shines on his skin, he almost looks angelic, like my own personal guardian angel. And I want him to save me. But I don't want to ask. Pushing my heartache and despair, my fears and crazy tendencies on Xander would be selfish. I could never do that to him.

"I knew you were strong enough to do this," Xander says, parting his lips into the lopsided smile I love to kiss.

His words sound so familiar, like he knew exactly what Lila used to say to me when I did something I swore up and down I'd never be able to do. They're comforting and reassuring and exactly what I need right now.

Lila would be proud.

"You got this, girl," Lila said, taking my hands into hers when I started to chicken out during my first driving lesson with Dad. She looked me dead in the eyes, her smile nothing but a straight line on her face as she pressed her lips together.

"I can't. I'm afraid." I licked my lips, my tongue feeling

like sandpaper in my mouth.

"You're going to do great." She opened the driver's side door to Mom's Mercedes and nudged me toward it.

Dad smiled from over the roof. "Listen to her, kiddo. She knows what she's talking about."

My heart dropped in my stomach like a heavy stone. I'd never been behind the wheel of a car, and I was so scared of hitting something. I didn't want to piss Mom off if I accidentally totaled her precious ride. I also didn't want to ruin my chance at freedom. Driving had been my dream since I started high school.

"All right. Get in, cupcake," I said to Lila, and she hopped in the backseat.

"Should I wear a helmet?" Dad asked as he slid in next to me.

My mouth dropped open, and I banged my head against the steering wheel. If he didn't quit joking, I thought I would really fail. I shifted my eyes to his. "Maybe," I said, forcing myself to smile. "Can't tell for sure."

He laughed, the deep sound reverberating through my bones, giving me the courage to start the engine. I backed out of the driveway, slamming the brakes when I exceeded five miles per hour, jerking the car sporadically. Lila giggled in her hands and smiled at me as I looked over my shoulder. She winked at me, and I let out a breath when I eased onto the empty street.

I clutched the steering wheel for dear life, my knuckles paling. Dad didn't help much with his death grip on the grab handle. Only Lila's constant giggles kept me from pulling over and quitting.

"I knew you could do it," Lila said, squeezing my shoulder.

I drove down the block and turned right on Sacada Circle, slowly making my way around the neighborhood. The Saturday afternoon was quiet except for the hum of the engine, and Dad finally relaxed when he realized I wasn't going to kill us going twenty-five miles per hour on the straight stretch of road.

"Caleb's going to be so jealous when he finds out you rock at this," Lila said when we pulled back into the driveway.

I laughed and put the car in park. "He's going to be pissed when he finds out you took me first." I patted Dad's knee.

He swiped his big hand across his forehead. "That's why this is going to be our little secret." He winked and turned to face Lila. "Do you have your permit with you?"

Lila bounced in her seat and shook her purse. "You know it!"

Dad pressed his lips together and waggled his eyebrows. "You want to go for a spin?"

Lila opened my door in a matter of seconds and yanked my arm. "You heard the man." She pulled me out and wrapped her arms around me. "You were awesome, Cee," she said into my ear. "But step aside, babe. I'm ready to rock n' roll."

I lifted an eyebrow, and she laughed, pushing me toward the backseat. "Lila just informed me she wanted to be a race car driver when she gets her license," I said, leaning between the front seats. "You still have time to change your mind."

"Quick! Toss me a helmet!" Dad said, wildly shifting his eyes.

Lila beamed another gigantic smile. "Don't worry, Daddio. I won't go faster than a hundred."

Thinking back, I don't think Lila went over twenty. It was the slowest ride around the neighborhood. I'll never forget how excited we were, and how big Lila grinned after she parked the car. I'd give anything to go back to that day and have Dad teach us what to do in unthinkable situations or to have had him take us driving a million more times. I sometimes wonder if he wishes he could—or if he regrets ever teaching me at all.

"We're here," Xander says, pulling into the parking lot of the hospital.

I glance up, wiping the burning tears from my eyes. I can't believe I did it. I can't believe I survived. It's a silly thought, but I felt like I'd die at any second. But now, as I sit in the front seat of Xander's car, I can't find the will to get out. I'm afraid of what I'll find with Caleb.

"Will you go in with me?" I ask after a moment. I know he isn't on good terms with my brother, but I'm afraid of being alone. Facing this alone. Not if he's willing to be here.

Xander nods, his jaw line tensing. "I'm here for you. Always."

The hospital looms on the other side of the packed parking lot, and the way the two towers reach toward the sky on both sides, it almost looks like a modern day castle with the rows of mirrored windows catching the sunlight and reflecting it back at me.

Instead of beautiful princesses trapped behind those glittering windows, the sick and damaged lie restlessly waiting to walk out the doors, or they pray that everything will just end. It's an awful feeling to be behind that glass, not sure whether you'll live or die, praying for both and ashamed to admit it. I'm ashamed those thoughts still haven't left me, and knowing that Caleb is in one of those sterile rooms, possibly thinking the same thing I did—I do—makes it so much harder to get my feet to move. How can I see him like that? I was never the strong one.

Xander waits for me to move before falling in step next to me. His hand rests on my lower back, not guiding me, but just supporting my unsteady legs.

A tired looking man smokes a cigarette near a small bench, and I'm tempted to join him, to come up with an excuse to not go in. He smiles and nods, not a friendly one, but one that says he wishes he wasn't here either.

The glass double doors swoosh open and cool air hits my face. The air reeks of cleaner and wilted roses. A small group of smiling people hover in the gift shop to the right, their arms loaded with bright pink balloons and flowers, and I remember that hospitals bring life into the world, too.

My Converses squeak on the shiny linoleum, and I freeze at the sight of a woman, covered in scabs and bruises, being whisked into the lobby in a wheelchair, the orderly not even glancing around as he wheels her by with a man trailing behind him.

Xander pats my shoulder and shuffles to the receptionist behind a long counter. He leans over and whispers to her, but I can make out Caleb's name.

"Coco!"

I hear Bridget before I see her, and my stomach twists the moment our watery eyes meet. She's a mess of runny mascara and frizzy blond hair and looks more distraught than I feel. Her shoulders jerk as she swallows back a sob, and it takes everything in me not to yell at her to pull herself together. That Caleb is my brother, and she has no right to breakdown before me.

I shove my hands in my pockets. "Where is he?"

"Come on. They're getting him situated in a room right now."

***

I hover in the doorway of room 5F and watch Caleb sleep. Dr. Boettcher spent the last five minutes informing me of Caleb's condition and how they drugged him with painkillers so he could get some rest.

I'm not sure what to do with myself. I sent Xander and Bridget to the waiting room, and wish I hadn't because Dad and Mom are still not here.

Shuffling into Caleb's room, I keep my eyes trained on his hands because they're the only part of him I can see that isn't swollen, bruised, and stitched up. His nails have a dark line of dirt under them, and I wish I had something to clean them with.

I let out a breath. "Why couldn't you let my last few days go by in peace?" My voice is no more than a whisper, but the words reverberate through me like I'm yelling into a hollow tunnel. "I was so scared."

Caleb doesn't even blink.

"Don't you think I've been through enough? I've already lost Lila, and I'm not going to lose you. I'm supposed to die first."

Tears burn in my eyes. "And what would happen to Dad? He'd be so lost if we both aren't here. I need you to live because I can't. I just can't."

A hand touches my shoulder, and I jump. I turn and meet Xander's sad eyes. My heart falls, the pain so sharp I suck in a breath. His eyebrows sink over his eyes, and his lips disappear into a thin line. He's heard everything.

And I don't know what to do. Kissing him won't fix this and there's nothing I can say to make this better. I'm not even sure I want to. He was going to find out my plan sooner or later, only I preferred later.

Xander grabs my arm. "Is that how you really feel? Like you can't live anymore?"

I press my lips together to keep them from trembling. "On the bad days." It's the only excuse I can manage. Because it's true. But I can't tell him that most days are bad.

"You could've told me. You should've told me." Xander tucks my hair behind my ear.

I look at the floor because I can't stand that he's unraveling my secrets. "Why?"

He tilts his head. "Because—because—God! I don't even know what to say, Coco. What you said to Caleb scares the hell out of me. How could you even say that?"

I don't have an answer for him. Not one that he'd understand. He's never lost like I have. He doesn't know what it feels like having to live my life without Lila. Or what guilt feels like. Or broken promises.

He didn't see the fear in Lila's eyes when the car closed in on us. He couldn't even imagine what it felt like believing that death was minutes away or what it felt like learning that your best friend died without you, without warning, without even considering that she was leaving you behind.

I swipe my hand across my cheek and turn away from him. My knees go weak, and I drop to the floor next to Caleb's hospital bed. Xander managed to make this awful situation about me when it needs to be about Caleb. Because Caleb is the one broken and bruised.

Anger creeps into my mind, and I can't stand being in the same room as Xander. I just need to be alone with Caleb, to be here with him like he's been there for me.

I press my face into Caleb's hand. "Thank you for the ride, but you need to leave."

"Please, don't do this. I'm trying to be here for you."

I crane my neck to glare at him. "I don't need you to be here for me. I don't need anyone. Just leave, Xander."

He steps closer. "Coco..."

I raise my hand. "Just go."

Xander's shoulders slump, and his face crumples. His mouth opens and shuts, like he wants to argue with me, but he doesn't. Instead, he shoves his hands into his pockets, spins on his feet, and walks out. And there's nothing left in me to want to make him stop. To beg for him to come back and tell him I was wrong. So I let him go. It's time for me to just let it all go.

Chapter 26

six days

ON DAY THREE hundred and fifty eight, one week after I decided to make a new promise to Lila, I was lying on my bed when Caleb quietly opened the door and strolled into my room. Instead of sitting on the edge of the bed, he pulled the chair away from my vanity table and placed it right next to me so his weight wouldn't shift me and cause me any more pain.

Though my legs were fine, my knee was still tender, and it hurt to stand for long periods of time. It hurt to lie down too, but the dull ache in my chest and stomach were more tolerable. And with the amount of pain meds I was on, I barely even noticed the ache in my face because I lost the will to do anything except stare at the loads of magazines and books Dad brought me along with the TV he made sure I could stream whatever shows I wanted to.

But that day, the day where Caleb entered my room bearing gifts, was the day that I knew for sure that I would keep my promise.

After a moment of sitting next to me, Caleb lifted a bag onto his lap, and I realized there were dozens of colorful envelopes practically spilling from the top. It was like my entire class had each made me a card while I was in the hospital, and Caleb was finally bringing them to me.

He carefully ran his finger through the first envelope and handed me the card. It was from a girl named Jenny Penn, and I had barely spoken more than a dozen words to her, though she sat next to me in Chemistry, or maybe English.

It was a simple card with a well wish and an apology for what I was going through like there was somehow a reason she needed to apologize. I tossed the card onto my night table, and Caleb continued opening them for me to read with neither of us commenting on how they all said the same thing, how basically the world felt sorry for me.

After grazing over a few more cards, I picked up one that had every open space covered in writing. It wasn't signed by anyone, just ended with the line, "It should've been you." I'd never forget that line, because I thought the person was right. I always thought that anonymous person, the only one who spoke the truth and put the blame on me for Lila's death, was right to blame me. Because I blamed myself.

Tears swelled in my eyes, and Caleb snatched the card right from my hands and shredded it while cussing up a storm. His face reddened, anger lowering his brows, and then he took the bag with the rest of the cards and tied it up before setting them outside my room.

"That person has no idea what they're talking about," Caleb said, coming back to my side to take my hand. He looked into my sad eyes, his own gaze glassy, and then he hugged me the best he could. "You know that, right?"

I didn't respond to him as the letter swirled over and over in my mind.

"Cee? They were wrong. This wasn't your fault, okay? The police said it wasn't."

I still didn't answer him.

He sighed a heavy breath and kept telling me over and over that we'd get through this. That Lila would want us to. And even when I still refused to say anything, he still remained by my side until I fell asleep.

But this time, he can't tell me this isn't my fault. As I sit by Caleb's bed as he sleeps from the painkillers, all I can think about is how he wouldn't be in the room if I had never agreed to dance with Trent at our party. He wouldn't be in this room if I had just kept to myself. If I had just given up sooner.

Because Caleb would be better off without me. He wouldn't have to worry about protecting me or standing up for me. He wouldn't have to worry about me needing him.

I thought that maybe, just maybe, I could survive a bit longer. Hang in and suffer. But how can I if every time something good happens to me, something bad soon follows, ripping it away. The police, Caleb and my family, even Lila's family might not blame me for her death, but it feels like the universe does.

Fighting against the universe seems impossible.

Giving up is just easier.

If I wasn't here, life would go on, and that would be that.

Just like it has done without Lila.

Just like I want it to do without me.

Chapter 27

five days

MY BACK CREAKS as I push off the chair I've been sleeping on. I'm alone in the waiting room, my hands frozen from the subzero temperature blasting from the vent. After a moment of looking around, everything sinks in again. My brother, Xander, everything. My heart aches in the worst way, like it's slowly being separated, torn between who I was before, who I am now, and who I'm going to be. If that ever happens.

A nurse pokes her head in the doorway. "Coco? Your brother's asking to see you. Your parents went for coffee, and he could use some cheering up, you know."

I run my hand through my tangled hair. "That makes two of us."

Her lips twist to the side. "I know this is hard, honey, but he's going to be okay. I hear he'll be released later today after a final evaluation."

I grab the arm rests and hoist myself to my feet. My back

screams as I straighten, and I almost fall back into the chair. I stretch my arms over my head and twist side to side before taking a step toward the door. "So, Caleb really did ask for me?"

Her brows crinkle. "Why wouldn't he?"

"I wasn't on speaking terms with him."

"I'm sure whatever happened is already behind you."

I shrug because it's the only thing I can think to do. I'm not about to spill my heart out to a stranger. "I guess."

The nurse smiles and lets me walk past her. The hallway leading to Caleb's room buzzes with energy. The hospital staff runs from room to room, and visitors linger in the hallway, anticipating some sort of good news or tensing for the worst.

Sitting up in bed, Caleb stares off into space. Machines hum, sending a familiar sinking feeling into my stomach, and I swallow hard to moisten my dry tongue.

I knock on the doorframe. "Some nurse said you wanted to talk?" My scratchy voice sounds like I need a drink of water, and it's as if I'm talking to an acquaintance and not my twin.

Caleb smiles before wincing. The fresh scab on his bottom lip splits open, and a tiny drop of blood splashes on his chin. He doesn't attempt to wipe it off before saying, "I had to see you for myself."

"What do you mean?"

"You haven't been more than a few miles from the house, and no train comes here. You drove." Caleb holds his small smile. I bet he's thinking it's a miracle. Maybe it is.

I shuffle across the tile and plop into a green upholstered chair. "I got a ride." I say it like it's not a big deal and shrug to make it seem that way.

His eyes shift to the IV taped to the back of his hand. "You trust Xander more than me."

I look him dead in the eyes even though he doesn't look back. "Not anymore."

"What happened?"

"Not going there."

"This about the other day? When you two were arguing?"

My jaw tenses. "You heard that?"

He nods.

"You were pretending to be sleeping?" I ask. I can't hide the annoyance in my voice. He heard everything I said, before and after Xander came in.

Caleb brings his eyes to mine. "I wasn't. You just woke me up when you came in, and I was in too much pain to even open my eyes."

I throw my hands up. "Great! Go ahead. Lecture me."

Caleb raises his eyebrows. "Do I look like Dad?"

"So, you're not going to try to change my mind?"

"Is that what you want?"

I push my hair out of my face. I want a lot of things—Xander to understand, my scars to magically disappear, to be able to see Lila again—but to be lectured by Caleb? No.

Caleb leans forward and grabs my hand. "Is it?"

"No." I sigh and slump forward until my knees knock the metal frame of the bed. "I just want you to be released so I can get out of here."

"I couldn't agree more. If frickin' Trent hadn't caught me

off guard, he would've been the one in here."

The reminder whooshes the air right out of me. It's my fault Caleb's in here. Just like it was my fault that I was in here, and why Lila never had a chance to be. A quiver builds in my chest and pulsates into my arms. I rest my head on Caleb's leg to get myself under control. "I—" I gulp for air as the words stick in my throat. "I need to get out of here."

Caleb's hands brush my hair. "I know what you're thinking and you're wrong."

"If it wasn't for me—"

He grasps my chin. "No, if it wasn't for my inability to keep my mouth shut, I wouldn't be in here. You didn't do any-thing wrong." He looks so sincere when he says it, but it still feels like a lie. Like he's lying to protect me, because that's what he always does best.

I shake my head, pulling away, until I'm wobbling on my feet. "I want to believe you..." My words trail into a whisper, and I step back, retreating to the door.

"Don't go."

"Bye, Caleb," I say, ducking past a nurse into the hall.

Caleb yells my name, but I'm already jogging to the eleva-tor. The door dings open, and I slide past a couple holding white carnations and lean in the corner, pressing my back into the cool metal wall.

An elderly woman shuffles in and glances at the row of but-tons marking the floors. "Where you heading?"

"Lobby," I whisper.

"Me, too." She presses her slim, wrinkled finger to the button and the door closes. "Gotta have my smoke."

I swipe my hand across my face. "I just need to get out of here."

***

With how packed the parking lot is, one would think the hospital was Disneyland and everyone was here for a good time. When in reality, it's more like a freak show at a carnival. The only shiny things are used to poke and cut people open with, and the bright lights? Well, they just enhance the ugliness of sickness and injury. The parades down the halls are almost always death marches and forget about costumes. The blood-covered staff doesn't count.

A circle of jittery smokers huddle together around the only ashtray midway through the parking lot, and I hold my breath as I pass them. If my last day was set for fifty years from now, I might have taken up cigarettes, but my skin is bad enough already, and I'm not sadistic enough to prolong my death like that. Lila would laugh if I told her that, especially after our two week stint as smokers.

"It's not that bad," I said, taking another drag off the cigarette Renee Mills gave me along with a half a glass of whiskey when I stepped onto the balcony of her dad's penthouse apartment during one of her many parties.

Lila's eyes followed the line of smoke trailing from my lips until it disappeared past the glare of the balcony light. I held the cigarette out to her, and she gingerly took it between her middle and index finger. "Give me your drink," she said, snatching it from my hand, spilling some on the ground.

"Girl knows what she wants." A guy laughed from next to us, but I couldn't keep my eyes off Lila as she brought the cigarette to her lips and inhaled. Her eyes watered, but she didn't cough, and I'd never seen anyone exhale smoke so elegantly, where she actually looked hot doing it.

She took a sip from my glass. "Everything looks weird," she said, taking another puff.

"Enjoy it while it lasts," the guy said. "It goes away after you smoke a pack."

Lila smiled at me. "Strangers always give the best advice, don't they, Cee?"

I rolled my eyes. Alcohol always brought out Lila's snarky side.

"It is sound advice," he said, taking Lila's comments in stride.

I laughed and took a sip of my whiskey, feeling it burn down my throat. It settled in my stomach, the burn warming my skin against the cool night.

"'Kay," Lila said, snuffing the cigarette out. "Then I'll only smoke a pack."

The next morning, on our way out, Lila swiped a pack of cigarettes off a table near the front door of Renee's. I didn't know she was actually serious, but Lila smoked a cigarette with me every day until the pack was gone, and I threw it away with every thought we had about the cute stranger with the terrible advice.

But now, standing in the hospital parking lot, I wish just for a second the guy would suddenly appear before me. Not because I want more of his weird advice, but because he'd probably let me bum a smoke. And I could smoke one for Lila this time.

"Coco?"

I shift my eyes away from the smokers and stop dead in my tracks, my memory disappearing. Xander leans on the tailgate of a beat up pickup truck with his hands shoved in his pockets. His puffy eyes show that he didn't get any better sleep than I did. He narrows his lips, frowning, and I can barely even look at him without wanting to cry.

I fold my arms over my chest. "What are you doing here?"

He rocks on his heels. "You can't get rid of me that easily."

I'm not sure what to say. He knows too much and part of me wants to say good riddance to him. The other part of me knows that it's harder to finish than to start over again. But where will that get me? There's not much time to start over.

I twist my lips to the side. "Is that so?"

He tugs a hand from his pocket and rubs his chin. "Want me to prove it?"

"Maybe."

Xander closes the distance between us, bends down, and swipes his arm against the back of my knees, scooping me into his arms. His lips gently touch my forehead and trail down my nose until they meet with mine. He lingers for a minute, touching his forehead to mine. Our eyes stay locked on each others, our lips touching. The world melts away, everything around us going fuzzy.

"You don't want to get rid of me," he whispers. "I can see

it in your eyes."

He's right. The last thing I want is to wonder what could've been. I have enough regret to last me a lifetime. "What else do you see?"

"I see how much pain you're in." He runs his finger down my cheek. Cupping my chin, he pulls me closer, our eyelashes almost touching. "It doesn't have to be this way, you know."

"It doesn't?" I bite back my sarcasm and anger. I've heard it all before, except now, it feels different, like Xander is right.

He kisses the tip of my nose. "No." He squeezes me against him like I'll disappear the moment he sets me down. It's tempting to try, to just fade away, but his eyes beg me to stay with him. I imagine what it would be like if I do. But what if how he feels about me is only temporary? It happens all the time. One moment you love someone and the next, you don't. It's reality, as certain as life and death. Nothing can stay the same forever. It's impossible. Unavoidable. Am I willing to risk it? Is he worth the risk?

"I don't know how to make it any other way." My words come out a whisper, and I'm not sure I even said them out loud until Xander closes his eyes and kisses me again.

"You have to let go." He winces when I stiffen in his arms. His fingers dig into my side, but not so tightly that it hurts, just tight enough so I don't fall, when he says, "Hear me out. Just listen to what I have to say."

I shift from his arms so I can see him straight on. "Go on, tell me Lila is dead, that she's never coming back. Tell me it wasn't my fault that I wasn't paying attention to the road, and it wasn't me who killed her. Tell me Lila wouldn't blame me, and I shouldn't feel this way, that she would want me to live. Go on, Xander, tell me." I don't know what I was thinking when I thought Xander was right, that what he could say would somehow be different. It's not. It's the same as always—unhelpful advice from people that don't understand and never will. Just empty words they think will somehow make me okay.

"Is that what you want me to tell you? Would it make you feel better?"

I'm taken aback by the tone of his voice. "It's what everyone else always says."

My stomach drops as he sets me on my feet and steps back. "Do I look like everyone else? Because I'm damn sure I don't." He throws his arms out before bringing his hands to the back of his head. He glares at the sky instead of me. "And you know what else?" He pauses and brings his eyes to mine.

I stare at the ground and wait for him to finish, because I don't know what else he has to say. Filling in the blanks got me in this mess just minutes ago, and I just want the mess to be cleaned up already.

"You need to stop treating life like a death sentence and be happy that you get to live at all. You're the lucky one because you're not the one who died. I'm sure if Lila had a choice, she'd gladly swap places with you."

I slap Xander without thinking, but all he does is take a step back out of my reach. "You don't know Lila," I say. "She'd never trade. She'd die for me." Tears burn in my eyes because she's not here to make that choice.

Xander tentatively shuffles forward and pulls me into a hug, and a sob rips from my throat, shaking my shoulders. He rubs his hand on my back, and I fall into him, barely able to remain standing. The hurt and grief swells so intensely it feels like I just found out that Lila died all over again.

"That's why you need to live. Live for Lila because she can't. Live for you," he says. "Don't choose this. I'm begging you."

All I can do is cry long, heart-wrenching sobs that I'm sure even the patients on the top floor can hear. Through my tears, I see the group of smokers gazing sympathetically at me, again reminding me of Lila, of the bad advice stranger, of our two weeks as smokers, and suddenly that memory that seemed so important, now doesn't. It's just a memory of one unimportant night, of a habit I never got addicted to, and of Lila, who I know in my heart would want me to start living again, who would want me to go on without her. Because I want to go on without her, too.

My tears dry, and I hide my face in Xander's sleeve. "I want to so badly," I say, rubbing the muddy day-old mascara from my eyes. "I just don't know how to stop thinking like it's the end or how to let her go."

Xander drapes his arms around me. "You don't have to let her go, Coco. You just need to start living without her."

The words sound strange coming from him, like somehow my boyfriend has been replaced with someone who has experienced life and loss and love. His words have lifted a bag of sand off my chest, and I can finally breathe again. It feels so good to breathe again.

"I don't know how or where to even start," I admit, sniffling.

"You're going to start with me right here in this parking lot. You don't have to go through this alone, Coco. I'm here for you no matter what. You just have to let me be here."

I glance at the hospital and the irony of starting over again here. It's a place where people are born and where they come to die. I've done both. A part of me died with Lila, but the part that still holds onto her memory lives. And I'm finally ready to live.

Chapter 28

life goes on

"I DON'T EVER wanna grow up," Lila said. "It seems like such a downer having to work all the time."

Mr. Thomas lifted an eyebrow. "That's why you should think about it now, so you'll choose to do something you'll love."

Lila rolled her eyes and grinned at me from her desk. She had been talking circles around Mr. Thomas for at least fifteen minutes since he'd scribbled *Career Day Tomorrow* on the whiteboard.

I raised my hand, forcing myself to keep a straight face. Mr. Thomas sighed and pointed to me. "Yes, Ms. Caraway?"

"What if I love being young?" I pursed my lips together to keep from giggling when the rest of the class began to laugh.

"Same," Lila said. "You wish you were still young, right?"

Mr. Thomas narrowed his eyes. "That's beside the point, Ms. Olivier."

"Then what is the point? You asked what we wanted to do when we grew up and maybe I don't wanna." Lila rested her chin on her hand, her eyes peeking out from behind her long bangs. "Maybe I won't."

"Of course you will. It's not something you can choose to opt out of. And now is the perfect time to start thinking about career choices. To make sure you do, I want all of you to write a one page essay about what you would like to be when you grow up."

I groaned just like everyone else did, but now that I think about it, Mr. Thomas was wrong. He said that Lila would grow up. He said it wasn't something she could opt out of. But guess what Mr. Thomas? She's not going to ever grow up and have a career. And another thing, people opt out of it all the time. I was going to opt out of it. Was. Past tense.

Anger rolls through me in waves, and it takes everything in me not to change my mind and decide to join Lila. I had to stop myself from marking an X on my calendar because I've grown used to doing it. It hurts to think that there is something else out there for me now that death is no longer an option, that I've taken suicide off the table. I haven't even thought about tomorrow.

A knock on the door breaks my train of thought, and I draw my eyes away from my calendar. Dad pokes his head in and offers me a smile. "You have a visitor."

I jump off my bed as Dad turns and leaves. Xander is right on time to pick me up for what he's declared as our very first normal date by car, which is true. There will be no family, no walking through the neighborhood, no cemeteries. Just us together, someplace normal without any drama, and I'm actually excited.

I check my makeup in the mirror one last time, then I swipe my favorite pink sweater off my vanity table and shrug into it. Skipping down the stairs two at a time, I hesitate when I don't see Xander. Yessica sits at the bar facing Dad, who's pouring a glass of soda. She's the last person I expected to be here.

She smiles at me and flicks her fingers in a timid wave. "I tried to call you." She turns on the barstool to face me.

"Sorry 'bout that. A lot has been going on."

She slides from the chair and swings her arms around my shoulders. "I'm glad Caleb's okay. Sucks that he's going to be bruised for prom."

I pull away. "Bridget cares more than he does. I'm just glad Trent and his friends were banned from prom. They're lucky we're not pressing charges. Caleb's upstairs if you want to see him." Trent and his friends weren't the only lucky ones though. Trent never even brought up the party and Xander. The only reason Trent got caught was because he was wasted while he jumped Caleb and it happened in public with Bridget. He's also not walking at graduation either. Serves him right.

"And risk Bridget thinking I'm trying to steal her man? No thanks. Actually, I wanted to see if you would like to hang out."

I glance at the clock. Xander should be here any minute. We've had so many ups and downs, love yous and breakups that I'd hate to cancel our date. But I'd really hate to pass on hanging out with a girl friend. It's been a long time since I've done it outside of school.

Yessica shifts and follows my eyes to the clock. I wonder who would be more understanding, her or Xander. *Xander, definitely Xander.* "What did you have in mind?"

"Well, prom's next weekend, and I don't have a dress yet. I was going to get one last weekend, but—" She crosses her eyes and smiles. "Long story. Damien and I broke up again. This time I think it's for good. So, I wasn't going to go, but then thought why should I let him ruin prom? I figured I have the ticket so I'd just go stag. Bridget said you may need a dress too, so I thought we could make an evening of it."

My first instinct is to turn her down because I didn't even think about going to prom. Also, the mall is a car ride away. The idea of zooming down the road in a death trap still scares the crap out of me, but it's been forever since I've been in an actual store and not one I found on the internet. I purse my lips and say, "I'll come, but I don't think I'm going to prom. I don't have a ticket."

Yessica grins. "You can get one at the door. Come on, it's our senior prom."

Senior prom. The only prom I'll get for the rest of my life. The life I'm now going to live. I tuck my hair behind my ear and shift my eyes to Dad, who's pretending not to be engrossed in our conversation as he puts away the dishes. "'Kay, I'll go, but only if the greatest dad in the world gives me an advance on my non-existent allowance."

Dad raises his brows and digs his wallet out of his pocket. "Whatever gets you out of the house."

The doorbell rings, and I smack my hand against my forehead. "Shoot! Xander's here."

I spin on my feet and jog to the door, open it, and fling my arms around his shoulders. "Please, please, please don't be mad."

Xander pulls back and shifts his eyes from mine to something behind me. "Hey, Yessica. Come to check on Caleb?"

"Please, don't be mad," I whisper.

"And succumb to the wrath of Bridget? I don't think so. Coco and I were just about to go to the mall." Yessica tugs her purse from a hook on the wall and slides it over her shoulder. "You do know prom is next weekend? You were planning on taking Coco, right? If not, she's my date."

I sigh and plead for Xander to forgive me with my eyes. I'm pretty sure I'm running out of chances with him.

"There's no one in the world I'd rather take," he says. He leans down and kisses my cheek before stepping back. "And since I'm here, how 'bout I drive you two there? Maybe buy you dinner if you don't mind?"

I could tell by the expression on Yessica's face that Xander had her hooked at, "Hey, Yessica." I couldn't have asked for a better boyfriend—not in a gazillion years.

Yessica smiles. "That would be awesome. Just remember, you're the third wheel, not me."

"Of course," Xander says.

The way Yessica jokes around with Xander reminds me of the way Lila would talk to anyone I was dating. During the few months I dated Scott Solomon, my first real boyfriend, and Lila dated Jared, we'd set some ground rules to make sure that we would never forget about each other like most other girls in our class did—the ones lost in love.

Rule number one was that we still had to call each other every day and talk for at least ten minutes, which was never a problem because we hung out most evenings anyway. Second, we would have Bestie Night two days a week and would never be the third wheel if we chose to let our boyfriends join us in the plans we had made with each other.

The rules were the best idea we had ever thought of because it meant that we'd never get upset or feel like our friendship was in jeopardy because of a guy. It worked for us, always, and now with hearing Yessica, I'd bet the same rules could apply for us.

Yessica steps outside, and Dad appears in the entryway and slides a wad of twenties into my hand.

"Thanks," I say before stepping outside and taking Xander's hand as we walk to his car. I let Yessica hop in the back, and I take the front seat, saying a little prayer as Xander checks his mirrors and pulls from the curb. I never thought this day would come. A day where I actually feel normal.

***

"Who says I'm going to prom with you?" I tease. "You haven't technically asked me again since I turned you down the first time."

Before I can stop him, Xander bends on one knee and grabs my hands in between his in the middle of the food court. My cheeks warm even though no one is paying any attention to us.

Xander smiles. "It would be an honor if you, Coco Caraway, would agree to join me in the festivities of prom."

It's the cheesiest thing I've ever heard in my life, and by the way his eyes crinkle in the corners, he knows it, but it's also the sweetest thing I've ever heard. How could I ever deny him? "I'll go with you if you'd just get up." I yank his hands, and he jumps to his feet only to lift me off mine. He kisses me hard, and the sounds of people ordering food and tossing food trays on the plastic trashcans disappear. The only thing left is the tingling sensation of our lips touching, the weight of his arms around my waist, and our hearts bumping against each other through our shirts.

It's a magical moment I haven't dreamed about in a long time. Since Lila and I used to fantasize about who would ask us, where we would eat beforehand, what our dresses would look like, if we would have sex.

My heart hurts for just a second. Our plans are now only my plans. I'm going to prom with Xander, and I won't ever share this moment with Lila. Instead of experiencing it with her, I'll be experiencing it for her. The thought is hard to swallow.

Xander notices the sadness in my eyes before I have a chance to chase it away. "I hope that look doesn't mean you've changed your mind." He kisses my forehead.

A smile slides on my lips. "Sorry. I was just—"

"Thinking about Lila," he says. He doesn't ask because he doesn't have to.

I nod. "Guilty. It's just, you know, we were supposed to do this together. Me and her."

"And now I will have to suffice." Yessica drops a tray of fries on the sticky table next to us. She plops down and places her feet on the swivel chair across from her.

"I'm sorry. I didn't mean it like that," I say.

"It's cool, Coco. Never feel like you have to apologize for missing your friend. What happened sucked."

Tell me about it. "Thanks."

We finish the fries and Yessica pulls me up from the table and away from Xander. "I hate to break it to you, but dress shopping is for girls only," she says over her shoulder as she drags me away. "Go find something to do and we'll meet you later."

***

Dress shopping with Yessica is almost the same as all the times I went dress shopping with Lila. As I watch Yessica try on dress after dress, I can't help remembering all the fun I had with Lila picking out dresses for our first official high school dance, one we chose to attend together instead of with dates just in case it sucked and we wanted to leave.

"You look so hot in that dress!" Lila said as she snapped a picture.

I twirled around for her, winking at our reflections in the mirror. "I think it's the one."

"Totally. Scott's going to ask you to dance for sure." At the time, Scott was the teacher's aide for my English class and it's how I met him before we shared a kiss later that year during

Jared's Chrismakkah party. Scott always smiled at me in a more-than-friendly way, and I desperately wanted him to think I was the hottest girl he'd ever seen.

I spun away from the mirror and pulled a deep purple halter dress from its hanger. "Try this on."

Lila stepped back into her dressing room. "You know me so well," she said over the door. "Jared isn't going to be able to take his eyes off my...best assets."

I laughed and watched her swing the door open. She looked absolutely amazing. The dress fit perfectly, and I was pretty sure no guy was going to be able to keep their eyes off her. Lila just had that way about her. She was like the sun in comparison to the planets. She could light up a universe.

"What do you think about this one?" Yessica asks, yanking me from my memories. She's wearing a flowing turquoise dress with a sweetheart neckline. Small glittering beads decorate the waistline, accentuating her perfect hourglass figure. The dress is beautiful, and I wish I saw it first.

"It's perfect!" My voice squeaks just a little, but my words are true.

"You really think so? You're not just saying that because it's the eleventh dress I've tried on?"

"Yes, really. You look stunning."

"And the dress you're wearing is amazing. I still can't believe it's the first one you tried on."

Turning back to the full length mirror, I stare at my reflection. I imagine Lila leaning against the wall behind me, agreeing with Yessica. I blink the oncoming tears away, and her image fades just as quickly.

She would've loved this dress. The deep burgundy color. The gathered fabric in the shape of a rose on my lower back, flowing to the floor. The rhinestones scattered across the soft tulle material, reflecting the light like tiny stars. I avoid glancing at my scars, focusing solely on the dress, because I refuse to allow myself to get hung up on something I can't control. I can't avoid showing. I will not be the one girl at prom wearing a jacket or long sleeves. I don't care what people think anymore. My scars are a part of me and a reminder of what happened. Not that Lila was ripped from my life. Not a reminder of death. But, a reminder that I lived. That I survived and will keep on surviving. For Lila. For myself.

"You think Xander will like it?" I fiddle with the halter straps, adjusting them to the same length.

"Well, duh! How could he not?" Yessica spins one more time before strutting back into the dressing room. "Now text him that we are ready to go before he decides to eat dinner without us."

I enter the dressing room and gaze at myself once more before sliding out of the dress. I still can't believe I'm going to prom and that I have the rest of my life to live.

Chapter 29

a fresh start

MY PHONE DINGS from the edge of my vanity table. I close my eyes and take a few deep breaths. It's a notification with instructions to my family about where to find the letters I never wrote. Yesterday was supposed to be the day I reunited with Lila, but instead I spent it at school and then with Xander. Just hearing the sound knots my stomach, and my hands tremble as I turn off the alarm and toss my phone on my bed.

"Straighten your shoulders, raise your chin, and take a deep breath," Lila said as I stared at myself in the mirror. "You got this, babe. We got this."

It was the first day of freshman year, and I was all sorts of nervous. Not because something big or special was supposed to happen, but because the first day of every school year always made me nervous. And the first day of high school was nothing short of terrifying. I wasn't ready to give up my summer freedom to jump into the fall prison at a school that I would be forced to attend for the next four years. I wasn't ready to be a little fish in the big ocean again after successfully surviving middle school. I just wasn't ready.

I inhaled a deep breath. "I could never do this without you, Lila."

She smiled. "Same! Thank God we'll never have to."

The memory of that first day of high school stings a little like all the memories that remind me of what I lost, about who I have to live without. But Lila's words resonate with me. While she might not be here, every little thing that made Lila who she was still remains with me when she can't.

At the end of the day, Lila met me in the center of the quad, a huge smile on her face, and then she threw her arms around me in a rocking hug. "We are so not small fish in a big ocean," she said, smiling at a group of cute boys. "We're totally mermaids."

My phone beeps again with a final reminder, pulling me from my thoughts.

It's no longer a reminder of what I've given up. It's a reminder that this is my fresh start.

Glancing at my door, I peer at the spot where my calendar used to hang. I refuse to acknowledge the days I've lived through anymore and the ones I'll be living through. It's easier this way—almost freeing. No timeline. No end date. No more reminders.

Today is the first day of my new life.

Chapter 30

another day

ANOTHER SATURDAY, ANOTHER day.

Lila would've been ecstatic. This would've been the Saturday we'd have talked about all year. It would've been labeled The Best Day of Our Lives, Part One, because prom was on the list of best days before graduation from high school, then college, our twenty-first birthdays, and our weddings. Now, it just seems like another day. The cemetery was the same as ever, and I still look the same despite sitting at my vanity getting ready for a supposedly magical night. One of many that I had planned with Lila.

"You know what would be magical?" Lila had asked me at the beginning of junior year. "If we moved to New York City." She flipped through the college brochures the guidance counselor handed us the week before.

I lifted an eyebrow. "Yeah, right. You despise public transportation as much as I do, and I doubt driving around the city in traffic would be any fun."

I thought she was crazy. We'd been to New York on a class trip the summer before we started high school, and while it was a blast hanging out with a group of boys from Pennsylvania, we complained about the June humidity and the way the grates on the sidewalks smelled like rotten eggs when you strolled over them. Not to mention I blew through the five-hundred dollars Dad had given to me and had nothing but a few cheap souvenirs to show for it.

Lila smirked and tossed me the brochure. "But I really think we belong there." She bounced on my bed. "Think of the nightlife, the shopping...the boys! It's all just so magical."

I laughed. "We'd be too poor to do any of that. We'd be living in a closet-sized apartment."

Her eyes sparkled. "A glamorous, closet-sized apartment!" Her voice was shrill with excitement, and despite the fact I never considered living in a big city, I was almost convinced that I'd love it as much as Lila loved the idea. We'd move as soon as we returned from our adventure abroad.

Maybe Lila was right. New York City might be the best place for me to move after graduation. I'd take the subway, live in walking distance to everything I needed without feeling trapped in my neighborhood, and I could forget this place. I could forget everything I hate about it.

You could forget Lila.

The thought brings tears to my eyes, and I blink them away as I stare at my reflection in the mirror. I could never forget Lila, but I can move on, live a life without her. I have to do it no matter how hard it is on the bad days, the good days like this one, too.

Xander should be here in an hour to pick me up for our dinner reservation at Le Kitchen where we're meeting Caleb, Bridget, and Yessica, who are all taking a limo. Dad frowned when I told him Xander was driving me, said I deserved a night of luxury with my friends, but it's still hard to shake my fear of vehicles. I don't know if it'll ever go away.

I push away from my vanity table. My face is flawless, coated in a layer of makeup, but the rest of me is peppered in scars. A shiny scar that trails from my left shoulder to in between my breasts glares at me in my vanity mirror. I don't remember what caused it, flying debris or glass, maybe when a bystander ripped me through the window, but it was one of the most painful wounds while healing. I sometimes still feel the pain, or the memory of it, and it burns as I slip into my burgundy, shimmering dress.

"You can't hide forever," I say out loud.

I frown as I spin. The dress isn't as gorgeous on me now as it was in the store. I look thinner, paler, and my scars seem darker. I want to call Xander and cancel, tell him I'm sick, but instead, I step into my black velvet, platform, peep-toe wedges, grab my black sequined clutch off my dresser, and head downstairs.

Mom sits on the couch with her feet curled under her. She's reading a gossip magazine and doesn't lift her eyes to look at me. I don't say anything to her either. Life is tolerable as long as we don't converse. It's just easier this way. I hate her less.

She drops her magazine on the coffee table before I have a chance to retreat to the kitchen. Her lips disappear into a thin line and then she shifts her eyes to her French manicured nails.

I lift my head. "What?"

"Your father told me you were going to prom." I guess someone would tell her since we haven't said a word to each other since she came home.

My eyebrows furrow. "Yeah." I want to rub in the fact that Xander is taking me, but it's not worth the fight. It's hard enough as it is to remain in control.

"You didn't buy a shawl?"

Heat creeps up my neck and into my cheeks. Tears burn in my eyes, but I refuse to cry. I won't ruin my makeup, and I won't give her the satisfaction of knowing that I'm not as confident as I'm trying to be.

"I don't need one," I mutter and turn toward the kitchen.

Mom laughs. It's not a fun laugh, but a high-pitched squeal that sounds manic and condescending. Her eyes narrow. "Don't be ridiculous. It's your senior prom. You need to be perfect. Photographs will make your scars look even worse." She stands up and walks to the hallway closet. "I may have something you can wear."

I shake my head. "No, it's okay, really. I'm fine."

Mom slams the closet door just as she opens it and spins to face me. A deep line sets between her eyebrows and strands fall from her chignon styled hair and into her face. With the way her wild eyes sweep over me, she looks unnerved. She's been cold for months, but something's different about her, and it scares me.

She steps closer and locks her hand around my wrist. "Stop having an attitude with me, Coco. I'm trying to help you. People are cruel, and they'll talk about you. Wearing the shawl will hide you enough that people won't notice."

"I don't care if they do," I argue.

"You should. Appearance does mean something in the world."

I grind my teeth. "You need to get over whatever problem it is you have with me. You've always been a little vain, but something is seriously wrong with you, Mom. Why can't you just leave me alone?"

"Because I'm your mother, and I know what's good for you." Her nails dig into the skin on my wrist, and I wince when she squeezes harder.

I struggle to pull my arm away. "You don't act like my mother. You don't know anything!"

Mom's free hand flies up and slaps my cheek. The sound resonates through me as stinging pain swells in my face, and I stumble and fall to the carpet while she's still gripping my arm.

She stands over me like a vicious stranger and glares with eyes so full of hate, I know she doesn't love me anymore and wishes I weren't here. She doesn't see her daughter, but some distorted version of the girl she used to care about. And I can see it slowly killing her inside.

I wiggle my arm to try and shake her hand off me. She's annoyed me, belittled me, pissed me off, and made me cry, but has never laid a hand on me or scared me like this until now.

I'm terrified she'll do something unimaginable, something that is out of my control. I've heard stories in the news of how a person can just break.

Tears drip onto my cheeks. "Please, you're hurting me, Mom. Let go. I'll wear the stupid shawl." I'll say anything, do anything, to get her to let go of me so I can leave.

Her eyes shift from the scars on my shoulders, arms, and chest, and then back to my eyes. In this very moment, she looks dead inside, and I see a memory of myself in her. We are both messed up and broken, and our relationship is irreparable. We'll never have what we used to. Mom will never accept me how I am because she's grieving and angry about the loss of who I was.

"Mom? Please, let go," I beg. "You're scaring me. Snap out of it. Stop staring at me like you're going to kill me."

Her grip loosens, and she blinks a few times. A hundred different emotions cross her face—fear, disgust, sadness, and self-awareness. Tears sheen her eyes, and she opens and closes her mouth. "What's happened to this family?" She's not asking me but throwing out the question to the universe. "I can't do this anymore. You need to leave. Take your things and get out of here." She lets go of me and brushes the hair from her face.

My heart falls into my stomach. "I don't understand."

She turns away from me, and I'm relieved she released me, but now that her words are sinking in, it's like my world, the world I was just starting to get used to again, is imploding on itself. *What have I done to deserve this? Why can't anything ever go right?*

I catch my reflection in the wall mirror. My mascara smears

under my puffy, red eyes, and a tendril of my freshly curled hair falls from my low side bun. My red cheek glares at me, and I feel as horrible as my mom thinks I look, and I just want it all to end.

She stops at the stairs. "I can't live under the same roof as you. It's too hard. It's not good for either of us. I can't live like this."

Shadows and tears blur my vision. "And I can't live at all!"

I rush to the front door and yank my mom's car keys off the hook. I'm out the door, jumping in the car, and reversing before she has a chance to stop me. When I hit the end of the block, the pain and fear sinks deep into my shattered soul. My chest tightens as a truck zooms past, and I push past the fear and force myself to keep driving. It's the only way to get away fast enough.

I drive past the cemetery and slow down as I near the street that changed everything. Valley View Road is a block away, and my knuckles turn white as I turn right onto it to go up the winding road where I feel like the best part of me died.

My breathing quickens, and it's hard to see through my tears as I ascend up the winding, two-lane road. On my left side is a brown hillside with dead brush that used to be green with life. On the right, far below, is a valley of trees and just past it sprawls small cities and towns as far as I can see. It reminds me of one of the last times I drove this way.

"Look at those lights," Lila said. "They are prettier than the stars."

We sat on the tailgate of Michael Thompson's dark blue

Ford F-250 and stared at the city lights glowing in the distance. We were on a double date with Michael and his younger brother Benjamin, and Lila declared that they couldn't take us to do something boring like watch another movie where we'd never get to talk.

We ended up at a look-out point a mile away from their mansion on the top of Valley View Road and were having a picnic on the bed of Michael's truck while listening to music from his stereo.

I leaned against Benjamin, his arms around my shoulders, and smiled as Lila's eyes reflected the pale glow of the full moon above us.

"You're so lucky that you can see them every night from your house," I said.

Lila twisted in Michael's arms and grinned. "Are they better there?"

Michael's shoulders shook as he laughed. "Want to find out? Our parents are out of town tomorrow."

"We can have a party," Benjamin added. I tilted my head toward the sky, and he kissed my temple.

Lila pulled away from Michael and jumped from the tailgate. She spun in the soft dirt and said, "Yes!"

I laughed. "It'll be amazing."

Lila grabbed my hands and swung them back and forth. "The best party ever!"

I never saw Benjamin or Michael again. They went to a private school, and Michael would be away at college now. I don't like to think about them anyway and probably never will.

Everything I've ever had before the accident is just a memory now.

I park Mom's car on the soft dirt of the empty look-out point. The valley isn't as pretty during the day. There's a light haze of smog clouding the view of the cities spread out in the distance and this spot has lost all its excitement and magic since the last time I was here.

I get out, slam the door harder than necessary, and tip-toe over the soft dirt. It dusts over my velvet shoes, and I hold up my dress to try to keep it from getting ruined. I walk along the paved shoulder next to the guardrail and keep moving up the hill. The look-out point is the last spot to park before having to travel to the small community at the end of the road, and it's not where I was heading.

I stomp the quarter mile distance to the place of the accident. The memory of scraping metal echoes in my ears, and it feels like I'm fighting for my life all over again. A small wooden cross sticks in the ground next to the guardrail, and my eyes sting with tears when I see Lila's name etched in the wood.

I hate it. I hate everything about it. It's just another reminder of my best friend and how she left me here to live life without her. It's a glaring sign for the poor girl who lost her life too soon. It's worse than her gravestone. This little wooden cross marks the exact spot Lila took her last breath, the spot where her promise was broken, the spot that I hate most in the world. I don't want people to remember this horrible spot. I want them to forget. I want to forget.

I yank the cross from the ground and chuck it as far as I

can into the valley below. Wind roars in my ears, and I don't hear it hit the ground. All I can focus on is keeping myself together, the quick pounding of my heart, and how raw I feel being here in this moment.

I dig my fingers into the metal guardrail and look over the edge and the sudden drop. It could be so easy to forget now. I wasn't supposed to be around anymore.

You'll get through this. The memory of Lila's voice echoes in my head.

I close my eyes and count to three. I will get through this. I want to get through this.

My phone rings from my clutch lying in the dirt at my feet. I scoop it into my hand and tug out my cell. I consider not answering because I don't know how I'll explain any of this. I hate that I'll have to. But I wouldn't have it any other way. Moving on is my only option. I just wish it didn't hurt so much.

I bring the phone to my ear. "Hi." My weak voice shakes, and I barely hear myself over the wind.

"Coco? Where are you?"

At the sound of Xander's voice, I start sobbing. A shudder wrenches through me and nearly breaks me in two. I clutch the guardrail as a wail rips from my mouth, and I cover my face with my hand and sink to the ground. Everything about today is ruined.

"Let me come to you. Where are you?"

I pull myself together and sniffle into the phone. "Take Valley View Road past the look-out point. You'll pass my mom's car."

"I'll be there soon."

***

I sit at the table in Xander's kitchen while his sister Elaina fixes my mussed hair. A hot curl falls over my ear, and I wince but don't move. I managed to fix my makeup with the few products I threw into my clutch, and Xander's mom tries her best to clean up my dress and shoes.

Christian taps on the door frame, and I draw my eyes from the hand-held mirror to look at him. He smiles despite the pity in his eyes and shuffles across the kitchen to slump into the chair across from me.

"I spoke with your father, Coco, and he would like for you to stay here with us tonight."

My heart aches, and I blink the oncoming tears away. "So, my mom won." I wish it were a question. For once I want Dad to really take my side instead of playing the mediator, but it looks like I've lost this time. He's not even that. He chose her.

I imagine curling up and disappearing. I wonder what Caleb would say, how he'll react, and who he'll choose in the end. I can only hope it's me, but after all our ups and downs, it wouldn't surprise me if it were our mom. *His mom. She doesn't want to be your mom anymore.*

A hand touches my shoulder, and I shift to see Xander standing next to me. I didn't hear him come in the kitchen. I can barely hear anything over the destruction of my life.

He shares a look with his dad, one that looks like they've talked about me already, and he may have told him everything.

"My mom's almost done with your dress," Xander says.

His dad looks between us. "Maybe you two should stay here instead. We could do something fun."

I shake my head. "That's what she'd want. I'm not hiding anymore. I'm trying to live."

Christian's brows furrow, and he bobs his head. He excuses himself, pulling Xander with him, and Elaina finishes my hair. I look even better now than I did, and I can't help the smile crossing my lips. It feels strange to smile because of how much sadness swells in my chest, but I do it anyway.

Fake it until even you believe it's true. I chant the words in my mind over and over again. It's what Lila and I used to tell each other when we weren't confident or needed to get through something hard.

Holly brings me my dress and shoes, hugs me and tells me that she's here for me, and then I change in Xander's room. I peer at myself in his door mirror and hold my head up high. I see my old self sparkle in my eyes and can picture how bright Lila's smile would be if she were here.

"You deserve to be happy," I say out loud. "Lila would not only want you to, but she'd expect you to. You know that." A knock startles me, and I turn toward the door.

Xander pokes his head in. "You look amazing."

I glance at the mirror one last time. I don't see my scars anymore. All I see is me.

Chapter 31

a new day

THE MUSIC PULSATES through the air, and Xander spins me. Colorful lights flash across my vision, and I feel so free and alive, like I'm away from my depressing reality. It's a feeling I didn't know I missed so desperately that I wish I could freeze time so it'll never end.

I peer through the crowd of dancers and watch as Bridget sways in Caleb's arms. He hasn't mentioned anything about Mom, and I don't even think he knows. I'm not going to tell him either. He's having such a good time; there's no way I'm going to ruin it for him. I just want him to be happy. It's what I always want for him despite everything.

The upbeat music shifts into a slow song, and Xander wraps his arms around my waist. I rest my head on his shoulder and breathe in his woody, citrusy scent before tilting my head up to kiss him. I sink deeper into his arms and let the music carry me away in my memories.

"You'll love this one," Lila said.

She handed me one of her ear buds and turned the volume up on her iPod. A pop song played, and she closed her eyes and danced while still sitting on my bed, swaying back and forth, getting lost in the music. I didn't move but just listened to the smooth vocals and repeated each lyric in my head.

When it ended, I stole her iPod and put the song on repeat until I knew all the words. We danced together, each with an ear bud planted in our ears, and sang at the top of our lungs.

"This should be our song," I said.

Lila beamed a bright smile and winked. "It already is, babe."

I laughed and sang my favorite line. "I don't care what they say 'cause we're on top of it all. No one will stop us now. We'll never fall. When it's just you and me, we can take on the world. Nothing will stop us now. They'll never stop us now."

Lila stopped and looked at me. She grinned and took my hand. "Come on, let's get out of here."

I giggled and let her drag me. "It's almost midnight. My parents aren't going to let us out now."

"They'll never stop us!" she yelled.

I laughed and covered her mouth. But she was right. No one stopped us. When we were together, nothing could stop us.

Xander kisses my temple and pulls me from my thoughts. His green eyes shine when I look into them, and he whispers, "You're perfect to me."

My bottom lip trembles and he stops dancing and studies my face. He runs his thumb across my lips, and I reach up and grab his hand and hold it between mine. I tug him from the dance floor and out onto the balcony that overlooks a sprawling golf course.

"Xander," I say. The words burn in my throat, and it's hard to find the nerve to say them out loud. So much has happened in our short relationship; I'm not sure I want to mess things up by saying something he may not understand. "I'm falling in love with you…"

"But?" He knows I'm not finished even though the words are lost on me.

I sigh. "I'm terrified of what's going to happen after tonight. I feel so broken and unsure. I thought about what it would be like to die today before you picked me up. I thought how fitting it would be to die where Lila did. It's just so hard. I do want to live, but it's hard not to think about what it would be like if I just didn't." As the words spill out of me, it's like the weight of the world that's been crushing me for so long has finally been pushed off me. Hearing my words out loud strikes me to the core, and I know I can't just keep ignoring the dark cloud thundering over me, hoping that it goes away on its own.

He rubs his hand across his forehead before meeting my eyes. I can't tell what he's thinking. It's like a thousand emotions roll around his head, and he doesn't know what to say.

He touches my chin. "Thank you for trusting me."

I frown. Those aren't the words I was expecting him to say.

"What?" he asks.

I puff air through my lips. "It's just—I was expecting you to make up some excuse to leave."

"Is that what you want?" he asks.

"I just want to be okay again," I say.

He nods. "I want you to be okay, too."

***

My cell phone vibrates on Xander's nightstand. I roll over and grab it, and watch Caleb's picture blink on the screen. The events of yesterday come flooding back to my memory, and I turn to press my face into the pillow. Prom was one of the Best Nights Ever. I didn't tell Caleb what happened because at least one of us deserved a worry-free night, but I'm sure he knows now. It's why he's calling.

I don't answer it.

I don't want to think about home.

Instead, I click through the photos on my phone from last night. I swipe through them and stop on a close up of Caleb and Bridget I didn't take. Their cheeks are squished together, and Caleb smiles so big that his eyes almost squint closed. They look so happy and carefree. It's exactly how I want to feel, always.

The next photo is of Yessica and me laughing on the dance floor. Xander grins just behind me while I tilt my head toward the ceiling with my eyes closed. Yessica holds my shoulder, half bent, clutching her stomach. We're both so happy; I wish I could remember what was so funny. I'll caption it Best Prom Ever.

I swipe to the next photo, and my heart hammers in my chest. It's another picture I didn't take. It's of me sitting on Xander's lap at our table. My arms are slung around his neck, and his hands are twined together around my waist. I'm gazing down into his eyes, and he's grinning with his sexy lopsided smile. It's an intimate moment, captured forever, and I'm glad it was taken.

It was a few minutes after I bared my soul to Xander on the balcony and just minutes before we left for the night. It was the moment I was certain everything would fall into place as it should and in the end, I'm the person I can live with. Want to live with.

A text message alert pops up over the picture, and I sigh.

I open the message from Caleb.

Caleb: *R U ok?*

Me: *Yes.*

Caleb: *Come home.*

Maybe he doesn't really know what happened or maybe he's on my side for once. I still haven't heard from Dad, and I wonder if he's thought about me and how I feel. I wonder what he told Caleb...I wonder what Mom told both of them. Lies, I'm sure.

Me: *Can't. U come here.*

Caleb: *K.*

I set my phone back on the nightstand and roll off the bed. I notice a pair of workout shorts and a T-shirt laid out across the desk that I bet Xander brought in while I was sleeping, along with a one-piece bathing suit.

A note sits on top of it all with the line, *Breakfast by the pool,* scrawled on it. I smirk while carefully folding the note before putting it in my purse, and then I get dressed. I pull my hair back into a ponytail and glance at my makeup-less face in Xander's door mirror. *No one will care. You're fine as you are.* I offer myself a smile in the mirror when Lila's voice reminds me that it's a new day for me. Better yet, it's a new life. My new life.

***

"Someone's here to see you, Coco," Holly says from the sliding glass door.

I set my fork down and watch as Caleb steps onto the patio. He gazes around the backyard, taking in the clear pool, the blooming rose bushes, and the cactus garden along the fence. He's wearing a black T-shirt and white plaid shorts, and his brown hair is mussed like he didn't bother to style it when he rolled out of bed this morning. He meanders around the pool and glances at Xander's sisters sunbathing on the lounge chairs.

Christian clears his throat. "Come on, Xander. Let's help your mom clean up."

Xander kisses my forehead before sliding from the picnic table and nodding to Caleb as he passes. Christian stops and introduces himself and points to the breakfast food, sitting in warming trays at a small table behind me.

"The plates are on the end," I say as Caleb strolls closer.

He shakes his head. "I'm not hungry, Cee."

"Suit yourself." I take a bite of scrambled eggs.

Caleb slides onto the bench seat next to me and rests his elbows on the table. He's quieter than usual, and I can see a hundred thoughts zooming through his mind through his sad eyes. I set my fork down and shift to face him. We just stare at each other, neither of us initiating the conversation. It's a painful silence, the kind where people push boring small talk to fill it, but I don't want to waste time on the mundane. *Get it over with, Coco.*

"You talk to Mom?" I ask.

Caleb's lips twist to the side. "I couldn't. Dad took her to a mental health rehab center near the coast. He didn't tell me much but said something happened between you and her. What did she do, Cee?"

I close my eyes. I'm taken aback that Caleb asked what she did to me and not the other way around. I don't know if I can tell him. I don't want to relive yesterday afternoon all over again. I don't want Caleb to hear about it either. He's spent so much time over the last year trying to protect me. Now it's my turn to protect him.

"It's nothing, Caleb," I say.

He grabs my hand and holds it in between his. "I always know when you're lying. You can tell me."

I drop my gaze to the ground. "I just want to forget it ever happened, 'kay? I'm holding onto enough baggage as it is, and it's hard enough to carry."

"You don't have to do it alone, Cee."

I press my lips together and bring my eyes to look past him at the calm, clear pool. "I know and I'm not. I know you guys are all here for me and I know I can get through it."

He leans over and hugs me. "Good, because I don't ever want to lose you."

***

Dad kisses my forehead. "I'm taking care of everything, kiddo. I'm so sorry for all this. I should've done something sooner." He pulls me in for another hug and then pulls away to sling an arm around Caleb's shoulders. "You two are my world, you know. I'd take all the bad things and keep them to myself if I could."

A tear slips on my cheek. "It's not your fault, Dad."

"It's not yours either," he says. "And I promise I'm not going anywhere anymore. My family is most important to me."

I rub the back of my hand across my cheek. "What about the company?"

"Don't worry. It's all taken care of. It's time to focus on us right now, all right?"

I nod. "And Mom?"

He sighs. "She needs to focus on herself."

We sit at the table, a box of pizza between us, and I finally open up to my family. Tears pour down my cheeks as I tell Dad and Caleb my version of what happened between me and Mom yesterday. I continue on and tell them about my dark thoughts and how they consume me. I tell them how hard the year has been on me and how I spent almost every day crossing off my calendar. I tell them about how I planned to join Lila and how even though I'm ready to live that I'm afraid. I'm afraid because the thoughts of giving up are hard to keep away.

Caleb stares at his plate of untouched pizza, and I feel Dad's heavy gaze on me. I can't bring myself to look at him. I know hearing everything was as painful to him as it was to me, but maybe even more so for him. I've been carrying the thoughts for so long, it's all I know. The small bright spots of happiness always feel so strange to me. They remind me of Lila.

Dad pushes from the table and comes around to hug me. His shoulders shake in silent sobs, and he kisses the top of my head. Caleb grabs my hand under the table and squeezes it. Love radiates from my family and wraps me in a blanket of strength, hope, and relief.

"We're going to get you help, kiddo. There's no shame in it, okay? Everyone needs help sometimes." Dad pulls away and straightens his shoulders. "We're here for you."

I didn't know it before, but they've always been here for me. I just couldn't see it past the black fog that hung around me. My own shadowed mind made me feel like I was alone, like I had to be alone, that I deserved to be alone.

I've always been my worst enemy. Not the accident, not the horrible aftermath of finding out I lost Lila, not even my mom. It's always been the thought that I'm different, not just physically, but that Coco Caraway died and I was a cheap replacement carelessly put together again. But I can't let circumstances define me anymore. I'm not a replacement, and I didn't die in that accident. I lived. I'm still living.

We're going to get through this. Lila's voice trickles into my memory, reminding me of all the times she helped bring happiness into my darkest moments.

"Now, don't be sad," Lila said after the Worst Breakup Ever, Part Two. She petted my hair, and my tears spilled onto her shoulder. I thought my life was over then, because my heartache felt so permanent.

"If I could stop being sad, don't you think I would?" I asked. I pulled away and glared at her through my dark, wet eyelashes.

She stared at me with her coffee brown eyes. "Well, I don't want you to be sad."

I huffed. "You can't always get what you want, Lila. Hasn't anyone ever told you that?"

She raised an eyebrow but didn't respond.

I laughed. I couldn't help it. It was rare that she was caught off guard, and I had surprised her.

She grinned and shook my shoulders. "See? I *do* always get what I want."

I rolled my eyes and threw my pillow at her. I don't know how she did it, but she was capable of making everything right in the world. She had a smile that made people smile even if they were angry. Her essence shined so brightly that she'd never go unnoticed. It was just how she was.

How she still is to me. How she'll always be.

***

Xander tucks my dark hair behind my ear. His sun-tanned skin enhances the emerald green of his eyes, and they sparkle in the porch light. Twilight morphs into night, and the world is aglow in soft pastel purples and blues. The neighborhood is quiet, and the only sound I can hear is the low hum of the TV through the open window.

"Want me to go with you? I can wait in the car or something," Xander says.

I shake my head. "My dad and Caleb are taking me." I

twine my fingers through his. "Let's hang out after though. Somewhere fun."

It only took Dad a phone call to Holly to get a recommendation for a therapist, and lucky for me, Dr. Fuller had a cancellation for tomorrow afternoon. She won't be the first therapist I've seen, but maybe now things will be different because I do want to get better. I want to finally heal.

"I know the perfect place," Xander says.

I raise my eyebrows. "Where?"

"It's a surprise." Xander kisses me, and I sink into him.

Before I met Xander, I let the past and my scars define me. But now, I won't let them. Not even my family, the accident, or Lila can define me. Only I can.

I don't know if Xander and I will be together forever. Things are supposed to change. We could grow together or apart, but I'm not going to worry about that. Life is what is around me right now. It's fickle and funny, sometimes short, but always filled with possibility.

Epilogue

a new beginning

I STAND OVER Lila's grave. It's different, emptier now, and I stick a bouquet of white lilies into the in-ground vase. Weeks have passed since my last visit, and the cemetery doesn't have the same peacefulness I sought after.

"I'm sorry I can't come here like I used to, Lila, but I know you don't really give a crap. It's always been for me, you know." I fold my legs under me and sit on the warm grass. "I have so much to tell you, and even though I know I could say it anywhere, I wanted to come here. Mom's moving in with Aunt Kelly in Arizona. It's hard not to think it's my fault, but Dad swears it's about them and how they grew apart as a couple. It was hard on Caleb, but he's managing. He'll be fine when he starts college in the fall." I rub my fingers along the soft, white petals of the lilies. "I'm taking the year off, just like we planned. I even get to go to Europe."

"Coco?" Xander calls from his car. He leans against the

Mini Cooper, wearing black slacks, a button-down, and a deep green tie that matches his eyes. "We have about twenty minutes."

Smiling, I wave my hand. I shift my eyes back to Lila's headstone. "Can you believe I'm graduating today? I never thought I'd be doing this without you."

I press my lips together and take a deep breath. I dig a photo of Lila from my bag, the last one I took of her, and stare at it. It was the day of the accident, and we were sitting on the bench swing in my front yard. We were talking about the party we never made it to, and she couldn't wipe the smile off her face. The golden sunset splashed her in warm light, and I snapped a picture.

"I think someone accidentally gave me a halo," she said.

I laughed. "You totally deserve it, angel."

She winked. "Not after tonight."

I flip the photo in my hand. I never captioned it. I couldn't. I didn't know what to write before. I swallow the lump in my throat and pull a pen from my purse. "I'll never stop missing you, Lila," I say after a minute.

I pull the cap off the pen and scribble on the back of the photo in bold letters.

My Angel, The One I Live For.

I won't miss you because I'm always here. It's time to move on, Cee. Her voice echoes in my mind, and I take comfort even though it's my own imagination. I know that's what she'd say. While Lila couldn't keep her promise to live, she kept her promise to be my best friend always.

I push to my feet and bend down and touch her cool grave-stone once more. "You're right, Lila. I know we were always about moving forward, it was just so hard to do it without you, but I've learned how to do it on my own now."

A hand touches my shoulder. "Ready?"

I nod and take Xander's hand. "More than ever."

***

"Caleb Caraway."

Caleb strolls on the stage in front of me and raises his arms into the air, pumping his fists. He turns and bows dramatically, making the crowd break out in laughter through their cheers. I smile, watching him exit the stage to wait for me on the other side.

"Coco Caraway." The crowd cheers again, and I stroll up to the podium and wave at Dad, Grandma, Aunt Kelly and Uncle Stefan, and even Mom in the stands. I look up at the bright blue sky, grinning, before shaking Mr. Somers' hand and walking to the stairs to meet Caleb.

He jogs to me and lifts me off the ground, spinning me around. "I didn't think we'd ever make it," he says, setting me on my feet.

I laugh and flash my empty diploma folder. "There's still time not to. I can't believe they mail these things to us."

I go back to my seat as the rest of my class files through and wait for them to announce, "Xander Romano."

I cheer as Xander accepts his diploma and a handshake, and then waves to his family in the audience. Raising my arms up, I cheer louder than anyone, and he jogs toward me in the front row with a heart-melting grin.

He wraps his arms around me, and I kiss him until Caleb clears his throat behind us. I glance over my shoulder and laugh, pulling Xander to sit with me in my chair despite the glare from one of the teachers.

I tune out the rest of graduation, and when they announce our year, I kiss Xander again. It's surreal to be standing here on graduation day. The cheers ring loud in my ears, the sun beams hot on my robed shoulders, and a smile crosses my face.

This is my new beginning.

Dear Reader,

I chose not to finish this novel with *The End*, because this isn't the end of Coco's story. If you've ever contemplated suicide, I want you to know that suicide is not an option. This isn't the end of your story, either. If you or someone you know is considering suicide, please, please talk to someone you trust or call the National Suicide Hotline at 1-800-273-8255 or text message the crisis text line by texting HOME to 741741. As someone who suffers from anxiety and depression, I want you to know that you are not alone. Never be ashamed to talk to someone. Never be ashamed to ask for help. You are loved. Always loved.

XOXO,

Ginna

Acknowledgments

LIFE AFTER LILA was one of the hardest books I've ever poured my heart into. I started writing it over six years ago as a way to cope with depression. I stopped after I got halfway through and just couldn't finish it, but Coco had never left my mind. Then in 2015, after a series of terrible events, I picked up Coco's story again because I had the sudden need to finish it. And then it sat. It sat for a whole year before I revisited it. I went back and revised it a dozen times, and then I summoned my bravery to send it to my trusted beta readers, Sarah Collier and Amy Holliday, who were so very helpful in making sure I conveyed the story I wanted to. So, Sarah and Amy, I owe you many thanks! Also, another thanks to the rest of my team. Thanks to Katie Harder-Schauer and Jan Moran for always making my books the best they can be. You two rock!

I also want to thank Nikki Godwin for being a listening ear and for helping me write the dreaded blurb. Nikki, you are truly incredible, and I don't know what I'd do without you.

A shout out to Jamie Hall, my sister-in-law and my go-to for plot problems. Thank you so much for always making time to talk through my books with me. Thank you for letting me capture some of your essence in the relationship between both Coco and Lila and Coco and Xander. And lastly, thank you for saying yes to my brother when he asked you out. Thank you for saying yes when he asked you to marry him. You are more than just a sister by marriage. You're one of my best friends, and I'm so lucky to have you in my life. I'm pretty sure Eric has already told you that a million times over the years.

Another thanks goes to my parents. I know raising five children hasn't always been easy, well, I know it's been down-right difficult at some points, but you've all done exceptionally well if I do say so myself. Thank you for instilling in me the ability to see through someone to all the good stuff in their heart, mind, and soul. You are the best!

Thanks to the rest of my family and friends for your love and support. You mean the world to me and have been nothing short of amazing my entire life and through all my life's stages. I love you!

And lastly, thank you to my readers. Without you, my stories would stay hidden on my computer forever. I'm glad you make it possible to share them with the world.

About Ginna Moran

GINNA MORAN IS a writer from sunny Southern California. She started writing poetry as a teenager in a spiral notebook that she still has tucked away on her desk today. Her love of writing grew after she graduated high school and she completed her first unpublished manuscript at age eighteen.

When she realized her love of writing was her life's passion, she studied literature at Mira Costa College in Northern San Diego. Besides writing novels, she was senior editor, content manager, and image coordinator for Crescent House Publishing Inc. for four years.

Aside from Ginna's professional life, she enjoys binge watching television shows, playing pretend with her daughter, and cuddling with her dogs. Some of her favorite things include chocolate, anything that glitters, cheesy jokes, and organizing her bookshelf.

Ginna Moran loves to hear from her readers so visit her online at www.GinnaMoran.com. You can also find her on Facebook, Twitter, Instagram, and Snapchat (@GinnaMoran). To stay up-to-date on new releases, sign up to her newsletter. You'll not only get a FREE short story, but you'll be able to participate in monthly giveaways!

Ginna Moran is currently hard at work on her next novel.

MORE BOOKS BY GINNA MORAN

Destined for Dreams Series
Destined for Dreams (Book 1)
Destined for Despair (Book 2)
Destined for Death (Book 3)
Destined for Love (Book 4 Novella)
Destined Together (Short Story Anthology)

FINDING NATE SERIES
Altered to Kill (Book 1)
Stolen from Me (Book 2)
Bond to Break (Book 3)

DEMON WITHIN SERIES
Tainted (Book 1)
Crushed (Book 2)
Haunted (Book 3)
Scorned (Book 4)
Revived (Book 5)
O Unholy Nights (Christmas Short Story Anthology)

Falling Into Fame Series
If This Was a Movie (Book 1)

Spark of Life Series
Diving Under (Book 1)
Treading Water (Book 2)

STANDALONES
Life After Lila